## ACKNOWLEDGMENTS

First of all, I'd like to thank my critique partner Angie Fox, my agent, Laura Bradford, and my editor, Leis Pederson, for their hard work and dedication. I feel very blessed that I have such talented people working with me to bring my words to life. I'd also like to thank the staff at The Berkley Publishing Group for all their efforts on my behalf. Your work is greatly appreciated and never taken for granted.

I'd also like to thank fellow author Linnea Sinclair for tying a much-needed knot in my tail. I wrote a book I was proud of, but your guidance took it to the next level. I'm very grateful for your support.

I give thanks every day for my wonderful family and friends, whose enthusiasm and praise for the first book warmed my heart. That includes you, Uncle Jim.

Finally, I'd like to thank all those deployed, who served with my husband while this book was written. Stay safe and come home soon.

# 1

CYN ALWAYS LIKED WATCHING WOMEN MOVE, BUT THERE WAS NOTHING SEX-ier than an angry woman moving with a purpose. Commander Yara cut across the dingy pub with the swift efficiency and cold grace of a falcon.

*Perfect.*

He tapped his fingers on the crooked table. The staccato rhythm punctuated his thoughts as he watched his adversary from the corner of the Freedock bar. On the far side of the base from the military platforms, the Freedock, or Scum, as the base personnel liked to call it, was the dock for traders without supply contracts looking for surplus or to fill trade gaps with the Union base.

Perched high over the platforms, the pub had a nice view of the desolate oceans of rock beyond the atmosphere shields.

The sharp, metallic smell of cooling starships mingled with the scent of hot gear grease. It wafted into the pub in spite of the wheezing filtration system from where the automatic haulers shuffled empty freight containers like square-backed beetles. This was his world, and she had just stepped into it.

From the look on Commander Yara's face, she seemed keenly aware she'd just stepped in something. Cyn chuckled. She had a commanding enough presence in her uniform, but he couldn't forget his very first impression of her. She reminded him of a lovely pixie with short, flyaway green hair. Now that pixie was pissed.

This was going to be fun.

"What do you mean there's only one ship?" Her voice carried through the bar as she leaned toward the bartender, giving Cyn a healthy look at her ass.

He eased deeper into the shadows, kicked his boots up on the table, and enjoyed the show. He knew who he was messing with. He'd been studying her for months. She was a Union commander, next in line to the throne of his home planet, and the only thing standing in the way of the revolution brewing on Azra.

But right now, for all her power and prestige, she was nothing more than a traveler searching for stage passage in the Scum. Lucky for her, he was the only one around with a ship. He'd made damn sure of that.

The encrypted nano-link he'd injected into his ear buzzed.

Through the low hum of interference, he heard Quad Sergeant Nalora's voice as if she spoke directly into his head. He scratched his neck below his ear to try to adjust the damn thing. "You got her yet?" she asked. Even though she was somewhere on the base, the link sounded weak. The temporary transmitter would probably cut out soon.

"I'm on her," he answered under his breath. His fellow revolutionary had risked much to help facilitate this meeting.

"Good, don't crack this out, or we're all dead."

"It's war, Sergeant," he warned. It wouldn't be pretty. It wouldn't be nice, and there would be blood.

Azra was at the brink. The lower classes were about to rise against the high cities, but so far, the upper classes knew nothing. He intended to keep it that way. Yara was the linchpin. She was the clear popular choice for heir to the throne. If the Grand Sister chose to step down, Yara would ascend peacefully as the new Grand Sister of Azra in a seamless transition that left no chinks in their security system, no opportunities for his people to strike.

He couldn't let that happen. He needed chaos. He needed a blood duel for the throne to crack open the Elite's defenses and hopefully their unforgiving control over the planet.

"Any news on Palar?" he whispered. Yara's rival had a solid following and a bloodthirsty nature, but a weak mind. She was just the sort of person who could start a war without knowing it, and he wasn't going to miss his opportunity to take advantage.

"She's edgy," Nalora admitted. "She's ready to take down the Grand Sister, but she doesn't have the guts to face Yara for the throne. Yara would thrash her without blinking. You may have to hold on to her for a while before Palar has the confidence to strike. You think you can handle her?" Cyn waited half a beat. "Don't answer that," Nalora added.

Cyn hadn't stopped watching the lovely commander. It was a shame that his plans couldn't include anything more than kidnapping. He didn't need complications, yet her wild green hair made his palms itch to touch it, smooth it. He wouldn't mind letting his hands smooth a couple of other things, too. It was impossible. He knew what it meant to be Elite. For as much as she looked like a pixie, the women that ruled his home planet were hard, brutal, power hungry, and cold. This one would be no different.

According to his information, Yara was a talented fighter, driven, focused, absolutely dedicated to her bloodline, loyal to the Elite, but untested in true war. He'd use that weakness to his advantage.

"Can't we just kill her?" Nalora grumbled. What was it about future Enforcers that made them so cavalier about handing out death?

"You elected me leader, so shut up and follow orders. If Palar strikes before I can deliver the goods and hack the com array, we're screwed. The timing of this has to be perfect." They only had one shot to breach the Elite security systems. Everything had to go according to plan.

"So you're going to use her like a piece in your game of chest?"

"It's *chess*, Nalora, and yes. We need to keep Yara talking with her allies on Azra. Palar won't strike while Yara's still a viable leader. She'll have to eliminate Yara from the picture. That gives us time to deliver the weapons and hack the array. As soon as we let it leak that Yara's been taken hostage, Palar will immediately challenge the Grand Sister. If we control Yara, we can start this war when we have the perfect advantage, like pushing a button." The static deepened. The nanos wouldn't last much longer.

"You play too many games." Nalora's voice turned icy.

"I'm good at games."

"You'd better be." He listened to the annoying buzz as the nanos in his ear fizzled out, cutting off his communication. It was one thing to lead trained soldiers used to orders. It was another to try to band together thousands of individuals burning with pain and rage and little discipline in their lives. Still, they all looked to him as their one hope for freedom. Kidnapping the commander would be comparatively easy.

Yara scowled with the cold expression of a future queen, but the Icanlen bartender's face remained as hard as her bald head. He listened carefully to their conversation.

"I am not going to pay some rankock-licking Earthlen scum for passage on a junked-together freight hauler that doesn't even look capable of flying through the atmosphere shield. When will another ship arrive?"

Cyn crossed his arms at the insult. At least his disguise was working. After living on Earth for more than a decade, he knew how to impersonate them. It didn't take much to hide his Azralen heritage, just some hair dye; some antique Earthlen eye lenses; his alias, Cyrus Smith; and the bracers that covered his Azralen coloring and traditional tattoos. Sometimes the low-tech route worked best.

He glanced through the dingy force-shield and down to the docks below. Steam rolled over the smooth black body of his I.S. Cruiser, illuminated by the glowing orange gravity generators. He'd busted the poor ship to make it to the base in time to intercept Yara, but it was more than capable of flying through the atmosphere shield.

"We're between trade cycles. Next ship is at least a month out." The bartender grasped the sanitizer hovering over the worn bar and resumed her cleaning as if she'd heard it all before, and didn't give a damn about any of it.

"*Shakt*," Yara cursed. Cyn smiled, enjoying her frustration. Now what was she going to do? She squinted as she looked around the dim interior of the bar.

"How can a Union base be completely devoid of any free-trade traffic?" she lamented.

How indeed. Cyn had pulled in a lot of favors to clear out the other transports, and Nalora had tied up the trade schedule with some perfectly timed rearrangements of the free-trade docking permission cycle. Because Yara's return home was considered personal leave, she wasn't allowed to use military resources to travel. Not that it would help. The military ships were too busy moving the fourth front to play chauffeur to a commander heading in the opposite direction. If she wanted off the base, she only had one choice—him.

An enormous feline strutted out from behind a bench in the corner. It twitched its large tufted ears while its dark coat shifted over its chunky build. It was the type of cat that could take down prey five times its size, and for this cat, that equaled a small hippopotamus.

*Crap, not a korcas.*

"NOT NOW, TUZ," YARA GRUMBLED, NUDGING HIM ASIDE WITH HER LEG. HER scout hissed, let out a low, irritated growl then he grabbed her by the ankle with his prehensile tail.

She hefted the overweight feline to her shoulder and stroked his swirling black and gray fur.

"Ona, give me patience," she prayed as she turned toward the dark corner of the bar.

A pair of black boots and the frayed cuffs of some old blue canvas pants from Earth propped up on a cracked synthwood table. Tuz growled and flicked his tufted ear against her cheek. She placed him on the floor and ordered a refill of whatever the guy was drinking from the bartender.

The woman pulled a bottle of amber liquid with a black label out from under the bar.

"You know anything about him?" Yara asked.

"Cyrus is safe enough," the bartender replied. "Could do worse. He doesn't like to take on passengers as a rule, but he has his papers and I haven't heard a word against him."

Yara flexed her fingers around the drink as she stepped back into the shadows of the bar.

The man in the corner leaned back in his chair with his arms crossed over his honed chest. There was nothing soft or tired about him. He bore no evidence in his body of long stretches of time spent in macrospace as he delivered his goods.

No, he was built like a cat, sleek muscle and lazy curiosity in his gaze as he watched her approach. She wasn't fooled. Tuz always looked like that just before he pounced.

"You Cyrus?" she asked, getting to the point as she placed the drink on the table near his large foot. She felt a tingle slide down her spine.

"Commander," he answered while tilting his head in a half-hearted acknowledgment of her authority. He had elegant, angular features roughened only slightly by the waving black hair curling around his ears from under his Earthlen ball cap. "What can I do for you?"

"Don't play games. You know why I'm here. What's your price?" The faster they got in the air, the better. As it stood, she wouldn't be able to leave the base until that night. If she didn't reach home soon, a bloodbath could ensue.

He leaned forward and wrapped his long fingers around the drink in a slow, deliberate fashion, teasing the crystal before surrounding it in the heat of his palm. Yara found her attention fixed on his hand.

"Is this an attempt to butter me up?" he asked as he took a slow sip. The rat was sharper than she initially thought. Yara watched the muscle in his neck flex then lifted her gaze to his impossibly dark eyes. All thought melted away as she stared into his eyes. Black as space and just as deep, they seemed full of sexual fire as they met hers with blatant challenge.

She wasn't used to men meeting her gaze. Azra was a female-dominant culture and men knew their place. Here on the Union base with the myriad of cultures and people, her rank and reputation kept others from looking her in the eye. Her stomach fluttered.

He lowered the glass. "If it was, I'm sorry to say you suck at it." A wicked smile full of sin and promise spread across his face as those dark eyes laughed at her.

Rankock licking was an understatement. She wouldn't stand for this. She couldn't let him get to her. Even as she thought it she realized he already had gotten to her. She tried to stifle her irritation, but couldn't manage to suppress it.

"Listen, you . . ."

"Rankock-licking Earthlen scum?" He tilted his head as he watched her. "I'll concede the Earthlen scum bit, but I draw the line at rankock licking. Licking rankocks isn't my idea of a good time, Pix."

Yara wasn't sure what *pix* meant, but she was certain it wasn't a term of respect. Her irritation blossomed into red-hot anger. "I don't know who you think you are, but I am still a commander on this base. You will address me as such or I'll watch you rot in confinement for a week."

The corner of his mouth twitched as he took another drink. "Yes, sir."

He placed the glass back on the table, never once breaking his eye contact. "I'm sorry. I don't take on passengers. You're out of luck." He leaned back into the shadows, giving her a reprieve from his gaze.

"Everyone has a price," she hissed, unable to contain her ire. Did he think he could just dismiss her? "Name yours."

Tuz leapt up on the table and glared at him with slanted yellow eyes only a shade lighter than hers. The table nearly tipped under the cat's substantial weight.

"No deal, I'm allergic to cats."

"Take a pill," she quipped.

"There's no pill for attitude."

*Great, he thinks he's smart.*

Tuz hissed, as if he agreed with her assessment.

"Tuz wouldn't disobey me," Yara stated. Her cat growled and swished his thick tail. Which wasn't entirely the truth, but she could be reasonably sure Tuz wouldn't kill the bastard. She just couldn't guarantee he wouldn't bleed a little.

Cyrus kept a wary eye on the cat. "Sixty thousand."

Yara felt as if she'd just taken a blow to the gut. "You're out of your mind."

"No, I'm the one with the ship and you're desperate." He downed the last of his drink and placed the empty glass between them. She found her gaze inexplicably drawn down to it and caught there a moment before she could snap out of it.

"How long will it take your ship to reach Azra?" she asked. She shook the image of his hand caressing the glass out of her mind and focused. He had caught her unprepared, but now that she was in the thick of it, she wouldn't lose control again.

"It should take four days to reach Gansai and one to repair the converter. After that, it's an hour-long macro-leap tops." He leaned forward, locking gazes with her again. Oh, he knew this was a battle, the filthy rat.

"Wait a minute. The converter on the macro-drive is damaged?" Her shock slapped her in the face, followed by the sting of disappointment. This would not be an easy trip.

"It'll be an easy fix. Don't worry, the transwave systems still work."

"You mean we have to travel transwave?" Her voice pitched up on the last word. She'd get there faster floating adrift in a pressure suit than using the outdated leap tech.

He shrugged. "You could hold your breath and try to jump, but I don't think you are going to make it off this base any other way."

"Fifteen," she snapped as she crossed her arms and glared at him. "You're not worth sixty."

"Are you sure?" He let the sexual suggestion drip with innuendo as he said it.

Elite warriors were supposed to remain celibate. Very few adhered to that rule. She had neglected it in her youth, and now her transgressions haunted the back of her mind. She had enough experience to recognize this game for what it was but not enough to numb her to it.

He watched her with a sinful look. "I know for a fact I'm worth forty-five," he added.

"I'm not paying more than thirty-five." She'd let his innuendos fall on deaf ears. "If the Grand Sister wants me that badly, she'll send transport herself. I don't need you."

"But do you want me?" The fringe of his dark lashes lowered, turning his gaze into a polished seduction. He smiled that damn smile.

Her dagger sunk into the worn chair with a satisfying *thunk*.

Yara enjoyed the look of surprise on the trader's face as he looked down at the dagger lodged just centimeters from the seam of his crotch, then back up at her. It was all the answer she felt like giving him.

"Do we have a deal?" She stood straighter and looked down at him.

The Earthlen slowly rose to his feet, forcing Yara to look up to meet his arrogant gaze. Again that annoying shiver rushed down her spine, and she felt a tingling in the backs of her thighs. Her heart beat faster with a sudden rush of adrenaline. She felt as if she was about to begin a long and difficult sparring match, one she wasn't sure she would win. Why did she like that feeling?

He smiled again as he offered her a hand. "I'll take you on, Commander."

YARA STOPPED BY HER QUARTERS AFTER AN AWKWARD FAREWELL PARTY hastily thrown together by some of her lesser officers. She doubted any of them would miss her. She was just another commander, and a new uniform would take her place. She suspected a third of the people there had never even seen her but were only there for the cold food and an excuse not to work.

At least Tuz had fun. He took a good chunk out of some poor lieutenant's leg.

Her scout blissfully scent-marked her single bag of belongings with the side of his face. Clothes, weapons—they all stowed neatly in that bag. She double-checked the room as a force of habit more than anything. Empty, gray, it was as if the years she'd spent living in this room made no impact on it at all, just like it had made no impact on her. She felt nothing as she shut the door on what should have felt like a home.

She'd been born, raised, groomed, and trained, her entire lineage preparing her for one single thing, the day she would take over the throne. She had no room in her life for anything else. Azra needed her now.

With a sense of foreboding, Yara accessed the stored messages in her com unit and listened one more time to the warning from one of her closest allies on Azra. The message was encoded, and she wanted to be sure she didn't miss anything.

Palar was planning to light the fire in the temple. If she initiated a blood challenge, she'd probably kill the Grand Sister, and Yara and her supporters would have to fight her and her faction to the death for the throne. She had to return home and show Palar she wasn't about to back down. She would inherit the throne peacefully once the Grand Sister decided to step down.

She wondered if the Grand Sister knew of Palar's plot and whether that was the real reason she was calling Yara back home. It made sense. The Grand Sister couldn't be serious about sending her on a bloodhunt for some worthless mudrat traitor. She knew her training partner's defection was a scandal, and that the Grand Sister was furious about it, but finding the traitor's brother, Cyn, and seeking justice through him was pointless. It wouldn't bring Cyani back.

Yara wandered toward the Scum, unsure how she felt about returning home. No matter how much she had been pressured into her position as one of the Elite, something didn't quite fit. She felt the weight of expectation, and it cut into her like binding straps tied too tight. But she didn't want a bloody coup to tear the Elite apart, either. Her planet needed her to be what she'd been bred to be. A leader. She would maintain the peace and order of her planet. Azra didn't need change; it needed consistency.

Perhaps when she assumed the throne, the emptiness would ease. It was probably nothing more than a need to fulfill her purpose. Doubt crept into the dark corners of her mind. What if it was something else? What if she assumed the throne and the dark emptiness never went away? She tried not to think about it. It didn't matter.

Tuz stalked along behind her, occasionally leaping forward to tag the back of her heel with a paw. They passed fewer and fewer people in uniform as they found their way through the maze of endless halls toward the far end of the base. She knew to keep moving. Tuz tended to launch a full-scale attack on her boot whenever she stopped.

The slick and polished halls of the Union base deteriorated to chipped slab floors with grimy walls as she entered the Freedock. The constant clatter of haulers shuffling shipping containers in the warehouses echoed under the large force shields. The shields arched like giant bubbles over the gravity generators on the rough ground below.

She still didn't understand. There should have been at least seven free-trade transports unloading supplies with hundreds of people milling through the halls on the way to processing and accounting, or the bar.

Her unease grew as she stared across the Freedock to the dark ship waiting for her on the other side. Her captain leaned against a landing strut, waiting.

She'd spent hours looking for something, anything, even a complaint of hull vermin against him. She found nothing. That alone was odd.

Her neck began to tingle, her skin growing sensitive as her heart beat faster.

She wasn't afraid of him.

If he tried to pull anything, she'd just kill him, or Tuz would.

He crossed his arms against his chest, his simple synthlin shirt gaped just enough for her to catch the edge of a scar on his chest. Who was he? In the modern age, scars were rare on people from tech, especially on Earth. That planet had at least a thousand-year history of seeking physical perfection through medical intervention. How did he get one? She had a sinking feeling it wasn't from a medical procedure. It was a mark of violence.

The muscles in her legs suddenly felt heavy and uncoordinated.

She still wasn't afraid of him.

But he made her nervous.

"Commander," he greeted with a nod of his dark head. The orange glow of the gravity generators reflected in the lenses of his eye shades.

Yara didn't like being unable to see his eyes. She didn't trust him.

She walked forward with a steady and deliberate stride. It would be fine. As soon as she reached home, she could put the Earthlen out of her mind forever.

"Captain," she responded, holding her head higher even though she felt flushed. She tried to tell herself it was only the radiant heat from the ship.

"Are you ready for this?" He smiled. It was a blatant invitation and an even more blatant challenge.

"Absolutely," she answered.

# 2

THEY DUCKED UNDER THE SHIP AND YARA CLIMBED A RUNG LADDER THROUGH the cramped vertical airlock. She pulled herself up into the back left corner of the cargo bay. Looking around with a certain amount of apprehension, she hoped the ship was livable. It seemed like too much to ask. A single stack of crates was strapped with military precision against the forward bulkhead with a closed door just to the left of the stack.

The outside of the ship seemed large. Why was the interior so small? What sorts of items did he trade in? Obviously he wasn't a major supplier for the Union.

"Impressed yet?" Cyrus asked as he picked up her bag and motioned to the bulkhead door ahead of them.

"Hardly. This ship is tiny." At least it looked clean. She inspected the area for signs of vermin as Tuz growled his disapproval and curled his long tail around his front leg. The lingering scent of stale joint grease and dust hung in the air.

"That's why I don't take passengers. You're lucky I took you on at all," he mentioned as he passed her.

"I should have talked you down to twenty."

Light glittered in his wicked eyes as he removed his shades. "It wouldn't have happened, Pix."

She turned to him. "I could leave this ship right now."

He shrugged. "No refunds. You know the way out." He flicked his hand at the open airlock hatch in the floor, daring her to back out.

Damn him. Damn him to the filth and darkness.

"You will not disrespect me, Earthlen." She felt the heat rise again, felt her hands shake. She had to control herself.

"Captain," he stated.

"Commander," she corrected.

"No, you will address me as captain on this ship."

"What?" He couldn't be serious. She refused to play these petty games with him. He should know his place. And this piece of junk hardly counted as a ship. It was less than half a ship.

"I think I made myself clear, Commander." He shifted her bag to his other hand, then opened the doors from the bay into converted living quarters connected to the command center of the ship by an open archway with an energy shield generator.

Yara felt as if she had taken a shock blast to the head. Handling venomous snakes seemed less hazardous than talking with him. Did he respect her authority or not? Was he trying to tell her it didn't matter either way? She felt like she was missing something, and she had the feeling that was exactly what he wanted.

Clenching her teeth, she entered the living quarters. Her nerves made her feel edgy as she carefully inspected the compartment.

Four bunks lined the sidewalls, with spacious storage lockers between them. She had expected old military blankets, or something equally as practical on the bunks, but each proudly displayed beautiful handcrafted blankets of soft foreign material. They swirled with deep red and black patterns, an intricate maze of craftsmanship.

They looked soft, inviting. A small but spotless galley sat in the corner with an antique water basin that had been scrubbed so clean she could see reflections in the smooth stone.

This wasn't a transport ship. This was his home. The conversion of the living space was personal, not simply functional. This was a ship made for a one- or two-man crew living and working in a single area. She had no place to hide from him.

"Which bunk?" She had trouble articulating the rest of her question as it dawned on her that she didn't know which one he slept in on a regular basis.

"Which one do you want?" he responded, placing her bag in the center of the polished floor and entering the open control center.

"I think I should sleep on a cot in the cargo bay." It was the best solution. She shouldn't be in here.

"I don't own a cot. You can sleep on the cargo bay floor, but I can't guarantee a smooth ride in transwave. You might get knocked around, so to speak."

Wonderful.

Tuz jumped up on the bunk nearest the galley and kneaded the pillow with his paws. Yara sat on the edge of it. The blankets felt even softer than they looked and smelled like fresh air and sun-soaked grasses. "Is this one yours?" she asked, wondering where the scent came from.

"They're all mine." He leaned against the archway to the control center and watched her with his shadowed eyes.

She shifted her weight, unsure what to do with her hands. She could picture him sprawled out under rumpled sheets. What did he wear to bed? She tried to keep herself from wondering if he wore anything at all, but the thought hit her before she could stop it.

She jumped up like a hot spark had gone off beneath her. "This will do."

"Is there a problem, Commander?" He smiled, just a twitch in the corner of his mouth and a glint in his dark eyes.

*Yes, I'm in your bedroom, you dirty mudrat.* "No, no problem. The sooner we leave, the better."


CYN SHOOK HIS HEAD AS HE EASED THROUGH THE LIVING QUARTERS AND EN-tered the cargo bay to shut the airlock hatch. The commander was a real piece of work. He had no doubt that she would be a cold and efficient killer when provoked, but he had never seen an Elite warrior with less of a handle on her physical reactions to her emotions. She probably sucked at cards.

She was uncomfortable in his ship. That much was clear. But why?

He hauled the hatch shut, dropping it in the floor, and engaged the wheel lock in a slow, thoughtful motion. He came from a long line of Elite women. His sister was Elite. They hadn't brainwashed her no matter how much they threatened her life. His sister broke away from them, whole and happy. His mother had been Elite until they turned on her like a pack of hyenas and banished her as a traitor for the terrible sin of getting pregnant. Yet his mother raised them with courage and love until she found a way to escape the shadows.

And then there was his aunt, the Grand Sister of Azra. The manipulative bitch. Heartless and ruthless, his father's tyrant sister was obsessed with her bloodline and maintaining her hold on the throne of Azra no matter the cost. She'd drugged his parents so they'd have sex, used the scandal to steal the throne from his mother, and then turned on her own brother when he decided to stand up for the woman bearing his children.

If that weren't enough, she'd tortured Cyn's sister in an attempt to make Cyani her heir to the throne. Fira intended to create a mindless puppet strong enough to meet any blood challenges but not independent enough to control Azra without her. Cyn was determined to make his aunt fall. For many, the revolution was about freedom, justice, and safety. He knew the suffering of the people he led. He had lived it, and he couldn't forget it. But this was about more than suffering. For him, it was personal.

So where did Yara fit in? His sister respected her but insisted Yara was as focused and cold as they came.

He didn't see it. The woman unable to sit on his bed was anything but cold and focused. There was a chink in that armor. What kind of woman would he find beneath it?

What could it mean for the revolution?

He shouldn't be thinking such things. He had a job to do, a plan to carry out. The time for plotting was over. It was time to act.

The hatch lock ground shut with a final clunk of metal locking into metal. They were stuck together now.

He stood and wiped his hands on his jeans.

"You ready, old girl?" he asked the ship as he pulled open the door to the living quarters.

He ignored Yara as he entered the control center and began the launch sequence. He barely glanced at the screens and consoles as he punched in coordinates from memory. Once the flight plan had been entered in the panels on the copilot side of the ship, he fell back into his worn pilot's chair, synched the ship systems with the base's launch program, and waited for the base to give the all clear.

"You have a last name?" he asked, knowing full well she didn't. The more ignorance he showed for the cultural habits of Azra, the better his disguise would be.

"What is it about Earthlen that makes them think everyone in the universe does things the way they do?" she responded. She climbed the step to the edge of the control center and stood with her stiff back to the archway connecting it to the living quarters. Her eyes fixed on the copilot seat, but she didn't make a move to sit in it.

"So you don't have a last name?" Verbally sparring with her was fun, like when he used to poke snakes with sticks.

"The Yar in my name denotes my family lineage. I'm a descendant of Yarini the Just, one of our matriarchs. The closest thing you have on Earth is royalty." She stood a little straighter. "How about your name. Does Cyrus mean anything?"

"It means I turn around when you call it." His alias had always served its purpose, but it was just that, an empty moniker. Cyn pivoted in his chair as clearance came through and then initiated the gravity disruptor. "You'd better sit down, Your Highness."

He wondered if she would consider him a prince if she ever found out his real name. He was the direct descendant of two matriarchs, Cyrila the Rebel on his mother's side, and Fima the Merciless on his father's. Few on Azra could boast such a powerful combination, but men who carried the bloodlines weren't seen as respected warriors, only breeding stock.

Yara took a seat on the bed nearest the copilot's seat, and Cyn slid his hand up the angrav controls, lifting them off the ground. He initiated the control thrusters and angled the ship for the shield breach. The ship shuddered as it pushed up out of the docks and through the atmosphere shield. The bubble folded over the ship, with the remnants of the energy shield sparkling over the visual sensors in a flashing rainbow of lightninglike discharges. The stars opened up before him, and Cyn set the computer on course.

The main thrusters engaged, pushing them farther from the small, desolate planet and through the fleet of large military starships space-docked above the base. Once they were well clear, Cyn engaged the transwave system.

The ship rattled as it settled into an uneasy stride. The stars around them blurred. It gave Cyn a headache, so he turned the viewscreen to information on the ship's systems before rotating his chair back around. They must have been on course for at least half of a standard hour, but she didn't say a word. He almost wanted to see how long she'd go without moving or speaking, but the silence was already buzzing in his ears.

"You like cards?" he asked, pulling a worn deck out from under the console.

"I don't play," Yara responded.

"Nassa, poker, hyped eights?" He cocked his head. "Maybe you prefer ralok?"

"I don't play," Yara turned to look at him.

"Ever?" Cyrus prodded, flicking the cards between his hands like a master.

"Ever." And she wasn't about to get caught up in his games, either. She looked down at Tuz in an attempt to halt the unwanted conversation with the nosey pilot. The start of the journey hadn't been half bad. It was quiet. If she had her preference, they'd ignore each other for the next four days, and this mess would be over.

Tuz lifted his head and pricked his ears and whiskers forward in the universal cat sign language that meant he'd discovered something interesting, edible, or twitchy. What was he after? Yara hoped it was something she could use to bust the Earthlen's trade permits, but they were already off port.

The cat jumped down off the bed and stalked under one of the other bunks.

"Get him, quick!" Cyrus shouted. Yara jolted to attention.

A loud snap echoed through the ship. Tuz exploded in a ball of spitting, fluffy fury. He streaked out from under the bunk yowling and hissing like his tail was on fire. Every single hair on the cat's body stood on end.

Yara tried to catch him, but he arched his back and took a swipe at her.

"What happened?" Yara grabbed the blanket from the bunk to wrap Tuz up. She needed to figure out if he was injured or not. Suddenly a small ball of pink and green light zipped past her head.

Tuz launched off the bunk in a tremendous leap. He swiped at the flying object in midair before catching an overhead support brace with his tail.

The flying ball let out a high-pitched whistle. Yara covered her ears as Tuz hung upside down from his tail, his paws flailing for the strange flying disc.

"Bug, calm down!" Cyrus shouted. Tuz joined in the ruckus with a loud wail.

The disc swooped down and circled Cyrus's head, while releasing a litany of clicks, whistles, beeps, and buzzes.

"I know, I know, but you shouldn't have shocked him," Cyrus said to the machine.

"What is going on here?" Yara lifted the blanket toward her swinging cat, but he wouldn't release his tail. His dark fur still stood on end as his large eyes narrowed on the chattering bot.

The swirling lights around the little disc swelled as it flew into the control center and touched the console in a series of quick taps.

"Damn it, Bug. Leave it," Cyrus scolded as he climbed up into the control center.

The ship shuddered and lurched as the living quarters began to move. Yara leapt into the center of the bay as angrav cases emerged from the sidewalls and slid into positions at the end of each bunk and over the storage lockers.

Cyrus looked exasperated and furious as Yara stared at the transparent panels in front of each case. Art treasures floated in the center of the dark cases, gorgeous works of craftsmanship and intricate design, but she didn't recognize what cultures they were from. They were not objects normally found in the honest trade markets, more like the collections of art thieves.

The machine landed on a small quilted pillow attached to the top of one of the cases. Six spindly legs emerged from the bottom of the glowing disc and hooked into the cushion. The metal contraption wiggled down into the pillow while fluffing it up with his spiderlike legs.

Was the machine snuggling?

The bot seemed to contemplate her with a small black "eye" protruding from the top of its smooth silver disc. It started clicking and buzzing again.

"She's our guest, and so is her cat, so no more static discharges, understood?" Cyrus rubbed his forehead then surveyed the room, before looking up at Tuz still hanging from the ceiling by his tail. "Can you get him down?"

"Come on, Tuz." Yara reached for Tuz with the blanket again, and this time he dropped into her arms. She wrapped him up tight, smoothing his fur as she tucked his head under her chin. "What is all this?" she asked, looking at the cases.

"Trinkets," Cyrus dismissed as he crossed the quarters to the galley. People didn't keep trinkets in special hidden compartments. He poured himself a drink into a dented cup and downed it before turning around. He flicked a lazy gesture at the bot on the pillow. "Bug, meet Yara. Yara, Bug."

The disc held on tighter to the pillow as his eye sank down

in a strange glare and the glowing aura of light around him turned mostly pink. He let out a grinding noise.

"That's rude, Bug." Cyrus walked over to the disc and stroked a finger around the front edge of the thing.

"That's A.I., isn't it?" Yara had a sinking feeling. Most artificial intelligence was illegal. To make matters worse, this one looked like Yeshulen tech. The Yeshulen weren't exactly on good terms with the Union. They had a nasty tendency to fire on ships without provocation. The Union didn't trade with them.

"Yeah, he's artificial. Intelligent is still up for debate."

Electricity arched out of the bot and into Cyrus's hand.

"Ow, damn it." Cyrus glared at the bot, then rubbed his hand as he turned back to Yara.

"So, are you going to tell me about the cases?" she asked, taking a closer look at a handcrafted vessel with intricate inlaid pictures of people gathering some sort of harvest and offering it to what looked like star gods.

"I thought you preferred not to talk." He retreated to the control center and focused on the viewscreen, like nothing had happened. Oh, great, now he wanted to be quiet.

Yara placed Tuz on the bunk and ordered him to stay. He hissed at her and crouched, keeping his eyes fixed on Bug.

"Leave it," she commanded. Her cat remained still, but Yara could see the tension in his shoulders and his puffy fur.

She had a bone to pick with the captain. She entered the control center and perched in the copilot's seat.

He tilted his head to look at her, but his expression was a mask of indifference. She knew better than to believe it this time.

"Are you a shadow trader?"

He leaned back in his chair with that infuriating look in his eye, like he wanted to toy with her again. "How do you want me to answer that?"

"With the truth," she stated. She kept her gaze locked with his, even though it made her uncomfortable. She had the feeling he could read her too easily. And there was something about the expression in his eyes that disarmed her. It was the challenge, the sheer defiance. An excited thrill of awareness tickled near her heart.

"That's not in my best interest," he responded, his lips turning up in the corner in his enigmatic grin. "If I am a shadow trader, I'm not going to hear the end of it for the next four days, and then I'm sure you'll try to arrest me when we reach Gansai. If I'm not a shadow trader, you'll be disappointed."

"Disappointed?" She had to hear his explanation for this one.

"You want to think the worst of me." He turned his attention back to the viewscreen and tapped on the console. "That's the way Azralen elitists are."

"You're damn right." She felt her irritation rise and the sudden need to defend herself.

"Yeah, well, don't be surprised if I surpass your expectations." He stood and left the control center. Ignoring her, he opened one of the storage lockers, removed a black case, and crossed the quarters into the cargo bay.

Tuz laid his ears back and growled but kept his stare fixed on Bug. The bot continued to cling to its pillow and stared back. Yara didn't have time to police the staring contest. She wanted to get to the bottom of what Smith was hiding. Besides, Tuz always won.

She followed Cyrus into the cargo bay. He had removed a floor panel and was working on the conduits beneath.

"What do you have hidden in here?" she asked, mostly to get his attention. She didn't like the way he dismissed her so casually.

"A cache of illegal weapons for a bunch of revolutionaries. I got a good price for them." His voice dripped with sarcasm.

Now he was just taunting her.

"What kind of trader are you?" It was a straightforward question, and she expected an answer.

He looked up at her, his long fingers stilling on the conduit. "The kind that likes to make a profit."

"At whose expense?" she responded.

"Is that another accusation?" He yanked hard on a wire, pulling it from its socket. "I don't appreciate being labeled."

"You trying to tell me you haven't already labeled me?" She was used to men from male-dominant cultures and the names they called her behind her back.

"You mean like rankock-licking scum?" Cyrus arched one brow. "Any other colorful names running through your head?" he jabbed.

"Maybe." She reached down and handed him his box of tools. This wasn't getting her anywhere, and it wouldn't make the ship go any faster or give her any peace during the journey. Perhaps she needed a different strategy when dealing with the Earthlen. "Are we going to spend the next few days verbally sparring, or should we call a truce?"

"Giving in?" He smirked.

"Never." She lifted her chin. "Just saving myself a headache.

Your company was infinitely more bearable when you weren't speaking."

Cyrus laughed. "I'll call a truce, but only if we're taking bets on how long it's going to last." He returned his attention to the conduit. "If you're hungry, there are dry stores in the locker next to the galley. Make yourself at home. You should think about getting some sleep. It's going to be a long trip."

Yara retreated into the quarters and remade the bunk she'd messed up in her attempts to catch her cat. Tuz refused to move from the bunk in spite of her prodding, so she relented and smoothed the blanket on top of him. Even covered, the cat didn't move, continuing the stare-down through the blanket.

Cyrus gave the lump under the covers a sidelong glance as he returned to the living quarters.

"Need some help?" he asked as he collected his tools and rubbed one of the strange black leather bracers covering his forearms.

"No." She sat on the bunk by the galley once more, and let her hand slide over the blanket. It seemed their little sparring match was done. So be it.

He had told her to make herself at home. He had no idea that that simple statement meant nothing to her.

Home, such a simple thing, and yet she never felt like she had a place that deserved that label. She ran her hand over the blanket again, then glanced at the bot and its hand-embroidered pillow.

A distant memory floated into her mind. She had a pillow once. It had a woven cover made from ciera blossom silks.

While artisans created intricate woven designs with ciera

silk, this one was chunky, rough. It was a child's practice at an adult art. Her friend Ceeli had given it to her, and it was beautiful.

The fact that she could remember what it looked like so clearly surprised her. She hadn't kept it very long. Her father found it and took it from her, then scolded her for befriending an inferior and forbade her from speaking with Ceeli again.

Yara lay down with her head on Cyrus's pillow. It felt soft and comforting, but she couldn't bring herself to take her boots off and get under the blanket.

She didn't know if she ever could.

Cyrus returned to the control center. He sat in his captain's chair and started scrolling through information on the viewscreen.

What sort of man kept vases and art pieces in secret compartments that no one would ever see? She glanced at the screen and noticed the text scrolling by at a very rapid pace. How did he keep up?

Maybe he had neural enhancers implanted. She wouldn't put it past him. There was no other way an Earthlen could process information that quickly. Certain members of the Azralen population could do it, ones with the catgaa gene. She wondered if there were any of the geniuses left. Only males in the Azralen population carried the full gene, and they had been persecuted by Grand Sister Firona almost a century ago. She wanted to cleanse the male population before they became *plagued by mental illness*. Yara had her own suspicions that Firona didn't want the men of Azra to develop an advantage over the ruling women. The catgar, as they were called, had a memory that processed information, then stored it like a computer. They never forgot anything that they learned, and their memories never faded.

Yara felt a chill tumble down her spine. What a horrible curse. If someone never forgot anything, then any pain they had ever known would still be as sharp as the day it was inflicted. How could a person survive like that?

# 3

THIRTY-ONE HOURS. IT TOOK THIRTY-ONE HOURS TO MAKE HER WANT TO KILL him.

"You have no idea what you're talking about," she snapped. "You've never even been to Azra." She had never met anyone that had gotten so far under her skin, like a logic parasite. They'd been arguing about politics for at least three hours, and she'd had enough.

She lingered in the archway to the control center, unwilling to enter that space but feeling like she had no other escape on the modest ship. If she retreated deeper into the living quarters, he'd probably let the conversation drop, but that would be a defeat, and she'd sooner fall to filth than let go of this one.

"You know what they say about absolute power." He shrugged as if none of this mattered to him, because it didn't.

"That it's efficient?" she offered. She could feel the heat burning under her skin as she crossed her arms.

He laughed at her.

"The bottom line is the Grand Sister has done more to protect Azra than she's ever done to harm it," Yara stated, turning the conversation back on point.

"How so?" His brow lowered, his expression subtle but lacking his earlier amusement.

"For thirty years she's defended our autonomy from the Union's interference. How many other planets have you seen that have become like Union drones, all hopelessly tangled in treaties and bureaucracies. They can no longer trade without the Union, no longer defend themselves without the Union. They're all puppets. They're losing the strength of their culture. If the Union fails, so do they."

"And here you are, Commander." He tucked his hands into the crooks of his arms, and kicked his feet back up on the console. The arrogant tilt of his head dared her to continue.

"I serve in the Union forces for the good of my planet, to maintain our trade agreements. For as strong as Azra is, the Grand Sister is wise enough to know we shouldn't be completely disconnected from our neighbors." Tuz jumped into the copilot's seat and started sharpening his claws on the arm rest. Yara didn't bother to stop him. Cyrus just scowled, though he looked like he was tempted to kick the cat.

"So you only isolate yourselves personally, not politically."

Yara's head began to throb. "What is your point?"

"I have to have a point?" He dropped his feet and leaned forward, resting his forearm on his knee.

"I'm done." Yara headed for the galley. She needed a drink.

Too bad she couldn't dig into that bottle he hid on the third shelf.

"You admire her, don't you?" Cyrus called after her.

"Yes." This conversation was over. She refused to give him any more than that.

"Do you want to be like her?"

Yara turned and stared him down. "I want to do what is right for Azra."

She didn't speak to him again for another thirty hours or so. Each one seemed to drag, endless and unyielding, as time must have slowed down to mock her. Not even sleep was a reprieve. As soon as she fell asleep, she seemed to wake up again, those hours of peace stolen away by some trick of time.

Now with her mind feeling like a bowl of lumpy mash, Yara reclined on the bunk behind the control center, her back pressed up against the sidewall and her feet dangling over the edge. She watched the scene before her unfold with resigned attention. After three days on the ship with little mental stimulation or entertainment other than her host's witty banter, she could no longer think clearly or find the motivation to care.

For all of Cyrus's verbal games, he'd been very respectful of her space and had never once touched her. It was almost as if he was using their argument to keep her at a distance.

Now they had once again degenerated to mind-numbing silence.

She was on edge. They had been in deep space, too far away from an array to communicate with Azra. Her rivals were probably plotting against her. All she could do was watch Cyrus try to beat Bug in a game of cards. It had to be the strangest thing she'd ever witnessed.

Cyrus stared at the cards in his hand, his expression serious and thoughtful. After a pause he looked up and said, "Go fish."

"*Bzzzzz,*" Bug grumbled as he flew away from his card stand to the sloppy pile of cards between them and picked one out. He flew it back to the stand and then his aura turned green as he concentrated on his new card.

Yara stroked Tuz as she watched the game, careful to keep a restraining hand firmly beneath his thick chest. Her cat had landed in the "mush pile" twice, trying to catch Bug. "This has to be the most insipid game the universe has ever seen," she commented.

Cyrus turned his attention to her and raised one dark brow. "I thought you didn't play games."

"I don't." She picked up a piece of crumpled paper and tossed it through the open bulkhead door into the cargo bay. Tuz chased after it, disappearing into the storage area.

"Why is that?" he asked. After the endless hours locked in the tiny confines of the ship, she'd learned how to read him pretty well. So far, his inflection was neutral, but this was the type of conversation that had gotten her into infuriating circular logic with him earlier.

He already pointed out that basing a system of government on physical prowess in war was an outdated way of thinking in the modern era then pulled apart every cultural idiosyncrasy Azra had. She was tired of defending herself and her people from his backhanded logic.

But then there were other times when he was nearly friendly. That was strange, a situation she wasn't used to handling. She didn't have many friends. Deep in her heart she wondered if she really had any, or if the people that seemed to enjoy being in her company only did so to gain greater positions of power.

"I never have played games," she admitted. "I've never had the time." It wasn't that she didn't have the inclination; her life was far too serious. Only sparring gave her a sense of enjoyment, but she wasn't sure if that counted as fun.

"Do you want to?" He smiled again. The man smiled too often and easily. She didn't trust it, but she found she craved it. Not that she'd ever admit it to him.

Now that they were nearing the port of Gansai, she was going ship-crazy. All in all, it hadn't been a terrible passage, but having her world reduced to four bunks, an empty bay, and an attractive man in a worn pilot's chair had taken its toll.

She frowned. Did she just think of Cyrus as attractive? She was going mad. He was an ass. At first the silence of the ship was comforting, but that last thought was clear proof it was driving her insane.

It was the little things that were getting to her. Cyrus had cooked for her the night before, then left her to eat alone. He'd returned to his pilot's seat. He spent most of his time there. She suspected he slept in the chair, too, if he slept at all.

She hadn't slept much either. Being in the bunk made her uneasy. Completely relaxing in his presence was out of the question. Tuz slept in the crook of her arm next to her chest, and she knew if anything came near her, the cat would take its head off.

But, for all of his verbal tricks, she trusted that Cyrus wouldn't harm her. She couldn't sleep because every time she tried to relax, she could picture him in the bed, his dark eyes sleepy and full of languid pleasure as her hand strayed over the scar on his bare chest.

She trembled.

"Yara?"

She returned her attention to the captain. "I'm sorry, what?"

"Do you want to play?" He leaned back, letting the hand holding his cards fall down near his thigh. Yara's eyes followed the cards and lingered on the worn material of his Earthlen jeans. She wondered what the material felt like. The people of Earth didn't wear the canvas pants out of tradition, or even style preferences really, but had maintained the fashion for generations simply because they *liked* them. The pants had caught on fast, and now several planets enjoyed them.

It was a foreign idea for her—liking something for no reason other than pleasure. She'd been given what she needed to hone her skills. She'd never been allowed to keep anything simply because she liked it, not even a damn pillow.

Her family had wealth, they had the lineage, but they hadn't produced a daughter capable of becoming one of the Elite in four generations. Her mother married her father after her father's sister won prestige as a rising star in the training class, but she ended up washing out the hard way. She didn't survive. The training accident left her mother disappointed in Yara's bloodline and her father insecure about his status in the family.

Yara figured out really early that nothing mattered but making it into the training. Once she made it into the training, nothing mattered except being the best in her class and becoming a full Elite. Now nothing mattered but being named heir to the throne. None of the others had the popular support Yara had. Now that Cyani was out of the picture, no one had her skill. She'd be the next Grand Sister, and perhaps her parents would finally be happy.

"Hey, Yara," Cyrus called as he thumped her on the arm.

Yara's thoughts snapped to focus as his hand settled on her shoulder then slid down to her elbow. His warm palm chased a fleeting tingle down her skin.

"Don't you dare touch me," she scolded, horrified that she broke out in chill prickles at his touch. She whacked him on the shoulder to make her point, then realized Cyrus would probably take her to task and call her a hypocrite for touching him while simultaneously chastising him for touching her.

"Are you back with me? You completely tuned out." He seemed concerned. "Do you have lag?"

"I'm fine, just tired." Maybe the trip was getting to her. Mild cases of lag caused depression, but severe lack of mental stimulation in the confines of a ship had been known to cause a series of mental illnesses from dementia to full psychosis in certain species. It was part of the reason people were so suspicious of traders. Some races were more susceptible to lag than others. Azralen were particularly sensitive to it. Her people needed exposure to natural light to survive. The artificial lights in the ship didn't help regulate their bodies.

Was she getting ill? Or was it something else?

The captain ran a hand over his face, and one stray inky curl fell near his brow by his dark eye. She was willing to bet he looked glorious naked.

By Ona the Pure, she was losing her mind.

"Come on," Cyrus ordered as he tossed his cards into the pile. "You need to do something. You're lagging out on me." Bug, who had been winning, chattered angrily at him.

Yara crossed her arms. "Where are we going to go? On a little stroll outside?" Since she had nothing else to do, she got up and followed him into the cargo bay. She noticed how nice his backside looked in those faded blue pants. She was sick; she was very, very sick. She looked away from Cyrus and turned her attention to her cat.

Tuz batted at a loose case strap dangling from the sidewall through the holes in one of the support beams that circled the vacuous cargo area like great iron ribs. Even her cat was going stir crazy. He had taken to stalking both Bug and Cyrus and "singing" during the night cycle. He yowled so loudly, it rattled the cases at the ends of the bunks.

Cyrus's boots clicked on the smooth metal beneath their feet. He detached a pair of handles from an older model angrav lift and tossed her one. The meter-long tube of metal felt cold and solid in her fist, and smelled like overused joint grease. It focused her thoughts and she felt the urge to smile at him.

"What are you suggesting?" She twirled the bar, spinning it behind her back and then over her head. It made a slight whistling sound as it sliced through the still air of the empty room.

Cyrus shrugged off his vest, rolled up his loose sleeves past the bracers he constantly wore on his arms, and then widened his stance. He slowly lowered his center, dropping his point of balance low to the ground.

Did he want to spar with her? The man was insane. She'd whip him before he could blink twice.

"You can't be serious." She twirled the bar again and then adjusted her own stance before finding a good grip on the makeshift weapon. She tested out her footing in the fine layer of dust. While it helped reduce friction when moving cargo, it would make sparring tricky.

"C'mon, Pix. You've been dying to beat me with a stick from the moment you met me."

Oh yeah, she was ready.

She smiled.

CYN HAD TO TAKE A STEP BACK. IT WAS ONLY A QUIRK OF HER FULL LIPS ON either end, but it was the first time he'd seen her smile where it didn't look like she was faking it. Her smile softened her features and made her haphazard hair seem playful. He had intended to get their blood flowing; he hadn't intended for it to pool in the places that were responding to her now. She was hot. Her smile made her pretty.

That was a scary thought.

*Keep control of yourself.*

The smile faded as she looked down at the bar in her hands. He didn't want to lose her interest. He liked her attention.

"What? Afraid I'm going to fight like a girl?" he teased. His heart skipped and sped up with a sudden rush of adrenaline as her competitive spirit burned in her golden eyes. That got her back in the game.

"I don't want to hurt you," she admitted. "Too badly, anyway."

Cyn chuckled low. Damn it. It was too bad he was in the process of kidnapping her. Sometimes he almost liked her. He kept his bar in a defensive position. He wanted her to strike first. It gave him a better shot at scoring on the rebound. Of course, he didn't know what the rules of this game were going to be. That was another good reason to wait for the lady to move first.

Circling to her right, he taunted her by opening up his defenses just enough to give her motivation to strike. He tapped the end of the bar against the cargo floor as he circled. The metallic *ping-ping* reverberated in the bay and rang in his ears. He needed to unnerve her, make her strike without thinking. Her posture wasn't as closed as his. She was underestimating him.

That didn't surprise him. The men of Azra weren't allowed to train to fight. They were confined to artisan positions in the middle class. In the high classes their worth was defined by their sisters' talent in the Elite training rituals. Women who washed out of the Elite sought men as husbands whose sisters succeeded in the trials in the hopes that their daughters would be strong. High-born sons were considered a waste.

What had started because of women's superior skill in arboreal combat morphed into traditions that served no purpose other than preventing men from ever gaining significant power in the ruling order. Tradition alone kept men inferior to women, reducing them to nothing more than walking sperm banks for maintaining female bloodlines.

Cyn had every intention of changing that. The men of Azra could fight. They needed to fight. They *wanted* to fight.

He wanted this fight.

Yara swung at him and he blocked. The clang of metal

striking metal echoed in the empty cargo bay. He broke her strike, dodged a second quick blow, and spun out to the left.

Yara pursued, using the momentum from a leaping attack to drive him back toward the crates.

Again, their weapons met with bone-crushing force.

Their gazes locked.

Yara felt the rush of adrenaline and a flood of something softer, warmer, in her blood.

"Feeling better?" Cyrus asked. He deftly circled his weapon, spinning hers off of his with a sharp grind of metal on metal, breaking the strike. She shifted her weight to maintain her balance as she focused on controlling her muscles and her heart.

She drew in a quick breath as he moved in to her. It slowed her reaction enough for him to turn and nearly strike her shoulder. She barely had time to crouch, spin, and block the attack. She felt the clash of the two bars in her taut muscles. He wasn't playing nice. He intended to knock her well enough for her to feel it for a week.

She had to be careful.

He wasn't bad.

"You sure you want to do this?" she asked.

"Absolutely."

They broke away and started circling again. Their feet fell in sync with one another, tapping in a slow rhythm accented by soft shuffles on the scuffed floor.

"How did you learn to fight?" she asked, genuinely interested in his answer.

"What is it about Azralen women that makes them think everyone in the universe does things the way they do?" he teased, throwing her words from several days ago back at her. He smiled then continued. "Earth has a long martial tradition created by men."

"But why did you take it up?" She changed the position of her weapon, and then as he adjusted his stance, she struck at him. Again, he blocked her blow with a skillful spin of his bar.

"Good exercise and the mental control helps fight lag." He advanced, his bar clattering against hers in a quick pattern of sharp strikes against her weapon. She was forced to retreat, unused to the style of attack.

"Fair enough." She stopped the next strike with a solid block, locking them together so they came face-to-face.

They lingered there for a moment and Cyrus's gaze slowly drifted to dwell on her lips.

Yara's breath stopped in her chest. He tilted his head just slightly. It was a provocative invitation.

"Don't even think about it," she warned, but she couldn't bring herself to back away.

"Think about what?" he asked as he edged his chin forward. She tilted her own head, exposing her neck to him.

"You know what."

She could feel the heat of his body in the cold empty space of the bay. Standing so close to him made her muscles feel loose and heavy.

"Earthlen aren't known for their mind-reading abilities," he murmured. "Why don't you spell it out for me?"

She whopped him on the side of the thigh with her bar.

"Ow." He hobbled away from her, clutching his thigh. Then he laughed.

"Why are you laughing?" She lowered her weapon in disbelief. "I just gave you a bruise that should be green for a week."

"I think I like the way you play, Pix." He shook it out, then brought his bar up.

"I'm not playing." She twirled hers again and jumped forward with another pair of quick strikes. It forced his weight back on his bruised thigh, but he didn't flinch.

Damn, he was strong.

She tried to swallow the lump in her throat. It felt like her pulse pounded in every centimeter of her body. It radiated out from a place just behind her navel and seemed to float by the time it reached her head. He made her feel *hungry*.

"Are you sure?"

This had to be lag. There was no other explanation for her completely losing her mind.

No, she couldn't do this anymore. She tossed her bar at him, and he caught it, immediately turning it into a fast spin before tucking it down and behind his shoulder.

"I think that's enough distraction for today," she stated. Sparring with him was dangerous. She needed to be careful. She had a lot more at stake now than when she was younger and more reckless. She'd been overconfident in her position with the Elite. She didn't want to end up like Cyori, pregnant and banished to the shadows just before she inherited the throne.

Bug zipped into the room, his aura pulsing bright green. He let out a sharp whistle.

Cyrus looked at his pet with his brow knit. "What?"

Bug spun around Cyrus's head at a dizzying speed as he let out a short series of clicks, then another sharp whistle.

The hairs rose up on the backs of her arms, and she felt the urge to rub the white falcon tattoos there. What was going on?

Yara knew a warning when she heard it.

Cyrus dropped the bars with a loud clatter and ran through the bulkhead door. Yara followed him into the living quarters. He launched himself into the pilot's seat and scanned the strings of code scrolling in front of him.

"Shit," he whispered, then shouted, "Brace yourself!"

A heart-stopping *boom* pounded in the air as the ship tumbled, throwing Yara into the sidewall by the beds. Pain lanced through her body as her shoulder and head smashed against the hard wall. She fell onto the bunk and grasped the edge while her head throbbed.

She held on. The room around her blurred as her eyes tried to focus, but it was no use. The ship shook with such force one of the lockers broke its tether bolts and crashed to the floor.

Cyrus braced himself and initiated the energy net to protect the control center. Tuz raced under her bunk.

"What was that?" she shouted at Cyrus above an ominous rumbling coursing through the ship. He was too busy punching commands into the console.

Another thunderous *boom* shook the ship, followed by a second violent round of shaking. Yara did her best to hang on as one of the panels that hid the cases dislodged from the sidewall. It smashed into her injured shoulder, sending a new wave of agony rushing through her body.

She felt herself go weightless, and then gravity reengaged but at a lower threshold than Union standard gravity. The swooping feeling made her stomach turn in knots, but she didn't have the luxury of giving in to it.

Cyrus jumped off his seat, pushed through the energy field protecting the controls, and ran to the galley, each stride looking like a leap. "Get your weapons," he commanded.

He ripped open a locker and grabbed a DEC pulse gun. Yara grabbed for her bag and pulled out a sono to complement the knife she always wore on her belt.

"What is going on?" Her heart raced. For all her Elite training, and her five years in service with the Union, she'd never seen live fire.

"We got tossed by an energy web. They're coming."

The lights flickered then died. Only Bug's glow illuminated the quarters. Suddenly Yara felt the heavy weight of gravity increase to a level far higher than Union standard.

Cyrus had the hard look of a soldier as dim red lights along the sidewalls started to glow.

The temperature inside the ship plummeted.

Yara felt the chill in the air seep into her skin and heart.

The unmistakable groan of metal reverberated through the ship as it lurched. Another ship had docked with theirs.

Every sound grated on her nerves as Cyrus took her hand and pulled her into the empty cargo bay.

"Keep to my back. They'll send the bots first, then the men. I'll take out as many as I can with the DEC. Shoot to kill." He brought the DEC to his shoulder and aimed it at the closed cargo ramp. "Bug, stay in the control center and work on getting systems back up. Keep the security link open so you can hear us." Bug flew back into the living quarters and Cyrus shut and sealed the bulkhead door.

Yara took a deep breath, and let it out slowly. The vapor curled around her face as she braced herself for attack.

"Tuz," she ordered as her cat stalked to her side. "Attack and kill."

He purred.

A hollow grinding echoed through the bay as the cargo ramp cracked open.

"What's out there?" she demanded. She needed to know what they were facing.

"Spiders." Cyn cocked his gun and fired the first shot into the void.

# 4

YARA FOUGHT HER TERROR AS NINE LARGE BOTS THE SIZE OF WOLVES PULLED their fat and dented bodies through the gap in the cargo ramp. Their glowing red optic sensors scanned the bay while scorpion-like tails whipped over their bodies. At the end of each tail a paralyzing shock charge glowed with an eerie light.

"Aim for the eye, and don't get stung," Cyrus shouted as he fired three quick shots off the DEC. Two of the bots tumbled back toward the ramp, their bodies crashing in a cacophony of noise as they hit.

The seven remaining bots hugged the edge of the bay, scurrying around the outer rim of the compartment. Four moved to the left as three shifted to the right to fill in the gaps in their loose arc. Yara fired at the one closest to the bulkhead door, but the blast dissolved into a sizzling web of fractured light spreading out in a dome in front of the metal creatures.

"Shit." Cyn threw his gun at one of the bots. "My DEC is out of charge and they're shielded against blasters. We need to bash them." He whipped two knives out of the bracers on his forearms and flung them through the air. The knives sank into the eyes of two different bots. Electricity shot out of the damaged scorpions as they collapsed on the deck in spasms, their legs flailing in the air like dying roaches.

Yara turned just as a bot pulled his tail back to strike. "Cyrus, look out!" Yara shoved him to the side as she gripped her own knife and force-kicked. Her heel connected with the hard shell of the machine's body. The tail swung dangerously close to her as it crashed back into another one.

Yara ran to the fallen scorpion and twisted her body to lure the bot to strike. She felt her shoulders strain as she bent backward to avoid the stinger, while simultaneously grabbing the tail and guiding the jab into the eye of the other overturned bot. Yara leapt back toward Cyrus, the sting of the discharge searing into her legs as both bots froze in a net of webbed lightning before sparking out.

"Bug! Reactivate the hatch locks," Cyrus shouted at the security link in the corner. "Yara, cover me."

Cyrus yanked up a floor panel.

The three remaining scorpions inched closer, stabbing their tails in the air. Yara could feel the numbing energy of the shock charges tingle over her skin. She gripped her knife tighter as Tuz leaned against the back of her calf. He hissed, the sound blending with the hum of the bots.

In the corner of her eye, Yara spotted the handles she'd used to spar with Cyrus.

"Tuz, handle." Yara reached her hand down and Tuz curled his tail around her wrist. With all her strength, she whipped the cat straight up into the air.

The motion distracted two of the bots, but the third struck at exactly that moment. Yara had to dive into Cyrus to prevent getting hit. He cursed at her then connected a conduit as Tuz landed on the far side of the room.

The cat pounced on the metal pipe, knocking it across the cargo floor and through the spiderlike legs of one of the scorpions.

Yara grabbed it, ducking under the glowing stinger as it flew over her head.

"Got it," Cyrus shouted as he kicked out, knocking three metallic legs off balance.

Tuz ran around the bay, looking like a black streak of shadow as the bots tried to follow him. They couldn't get a fix on her scout.

Yara leapt in the air, spinning the bar over her head as she landed to the side of one of the bots. She brought the bar down on top of the optic in a smashing blow that shook the bones in her arms and shoulders.

She didn't have time to lose her breath or focus. Counting on her training for survival, she charged after the one chasing her scout.

"Yara!" Cyrus shouted as a bot righted itself. She tossed him her knife, then gripped the very end of the pole and slashed it into the body of the creature ahead of her.

The blow knocked the bot into the crates strapped to the bulkhead. She had to dodge to her right as its tail whipped back at her. Yara flipped the bar into her hands and used the end to crack the stinger, then jabbed the bar with all her force into the optic.

She spared a glance back at Cyrus, just in time to see him sink her knife into the optic of the final bot.

Just then a hole opened up in the sidewall to the left. Cyrus ran at her and pushed her inside. She tumbled backward and down, crashing onto a grate below her.

"*Shakt*," she shouted, clutching her bruised shoulder as Cyrus landed next to her. Tuz jumped through the gap just before it closed, landing on Cyrus's head.

"Damn it, get off," he tried to grab her cat by the scruff, but Tuz sank his fangs into his hand.

"Tuz, let go," she commanded.

Tuz growled and leapt down to her. The light from the open hatch went out, throwing them into complete darkness.

Tuz activated his collar, illuminating the room in a pale blue light. Where were they? "What in the name of Fima the Merciless is going on?" she shouted.

"Keep it down," Cyrus ordered as he pressed his hand to a nasty scratch on his forehead. "Spiders are pirates, bloody opportunistic mercenaries. They send the bots in to paralyze any crew, then ransack the ship for anything they can sell, including people. They usually hit weak trade vessels too poor to travel by macrospace or defend themselves. They aren't planning on us fighting back."

Yara looked around the cramped hole. They were in a protected pocket built into the side of the ship. Unlabeled shipping crates rose in tall stacks wedged between the solid frames of the ship.

"With what?" Yara whispered. "I only have one sono, the DEC burned out, and we left all our knives up there."

Cyrus placed his fingertips on a lock, and opened the top of one of the crates. He pulled out two projectile rifles and tossed one to her. Yara nearly let the thing clatter to the grate. It felt hard and dirty in her hands. With a long barrel and the worn black casing of a highly efficient discharger, it was a weapon of deadly practicality, a cruel and bloody thing.

"These are illegal."

"I don't think Spiders are going to turn us in to the Union for breaking arms treaties." Cyrus snapped an ammunition charge into the rifle. "Listen to me. They will kill us if we don't get them to back off. Bloody them, and they'll do a little profit analysis in their head. They don't fight well as a group, and if the ones coming in think they won't make it back out, they'll go find an easier target."

"How many?" Yara asked as she gripped the rifle tighter.

"I don't know. If we can take out more than ten, we should be good." Cyrus pointed above them. "Climb up to the top-load hatch on this side. I'll be on the far side. That will get us above them, and we'll catch them in our crossfire."

Yara saw him for the first time in a new and uncertain light.

He wasn't lying when he said he was smuggling illegal weapons. He was no honest or harmless trader. He had every intention of spilling a lot of blood to protect what was his.

Her hands shook with the letdown of adrenaline and her dawning horror.

"Do you know what they're armed with?" she asked. She had to keep her head clear and rely on her training.

"Anything you can buy on the shadow markets, which includes things a lot nastier than projectile weapons. We have to shoot first or we're dead." He held no apology in his hard expression. His dark eyes, made even darker by the deep shadows, turned as deadly as the rifle in his hands.

Yara felt the chill slide down her back.

Cyrus cocked his gun, the sharp click echoing through the dark. She watched the muscle in his jaw twitch as he reached back into the crate and pulled out several long knives. Their sharp blades gleamed in the dim light. "If one of us drops for some reason, stop shooting. The ricocheted projectiles are going to get nasty. We'll have to go in with these."

"That doesn't sound like good odds," she commented.

"Don't fall."

Yara tested the weight of a half-meter blade. It was as nasty and cruel a weapon as the projectile beside her. Blades injured. They cut and bled. And yet she had trained with them from the time she was three.

But she had never used them in earnest until now.

Without saying a word, he was pointing out her hypocrisy once again.

She checked her sono. It was a cold, clean weapon. A guilt-free, no-mess solution. The end result was the same, and so it was no kinder.

Blaster or knife, she had to come to terms with the idea that whoever was up there was going to kill her, if she didn't kill them first.

She arranged her grip on her sono so she could more easily fire.

The freezing air seeped into her skin as she listened to the footsteps on the floor above them.

Cyrus offered her a hand then pulled her in close. His warm breath caressed her cheek as he whispered in her ear.

"Climb up the rungs between the stacked crates behind you. Take Tuz. When the hatches open, start firing. It needs to be a bloodbath, or they won't retreat." His fingertips brushed her hair, and she placed her hand on his chest for balance.

She could feel the harsh ridge of his scar beneath the material of his shirt.

"Yara?" he continued. She met his hardened gaze. "Don't hesitate."

She nodded.

With practiced stealth, she climbed up the rung ladder as he disappeared into the darkness. Tuz clung to her shoulder, his claws digging into the fabric of her shirt.

Voices sounded muffled and tinny through the sidewalls. She didn't understand the language, but the confused tone was unmistakable. Their prey would be wary.

Would she have the strength to act?

She thought about her old training partner, Cyani. Her rival beat her more times than not when they sparred, and for the first time, Yara realized why. Cyani knew what it was like to fight for her life.

"Wherever you are, Cyani, thank you," she whispered. She knew what to do. Cyani had shown her. *Don't hesitate.*

Yara reached the hatch and perched on the top of the stack of crates to her right. The hatch was large enough to push smaller top-load crates into the secret compartment. She'd be too exposed once it opened. Pressing her back as far as she could into the closest frame, she waited. Each noise echoed in her ears and made her heart stutter in her chest. She had never felt the rush of such stark terror. She fought to control herself, chanting training mantras over and over in her head.

*By Isa, my hands are swift. By Esana, my eyes are clear. By Fima, I have the will to strike and kill.*

She lifted her sono, ready to fire.

The hatch doors released, clattering to the floor.

Cyrus's gunfire filled the bay, the staccato shots ricocheting off the sidewalls as they embedded themselves in the dirty group of men. The men scrambled, gathering weapons and looking up at the open hatches even as they shouted and fell, blood bursting from open projectile wounds.

Yara focused, aimed, fired, repeating the pattern over and over. Some fell. She couldn't tell how many she hit. They collapsed to the cold floor. She didn't have the luxury to think. She had to wedge herself to the side of the open hatch and hold on for her life as a shock blast fired through the hatch, crashing into the fuselage behind her. The spent energy made her skin tingle and go numb, but she turned and fired into the fray below.

Tuz leapt out of the hatch with a terrifying war-scream and landed on the head of one of the men. The man's shout was cut short as Tuz's thick tail wrapped around his neck, choking him.

One of the pirates raised a blaster to her scout, and Yara fired on instinct. She missed. The pirate shot at Tuz, but her cat leapt just in time. She had to get him out of there.

Yara held her breath and jumped.

She landed on the ground, immediately swinging her blade. It cut across the back of the thigh of one of the men, as she fired her sono at the pirate rushing toward her.

"Yara!" Cyrus shouted.

She leapt and wielded the blade beneath her, feeling it connect with flesh again. Time seemed to slow, and her body felt heavy and weak as her muscles moved from instinct honed by years of repetitive motion and training. Her blade couldn't swing fast enough. She couldn't strike hard enough. The room sounded like it was filled with water, the only clear sound the constant drumming beat of her heart.

She fired her sono again. In the corner of her eye she saw Cyrus drop into the thick of the crowd. He became a blur of deadly motion as his blade whipped through the air. "Bug!" he stabbed one of the pirates in the chest. "Initiate defense charges!"

Sono blasts reverberated in the bay as Yara ducked. Tuz darted through the crowd, his claws and teeth sinking into the calves of the pirates, distracting them whenever they focused their wild eyes on her.

She caught sight of one at the ramp. He started to enter, then turned around.

"Cyrus," she shouted. He turned and saw the pirate retreating, but one of the mudrats stabbed a blade into Cyrus's thigh. He roared and swiftly cut through the man's arm.

Her distraction cost her. A ripping burn lanced into her shoulder, tearing her nerves as she watched a bright splash of blood fall to the floor. Her breath slammed out of her lungs as she fell forward onto her hands.

Her vision blurred, but she rolled and fired at her attacker. She didn't know what hit her but could feel her blood rushing down her arm.

"Yara!" Cyrus shouted.

She barely comprehended the fall of bodies or the smell of

death as she fought back to her feet, grabbing her blade in her weak hand.

Tuz screamed, the haunting sound distracting their attackers as more of the wounded crawled back through the gaping ramp.

Cyn rushed forward, desperately grabbing one of the blasters off the floor. He fired, dropping any pirate still moving, as he fought to reach Yara. She tried to swing her blade, but her bloody arm fell back to her side.

"Get the fuck off my ship!" he shouted, his rage burning as intensely as the pain in his thigh.

He shot another one in the head. The pirate spun as he fell, flinging blood in an arc against the sidewall.

The pirates threw their bloody bodies back through the open ramp, dragging several of their fallen with them.

Good, less for him to clean up.

"Bug, fire charges now," he shouted. Bug's affirmative whistle broke through the speakers in the security link.

He couldn't give them time to regroup.

The emergency lights flickered, then dimmed, covering him in shadow.

Cyn accessed the control panel at the back of the bay and secured the ramp.

Blood soaked into his jeans, trickling down into his sock. He spared a quick glance at Yara. She swayed, but remained on her feet, kicking weapons away from the fallen.

"Damn it, Bug, hit the charge."

A series of loud explosions rocked the ship, and the ship groaned as it peeled away from the clutches of the pirate's docking link.

"Jump us forward," he ordered. Bug's loud beeps rang through the speakers. "I don't care what it takes, just do it. Yara, you okay?"

She turned to him, her eyes glazed. The blast wound cut through her shoulder. It looked ugly, like some beast had chewed a chunk out of her muscle. Blood dripped off her limp fingertips onto the slick floor. He had to stop her bleeding before they both passed out.

Pressing a hand to the wound on his thigh, he limped to her and lifted her good arm over his shoulder. She accepted his help without protest as he opened the bulkhead door to the living quarters and helped her to a bed.

"We don't know if they're all dead," she stated, closing her eyes briefly, then shaking her head and blinking as if trying to wake herself up.

He wiped his thumb over her forehead, smearing a trickle of blood there. "Tuz will take care of them. Are you wounded anywhere else?"

The ship shifted beneath his feet, and he nearly fell over. His limbs ached, his head screamed, and amidst all of it, a choking feeling clenched in his chest. He didn't have time to wallow in ugly memories. He had work to do.

Using every milligram of mental strength he had, he focused on the task at hand.

"I'm okay," she insisted.

"That's a load of shit." With a knife, he sliced Yara's shirt away from the gaping wound. The torn and singed muscle wouldn't pull together and heal easily. He'd have to use a knitter. "This is bad."

He had to stop the bleeding fast. He threw open one of the

lockers and swiped all the contents onto the floor. He found his med kit and tossed it onto the bunk, then opened one of the cases and pulled out a large jug of kiltii water.

"Drink as much of this as you can," he insisted as he pressed a bandage into her wound and then poured some of the water on it. He tied the bandage as tight as he could, then found his cup and filled it with the water.

"Are we safe?" she asked before downing the glass of elixir and coughing. The jarring cough made her shoulder bleed worse.

"Don't know." He inspected a cut at her hairline then let her wispy hair slide through his bloody fingers as he reached for his med instruments.

He took a deep breath, then let his mind loose. Shifting through the waves of information flowing through his consciousness, he plucked out the relevant medical data on repairing flesh wounds, and brought it to the forefront of his mind.

"Bug, are they following?" he asked.

"*Pip!*"

"Let out a cluster of mines just in case." Cyn grabbed the med sterilizer. His leg throbbed.

"The next time your cat decides to drop into a crowd of bloodthirsty pirates, could he at least be considerate enough to get hurt, too?" Cyn grumbled. He had to keep her focused on him. "At least there's some good news."

"Yeah?"

"I think your lag is gone."

She huffed, but the corner of her mouth twitched.

He took a quick drink of the kiltii water himself and shuddered as a rush of heat poured through his body. The plant extract in the water healed injuries quickly, but not quickly enough if he couldn't stop her bleeding.

He filled the cup again. "Drink it," he commanded.

"What is it?" she asked as she drank more of it and groaned.

"It speeds healing." He filled the cup one more time and handed it to her before untying the bandage. The raw flesh looked pink for only a second before blood seeped out of the torn tissue. He ran the sterilizer over the wound and grabbed the knitter.

"I'm sorry, Pix. This is going to suck."

Holding her as tightly as he could, he initiated the knitter. The small instrument glowed bright blue in his hand as he touched it to the wound. The skin around the knitter turned white and sizzled as the smell of burnt blood filled the room.

Yara screamed.

Her hands gripped his thigh and arm, squeezing so tight, her nails cut into him through his blood-soaked jeans.

"Hang on, baby," he whispered, holding tight to the knitter even as her blood flowed over his hand. Every muscle in her body had contracted with the pain. "It's almost over."

He felt a forceful thump at his back, as knifelike claws dug into his shoulder.

"Bug, get Tuz!" he shouted. All he needed was for her scout to kill him.

"*Werp, wheeeeeeeeeee!*" Bug fired off discharges at the cat. Tuz yowled and leapt off Cyn's back.

Cyn concentrated on the wound as he used the knitter to pull the gaping flesh back together, leaving a clean but ugly scab over the hole in her shoulder.

Yara grabbed his forearm, clinging to his bracer. Her glazed eyes locked with his. His own memories of being knit without tranqs overwhelmed him. God, she was in so much pain.

He could feel the stabbing, burning as if he were feeling it in the moment, not years ago.

Finally he turned the thing off.

Yara inhaled, her breath filling her lungs with a shaky hiss.

"You okay?" he asked, offering her another drink.

She nodded and tried to take the cup, but her hand shook so badly, she couldn't lift it.

Cyn wrapped his hand over her elegant fingers and let his palm slide over the soft skin of the back of her neck as he lifted her toward him. He helped her bring the cup to her lips.

When she finished drinking, he let her hand fall but kept ahold of her neck. The woman had guts. He felt the knot in his stomach tighten.

Her beautiful golden eyes blinked slowly, as a drop of moisture from the kiltii water clung to her full lower lip.

He found himself transfixed on that drop of water, longing to taste it. He could feel the adrenaline in his blood beginning to wane. The shaky loose feeling in his body overtook his senses. He wanted to taste her so badly.

"You did good," he murmured. She was glorious. She lived up to the promise of her royal blood. She'd been amazing. His body burned with battle lust. It would be so easy to fall down on the bed and pull her into his aching body.

He brushed his thumb behind her slightly pointed ear and leaned closer, inhaling the scent of her hair, hoping it would wash away the scent of death and blood all around them.

She didn't pull away as his cheek brushed hers. He leaned back just enough to look her in the eyes again.

Her expression had softened with relief, relief and something else, something raw and potent.

He held his breath, leaning in until his lower lip barely brushed the warm skin of hers.

She stiffened.

This was wrong. *She is the enemy.*

Damn it, he couldn't do this. Cyn pulled away, letting her fall gently back onto the pillows. She watched him with those sex-honey eyes as she pressed a protective hand over the wound above her heart.

Ona help him, he wanted her.

What was he going to do?

# 5

YARA FELT HER HEART BEAT WITH A STEADY, ACHING RHYTHM. SHE LET HER hand linger over the wound as Cyrus pulled back, but remained sitting on the bed.

He had almost kissed her.

*She wanted it.*

Ona be blind, she wanted him to kiss her so bad she could feel the ache of it deep in her belly. Weak and shaking, she reclined on the bed and tried to steady her breath.

She watched his expression change, subtle shifts in his shadowed eyes. His thick fringe of dark lashes only made his eyes seem deeper and more mysterious, and the smear of blood across his cheekbone woke something primitive and wild in her.

The man was glorious, and she was attracted to him on a

visceral level. Damn it. She stared at his lower lip, the slightly rough contour of his chin and jaw. What would that jaw feel like brushing against the tender skin of her cheek? How would his lips taste?

She dropped her gaze to her lap, but he still hadn't stood. The pressure of his weight on the bed tipped her thigh against his lean hip.

Her body felt like it was on fire as she took her thoughts further. He would never be submissive in bed. Even if she managed to tie him down, somehow he'd dominate her. It was his nature. He wouldn't surrender. That much was clear. He had soaked his ship, his *home* in blood, and never once backed down or gave in to fear.

A wave of dizziness forced her to close her eyes as a rush of adrenaline made her limbs tingle.

She had to get off of his ship.

"Yara, are you okay?" he asked.

"No," she answered, letting him interpret that however he wanted.

He finally stood, pulling his heat with him as he lifted the overturned locker and cleared a path to the bed behind the pilot seat with several stiff sweeps of his foot. "Take off your shirt, clean off the blood in the cleanser, and then you need to rest."

Yara pulled her aching body upright. The echoes of pain throbbed in her shoulder and ribs as she tenderly peeled her blood-soaked sleeve off her wounded arm. She struggled to get it over her head, but finally managed to get the ruined shirt off, leaving her in nothing but her support.

Cyrus's eyes fixed on her cleavage. She scowled at him and covered it with her hand. "Do you mind?"

"Not at all." His wit lacked its usual warmth and he turned away from her to clear off the other bed. She could see the frustration bunching in his shoulders.

Yara felt it, too. She stumbled into the small cleanser and fell to a seat. Resting her head in her hands, she enjoyed the feel of the warm air swirling around her. When the last of the sticky grime had lifted off her skin, she forced herself to stand and enter the living quarters again.

Cyrus sat on the edge of the bed nearest the pilot's chair, the covers neatly turned down. "Come here," he instructed, his voice clipped and cold. She was too exhausted to argue. It wouldn't be much longer and she'd pass out to heal.

She eased onto the bed as he offered her a soft black shirt. "Thanks," she murmured as she tried to pull it over her head, but she couldn't lift her arm. Cyrus slid the warm material over her back and gently helped her ease her wounded arm into it. The cool reserve in his demeanor didn't translate to his touch.

She fell back onto the soft pillows, while he tenderly pulled her boots off and tucked her legs under the covers.

With the rush of adrenaline gone and the pain still lingering, she felt empty and cold all of a sudden. Her thoughts felt scattered and sluggish, and a thick depression fell over her mind and body.

Cyrus pulled the blanket up. It didn't smell like the other one had. It smelled warm and slightly musty, like salt and heat.

He smoothed the blanket near her hip.

"This is your bed, isn't it?"

"Yeah." He shrugged as if the answer didn't mean anything to him, but the way he stroked the blanket said otherwise.

Yara relaxed her neck and let her heavy head sink deeper into the clean pillow. "It's nice," she offered.

"Thank you."

She didn't say anything for a long time, and he didn't seem in a hurry to move either. The stillness of the ship and his presence were comforting as her mind tried to sort through the horror she'd just witnessed.

"Am I going to scar?" She tried to keep her eyes open but couldn't. Her shoulder still throbbed, but the pain had lessened to a dull ache. The heat in her body felt like it was radiating out in waves. She couldn't get the images of dying men out of her head. Their faces haunted her.

"Probably." His voice sounded melodic in the peaceful quiet of the ship. She could hear the low hum of the systems, punctuated by a pip or chirp from Bug. Somehow she knew he wasn't talking about her shoulder, but something much deeper.

"How many have you killed, Cyrus?" she asked.

He rose from the bed and retreated to the control center.

"Do you know?" she asked. Staring overhead, she tried to determine how many she had killed in the battle. Her memories were like a jumble of noise, visions of faces and blood.

"I know." He answered with clear and simple conviction, and a note of melancholy that matched her dark mood. "Get some sleep, Yara."

YARA WOKE TO THE GROWL OF HER STOMACH, FEELING HUNGRIER THAN SHE ever had in her life. She ran a sleepy hand through the front of her hair and looked around the room with bleary eyes.

It looked as it always had—immaculate. She sat and questioned reality for a moment, trying to determine if the Spider attack had all been a crazy lag-induced dream.

A loud purr vibrated her feet. She looked down at Tuz, blissfully licking his claws. She'd never seen him so calm or content.

She reached out to pet him, when the sharp pain in her shoulder brought everything snapping back into crystal clarity. She sent a quick prayer of thanks to the Matriarchs. It was a miracle they were still alive.

She wrapped her stiff arms over her chest and inhaled the scent of Cyrus's shirt. Where was he?

Swinging her feet over the side of the bed, she let her head hang over her knees to regain her composure before trying to stand. The ship's lights had come back on, but the air was still cold enough to chill her skin.

She grabbed her com off the top of one of the angrav cases, and eased into the copilot seat. They were in a shipping corridor and had to be near Gansai. If they were close enough to an array, she'd be able to receive any messages from Azra. She linked her com to the ship's system and waited for it to connect. A small square of the viewscreen turned bright white, and then a message appeared.

"*Shakt,*" she whispered.

*Send communication immediately. Palar is restless. Rumors. Must return before fire is lit.*

She didn't have much time left before the coup broke out. Staying on the ship was impossible. There was no time for any more delays or repairs. She needed to be home or her peaceful ascension would be ruined. Tapping her fingers in rapid patterns on the screen, she relayed a simple reply saying she'd be back within days, and urging her supporters to do what it took to keep control of her rival.

Her situation was becoming dangerous—for her, and those that supported her.

Then there was Cyrus, yet another reason she had to get off the ship immediately.

"There's hot soup in the galley," Cyrus called from the bay. A soft swishing noise emanated from the back compartment. What was he doing in there?

Her stomach turned at the thought.

With cautious steps she crossed the quarters to the bay and peeked inside. Cyrus hummed to himself as he ran a glowing san-mop over the cargo floor. Several piles of scorpion parts lay sorted along the sidewall near the ramp, but other than the presence of the dismantled bots and some scorch marks on the sidewalls and the bulkhead, there was no evidence of a fight at all.

Cyrus folded his hands on top of the san-handle. "You'd better eat. Kiltii water works better on a full stomach."

"Noted." She leaned up against the doorframe. "How much longer until we reach port?"

"A couple of hours, tops." He resumed his mopping.

"And the status of the ship?"

Cyn didn't pause his cleaning to consider her question. He didn't like how anxious she sounded. In the course of one day, things had gone terribly wrong, and he had to figure out a way to regain control of the situation.

He still had a job to do. He had to keep her from Azra at all costs.

"The ship is functional."

"Did you sleep at all?"

Cyn threw one of his most charming smiles at her. "Worried about me?"

"No," she quickly denied, but her pale cheeks flushed cool pink.

"Your soup's getting cold." He didn't like the chill that ran down his back. Something was up with her.

And he was exposed. She'd seen the stash of weapons. She'd seen him in battle. There was no way he could continue to play Mr. Innocent.

He didn't know if he could continue to play the seducer anymore either. She'd responded to him.

He knew when a woman wanted sex, and she was oozing it.

Normally that wasn't a problem, but this game was turning dangerous.

As much as he wanted his attraction to her to be entirely physical, it wasn't.

That bothered him.

What could possibly come of this? Was he supposed to ask her out on a date after he destroyed all order on their planet? Yeah, that would go over well. He had to hand her over to the revolution, and then what? He didn't want to think about that. He shuddered. She wasn't supposed to be like this, like a real person. She was supposed to be a brainwashed Elite machine.

Could he hand her over to the revolution? It would be a death sentence, unless there was some way—damn it. He couldn't think too far past the start of the war, or he'd get sick. There was no other way. Azra had to change. His people were dying.

Cyn let the handle fall against the sidewall, needing the loud clang to rattle his thoughts out of his head. Why did the Yar family resemblance have to be so strong? Yara looked like her cousin. Yarlia had lived and died, and Yara didn't even know her kin had ever existed. That's how far apart their worlds really were, and he couldn't forget it. He picked up a piece of scorpion leg and tossed it onto the far pile with another loud clatter.

He *liked* her. That was the problem. Yara was interesting and not what he was expecting. His affection for the unexpected was one of his weaknesses, one he had to be aware of, or she could ruin everything. She was Elite. When it came to the war, she would give her life to protect the status quo.

If only there was another way.

She watched him from the bulkhead door.

"Eat the damn soup, Yara."

"Who are the weapons for?"

*Shit.*

He was half tempted to tell her. "That's none of your business."

"I can't believe you're smuggling projectiles." She crossed her arms, closing herself off.

"I can't believe you're bringing this up," he snapped back at her. "What's your problem?"

"I want . . ." She nearly shouted the words before she choked on them. When she regained her composure, she leveled him with a hard stare. "I want the people I deal with to be honest."

Cyn held back his chuckle of disbelief. That wasn't what she intended to say, but he'd go with it. "I didn't lie to you."

"Ha," she huffed. "It doesn't bother you that innocent people will probably die?" She rubbed the tattoos on her wrist as if the white falcons of the bloodline of Yarini the Just were clawing at her.

He resisted the urge to rub the snakes that marked him as a son of the Rebel. They were biting at him, too. "Innocent people are dying now. Someone has to stop it."

"So you're fine with stoking a war?"

"Sometimes it's needed, *Commander*."

Yara felt the heat of her temper rising in her veins. She just wanted to make it home so she could avoid the bloodshed of a messy transition of power. Why did the lure of the throne mean more to her rival, Palar, than peace? Cyrus wasn't helping things. Their little argument was an effective reminder of why she should never be attracted to a man.

She spun around and grabbed the pot of soup out of the galley then settled into the copilot's seat to eat it.

She wanted it to taste terrible and bitter. Of course it didn't. The bastard seemed to be good at everything.

If she'd tried to make soup, it would have congealed into a sticky gray mass and charred on the bottom.

The thick cream tasted rich, warm and comforting with just the right amount of exotic spice. It filled her with heat and pleasure.

"Damn it," she whispered.

Bug rose up off the console, inspecting the information on the viewscreen with his single beadlike eye.

"*Twip, errrrr, werp buzz EEeeeee.*" His aura turned bright green and swelled as threads of pink light wove in and out.

"We're almost there?" She reached out and switched modes for the viewscreen. In the distance a tiny blue planet glowed in the vastness of space.

Yara looked at the bot. After spending the endless quiet hours of transwave travel with Bug buzzing around "talking" to Cyrus, it scared her that she was beginning to understand him.

"Cyrus?" she called.

He entered the control center and claimed the captain's seat. With quick efficiency, he pulled the top of his hair back and tied it at his crown, leaving the rest to curl against his neck and ears.

Yara focused back on the viewscreen. She shouldn't be looking at him.

Tuz jumped in her lap and sniffed the pot of soup, then placed his front paws on the console so he could stare out at the stars. She stroked her hand down his gray and black coat. This nightmare was almost over.

"I can find passage on another ship once we reach Gansai," she stated.

"That's not a good idea," Cyrus countered with a hard edge in his voice.

"I don't have time to wait for your repairs." This trip had taken far too long already. She'd had enough.

"The repairs won't take long. Gansai is dangerous." He punched a quick set of commands into the console then turned to look at her. He crossed his arms and her attention lingered on the knives in the sheaths of his bracers.

"I made a deal, I intend to honor it," he argued.

"Honor." She didn't bother to hide her sarcasm. "You're a smuggler."

"Don't you trust me?"

"No." It seemed like a cruel thing to say to a man who had just fought beside her. Then again, if they hadn't been limping along in transwave for days on end, they probably wouldn't have been attacked by Spiders in the first place.

"There can be honor among thieves," he mused. "You're free to make your choices, but I'd be very careful whom you trust."

"I can take care of myself."

Cyrus looked like he wanted to say something but didn't. Instead he focused on the screen again as the planet slowly grew.

"Let me talk to my mechanic. I'll find out how long the repairs are going to take. If it is too much of a delay, I'll arrange for someone to take you the rest of the way."

"Fine."

Cyn pinged Xan's ship, relieved to find it somewhere on planet, though the versatile L6 Accipiter must have perched somewhere outside the city. He didn't see Xan's ship codes in the docking logs. He had to think quickly. If he couldn't convince her to stay with him on his ship, he'd need to find someone else who could keep her contained but still sending messages back to Azra so Palar wouldn't strike. Why did starting a war have to be so damn difficult?

Xan could keep Yara detained, but Cyn didn't like to rely on him for things concerning the revolution. Xan was his best friend and brother in all ways but blood. They'd fought and bled together. He'd saved Xan's life, but as a Hannolen, Xan wasn't particularly interested in the affairs of Azra.

Cyn didn't like this. He didn't like it at all.

He needed to keep his grip on Yara. She'd agreed to give him a few hours. He'd have to work quickly on Gansai. His best bet was to get Maxen on the job. The rat owed him a favor, and there was no one faster. The man was part machine.

The dark blue planet swelled, filling the viewscreen as Cyn adjusted the ship's trajectory to swing around to the largest land mass on the watery world.

On the edge of one of the continents, the clear ring of an asteroid impact remained on the scarred planet.

At one point it had been filled with civilization. Now the people were extinct, the remnants of one of their great cities turned into a hodgepodge collection of the culture and technology of too many planets to count. It was a vibrant port for pirates and privateers.

The Union left it to its own devices, knowing that sometimes the pirate fleets came in handy.

"Have you ever been to Gansai?" Cyn asked.

"No," Yara confessed as the ship sank lower, skirting just above the edge of the atmosphere.

"It's probably better if you don't leave the ship." He wondered what she would think of the arcades and the men who frequented them.

"I'm a big girl, I can handle it," she insisted.

Sometimes she could be so damn stubborn.

"Can you?" he challenged. "You don't even know what you're facing. Overconfidence can kill you."

"I'm not your concern. The only thing you should be concerned about is earning what I'm paying you."

The ship entered the atmosphere, and the friction fire danced over the viewscreen.

They dropped through the burning sky into the swirling clouds. Cyn concentrated on flying the ship through turbulent air. The port city rose before them, light gleaming off ancient ruins usurped by modern tech.

The ship flew over the stark hills as they approached the city. Cyn always entered the port with caution. Things never seemed to go according to plan on Gansai. He'd nearly died there twice, almost married once before he realized he was drugged, and at some point ended up hauling a load of shit, literally shit, halfway across the galaxy.

But the stakes had never been higher. He looked at the determined lift of Yara's chin. And his cargo had never been more unpredictable.

# 6

CYN LANDED THE SHIP IN A SMALL DOCKING PORT NEAR THE HONEST SIDE OF the forum. It would cost him to pay the dock security to protect the ship. He didn't have a crew to leave behind, only Yara. And she was the one thing he was worried about.

"Bug," he whispered as he entered his extremely complex locking codes into the ship's systems. The hiss of the pressure vents created enough of a cover for his hushed command. "Make sure Yara doesn't leave the ship. Get at Tuz if you have to."

"*Pip!*" Bug dipped and looped, then returned to his place at the copilot seat.

"I'm going out to find my mechanic. I'll be back in twenty," he said as he turned to Yara. He stopped cold as he watched her pack her things into a single bag.

"You going somewhere?" He stepped down out of the control center and crossed his arms.

"The situation's changed. I'm grateful for the passage to this port, but it's time for us to part ways." Her eyes darted to the side. He wanted to step into her personal space and challenge her, demand she stay, but he knew it wouldn't do any good.

"I'm only asking for twenty minutes. Let me talk to my mechanic. We'll see what he says, and then you can make your decision." He placed his hand on hers as she crammed a rolled-up pair of military issue boot socks in the bag. Her hand stilled and she lifted her gaze to his.

"Twenty minutes," he insisted. The light caught in her irises, shining like gold in the dim interior. Why did she have to be so damn beautiful?

"Fine." She dropped the socks and sat down on the bed.

If only he could pull out a roll of binding tape and make sure she stayed there.

He jogged to the airlock, spun the wheel, opened the hatch, then climbed down to the dusty ground before she could change her mind. Hopefully Bug would be able to stall her if he had to. He had to find Maxen, and fast.

The heat from the belly of the ship ratcheted up the temperature of the air around him as he jogged out from underneath the overheated metal.

Once out from under the ship, the cool air engulfed him like diving into a clear lake on a hot day. Blue gray clouds swirled overhead, remnants of a blanket of dust that plunged the world into a sudden ice age.

Cyn breathed in the temperate air, in spite of the smell wafting from a worn down cargo ship hauling some form of organic fertilizer. *Sucker.*

"Cyrus the Snake has returned," Polarx, the dock-master, greeted. The bald man smiled through his beard as he wiped a smear of grease from his brow with the worn red scarf he wore around his neck.

His worn shirt had yellow stains from years of sweat and little care for hygiene.

Cyn logged his payment into his com with a quick set of voice commands, then transferred the payment for dock security. "You know where Maxen is?"

"He owe you money?" the old man asked, rubbing his chin. "He's been hanging around the Dirty Link lately. Probably there."

"Thanks," Cyn said as he jogged into the busy street beyond the docks.

The crowded lanes of the old ruins were bustling with port workers unloading freight and hauling it down to vendor stalls in the forum. The calls of men haggling over shipments and prices rose above the hiss of pressure vents and the regular roar of ships lifting off from the docks.

Sunlight got lost in the thick clouds of Gansai, dimming the light and making the dry air feel sharp and cold. Cyn ran through the market to the arcades, enjoying the stretch of muscle and the natural light on his skin. It woke him up and sharpened his mind. He'd need it to deal with Maxen.

Nearing an old building that had been refurbished using the insulated siding of a dismantled warship, Cyn stopped and sent a quick message to Xan through his com. He nodded to a burly pirate leaning against the plasma-cut hole in the wall that served as a doorway.

Inside, drunken men lounged around, cheering, laughing,

and clapping for two holographic avatars screwing like mad rabbits floating over a glowing red projector in the center of the room.

The electronic moans and wails sounded ridiculous to him, and he ignored the computerized game pieces as they thrashed around in midair.

Cyn glanced at the two men controlling the avatars but couldn't identify them through the sensory shields over their heads. Others laughed as the players gyrated and flailed their arms around in order to make their game pieces move.

The female screamed and the crowd cheered, lifting their glasses in salute to the game. That's when Cyn spotted him.

Maxen didn't watch the games. Instead, he fiddled with a rusted cube of metal that seemed to be shedding small bolts and fasteners in his hands.

Cyn crossed the pub and slid into a chair at the table.

"Don't you owe me a drink?" Maxen greeted as he continued to fiddle with the chunk of antique machinery.

"Other way around," Cyn corrected. Maxen looked up at him through the shock of straight dark brown hair that constantly fell over his unnatural eye. The mechanical eye focused, the tiny lights and gears flickering with silver light in the artificial iris. Maxen smiled, deepening the scars at his temple and the pronounced one that cut into his upper lip.

"We can split a round and call it even," he suggested as he placed the cube on the table.

"Don't have time. I need your help. My converter is shot, and I got caught in a Spider's web on the way here. My life-support systems need to be recalibrated and I need a new adjuster." Cyn offered him the com so the mechanic could take a look at the diagnostic.

Maxen held out his right hand. The silvery metal of the artificial limb unfolded as naturally as a flesh hand, but a hole in the palm opened up to create a com port so the mechanic could pull information directly into his cerebral transplants. Cyn averted his eyes, knowing Maxen didn't like it when people stared.

"This is a mess," he acknowledged, though both his slanted real eye and the silvery fake one seemed to be staring off into nothing. "How long are you in port?"

"I've got twenty minutes."

Maxen laughed, his gravelly voice reaching over the din of the men watching the game. "What do you think I am?"

"The best," Cyn admitted, trying to charm Maxen into agreeing to the repair. Too bad it hardly ever worked.

The mechanic flashed a good-humored smile. "You're insane. What are you up to?"

"I've got a girl on my ship . . ."

Maxen laughed harder this time. "If you think I'm going to bust my gears so your pretty ass can get laid one more time, you'd better reassess the situation, lover."

Cyn rubbed the back of his neck in exasperation. "Listen, I've got to keep her waylaid and out of trouble for a little project I'm working on. Just come back to the ship and tell her the repairs will take no time. I'll stall her from there."

Maxen's natural eye gleamed with good humor, but his expression darkened. "I bet you will."

"Max," Cyn pleaded. He didn't have time to deal with

Maxen's frustrations with the opposite sex. He had enough problems. "Will you please just come back to my ship?"

"We have to go back to my shop and load my *only* spare converter onto a lift, and I'm not hauling it down to the docks without help." Max stood and straightened his shoulders. If Cyn didn't know the man was standing on a bio-mech leg, he never would have been able to tell.

"The faster we get going, the better," Cyn urged.

"Fine," he stated, pulling on the lapels of his long tanskin coat. "But this is going to cost you."

"I figured it would," Cyn grumbled.


YARA TRIED TO SIDESTEP THE ANNOYING LITTLE BOT, BUT BUG KEPT FLYING within an inch of her nose and zapping her with a small static charge. "Damn it, Bug, get out of my way," she insisted, swatting at him with the back of her hand.

The bot whistled so shrilly it forced her to cover her ears.

"All right, stop," she shouted above the screeching noise. "I need some sun. Is that okay with you?"

Bug stared at her with his single black eye, seeming torn.

When Yara saw the light break through the clouds on the viewscreen, she had nearly jumped straight through the sidewall to get outside, but Bug had stopped her.

"I'm sick," she pleaded. "I need the light."

The glow around the bot deflated as he floated out of the way.

*Yes!*

Yara ran through the ship and dropped into the circular hatch, climbing through the open airlock. Halfway down, she jumped, landing hard on the ground. The shock energized her muscles as she ducked under the belly of the ship and into a patch of sunlight near one of the landing supports.

Relief rushed through her as the warm light caressed her face and lingered in her hair. She took several long, deep breaths of air that smelled like dust and steam vents, but at least it was cold and fresh. She coughed. Apparently the manure from the cargo ship docked nearby was fresh, too.

Rubbing her eyes, she stretched, tempted to take off her uniform and let the sun soak into her bare back.

"Hey, ho ho," a man called to her. "What is this?"

Tuz landed with a thump on the ground and immediately took up his defensive stance near her foot. "Easy boy," she warned.

"I greet you." Yara held up her hand as a sign of peace as an old, bearded man waddled toward her like a territorial pelican in a grubby shirt. "I'm a stage passenger on Cyrus's ship."

"He doesn't take passengers," the old dock-master insisted.

"I know, not as a rule." She smiled at him, and he seemed to relax just a bit.

Slowly a grin broke over his round face. "Ahh, that Cyrus. I understand. I am Polarx, owner of these docks. Where do you travel?"

"Azra."

"Pah!" The man coughed out a hard guffaw. "All the way to Azra on this ship?"

"What? How badly is it damaged?" Yara's stomach began to sink.

Polarx's face twisted in a contemplative scowl as he pointed through the curling steam to one of the modules on the back of the ship. "The coils are shot on the converter. At least three days, and that's only if Maxen works through the nights. You'll probably be here a week. Ah! Would you like me to show you around?"

"A week?" She had suspected as much, but to hear it confirmed gave her a sick feeling. She looked around the busy docks. Large men hauled stacks of shipping containers on angrav lifts, shuffling through the dusty lanes like alien beasts of burden. Several ships rested in the large open area, while crumbling towers of stone gave way to a reaching skyline of patchwork metal buildings born from the cannibalized remains of old starships. "I can't wait a week."

Polarx rubbed his scraggly gray beard. "There's a Bacarilen ship in port. They do much business on Azra. I think they are heading that way."

"Bacarilen?" Yara felt the glimmer of hope spring in her chest. The Bacarilen took care of most of the shipping of foreign goods on Azra. Similar to the female-dominant culture of Azra, the Bacarilen were something familiar, something she trusted.

The old dock owner nodded. "Captain Brill is in port. Ah! She just unloaded several tons of refined morac ore from Azra and should be heading back with some light refiners from the Pasomlen."

Yara searched her memory. Brill, the name was familiar. Eventually she connected a face with it. She knew Brill. The woman was a fierce negotiator. Yara had been tasked with evaluating a standing contract with her four years ago before taking her position as commander for the Union. The Bacarilen captain was tough, a masterful trader.

"Where is the Bacarilen ship?" she asked. She couldn't believe her luck. This was her way out. She wouldn't have to face Cyrus again. She had a feeling he would try to stall her, just so he could play some more.

"Not here in my dock. No." The old man scratched his balding head, adding another smudge of grease to his already dirty face. "The Blackstock. It's on the other side of the forum past the mineral markets. Keep going that way." He gave a vague wave over his head. "You'll see them."

"Thank you." Yara ran back to the airlock and flew up the ladder into the ship. She grabbed her belongings off the bed and turned to leave.

Halting near the bed, she brushed a hand over the blanket, smoothing out a wrinkle.

She had to go.

After hoisting her bag over her shoulder, she trotted back to the hatch.

Bug zipped up and stopped right in front of her face. He made a low grinding noise.

"I'm sorry, Bug. Say good-bye to Cyrus for me. I left an EDI disc with his payment on it in the control center." She tried to step forward, but the bot went ballistic, pinging around the room letting out furious screeches and whistles.

Yara ignored it, even as it tried to shock her when she tossed her belongings through the airlock. She wasn't going to let a bot the size of her palm stop her from getting on that ship.

After climbing out of the ship, she jogged out of the docks toward the crowded streets beyond. Tuz leapt to her shoulder and balanced his weight as he sniffed the air and growled.

Yara caught a glimpse of the bot zipping over the gateway to the docks. She had to get out of there before Cyrus returned.

*Cyrus.*

She had to stop thinking about him. He was only attractive because he was so foreign, and she was half out of her mind with lag. Looking up, she wandered past a crowd of men shouting prices for bales of plant fiber to a trader clinging to a rusted vent pole as he pointed confirmations of orders to the other men.

Women here were in the severe minority. While the occasional female crewmate of the pirates or traders hung out of tavern windows or carried on business, the only females that seemed a part of the ragtag jumble of interbreeding foreign tech were the prostitutes waving from the only clean-looking building in the port.

Gansai was a man's world. Money, sex, liquor. Men's vices. She shuddered. Thank the Matriarchs the men on Azra weren't so uncivilized. The women of Azra had tamed them.

Yara wove through the crowds until she passed the great stacks of containers for the mineral traders. To the back and left, she could see docks just beyond a long narrow street.

A creepy feeling slithered up her back and made the hair on the back of her neck stand on end.

It was too still.

She walked forward but kept her sono ready as she held her head high.

Someone watched her, *assessing.*

She prepared herself for attack even as Tuz jumped down to the ground, his fur rising on his back. The smell of fouled water and rats caught in her nose as she passed a dark alley. This was the sort of place where pirates did quiet deals, deals best made in the shadows.

Did Cyrus frequent this place? Where else would he get projectile weapons?

She was right to leave.

Quickening her pace, she reached the gates to the far docks. A Bacarilen transport ship squatted on the far platform, while a crew of red-haired women worked to load the last of several shipping containers into the belly of the massive cargo bay.

*Thank Isa.* She wasn't too late.

Yara jogged to the ship and caught sight of the captain reviewing a holo image from a com.

"Captain Brill?" Yara nodded in greeting to the other woman, who looked up from her com in surprise. "I'm Commander Yara. I'm seeking passage back to Azra."

Any hint at emotion faded from the captain's well-tanned face as she pinched her lips tight. "I remember you."

Good. They had gone several rounds over that contract, but the captain had bent in the end. Yara stood straighter. She wasn't here to make friends. This was business, something she knew Brill understood. She was here to book passage. "When do you launch?"

The captain looked up over Yara's shoulder and squinted. Yara glanced back. A cloaked pirate stood in the shadows with his arms crossed. The creeping feeling slid back down her neck. The sooner she got out of there, the better.

"In two hours. Passage will cost you forty-eight." The captain clicked off her com and lifted her sharp chin. "That's nonnegotiable."

Tuz pressed up against Yara's shins, nearly forcing her to step backward. He growled at the man in the shadows. "Done."

"I should welcome you aboard, Commander." The captain waved a nonchalant hand to a hard-looking woman with a long nose and square face. "Take the commander up to my lounge."

"Captain, the launch codes are integrated and cargo—" the crewmate began.

The captain held up her hand. "Later. I have one more deal to negotiate. Take care of our guest."

Yara walked alongside the crewmate, down the ornately decorated corridors of the ship. She remembered the way to the captain's lounge from the last time she'd been on board. Brill had preferred to negotiate in familiar territory. Bacarilen traders lived exclusively on their ships. Yara hadn't given in to intimidation and had talked the captain down quite a bit from her initial contract. At the time it was quite a victory. Now it felt good to be away from the docks and the ill feeling in her gut.

Yara sank into a plush red seat that smelled like gin smoke and waited for the captain to return. Within hours, she'd be back on Azra and able to cut off Palar's coup at the knees.

Brill returned sooner than Yara expected. She strode into the room with an arrogant swagger and lit a sharp-smelling cigar. Without saying a word, the captain poured herself some white-lace sugar rumma, and steeped some Azralen ciera tea for Yara. The elixir Cyrus had given her was still making her extremely thirsty. Yara was glad for the drink. It smelled stale, but she was too thirsty to care. She took a long draught and placed it on the table between them.

The captain smiled.

Yara didn't like the predatory expression on the other woman's face.

"You know, the contract you negotiated cost me quite a bit over the last couple of years," she admitted.

What did she expect? Yara had done her job and had looked out for Azra's trade interests. Her arms felt heavy.

"It was a tough negotiation. I look forward to another round when the contract is up." Yara blinked. It was probably exhaustion. Tuz sniffed at her drink and hissed. The lights on his collar activated.

"Another round?" Brill chuckled. "I think I prefer to negotiate with Palar. She's been very generous and promised me much more profitable contracts as soon as she ascends the throne of Azra." The captain smirked as she stepped forward. Yara tried to stand but stumbled.

Palar? By Fima the Merciless, Brill was supporting her rival. This wasn't exhaustion. *Shakt.*

"Did you enjoy your drink?" Brill asked. "It should make your trip to Krona more comfortable."

*She wouldn't. No.*

"Tuz, run." Yara fell while her scout growled. "Run!" she shouted, before her strength completely gave out.

Tuz hissed. Yara watched as he streaked out of the lounge.

"Get that cat!" The words sounded distorted to her drugged senses as the room blurred then turned black.

# 7

CYN EASED THE CONVERTER ONTO THE BED OF A GROUND-RUNNER USING THE awkward controls of the angrav lift while Maxen gathered the tools he needed from his loft. Cyn winced as the nearly spherical polyhedron surrounded by a geometric web of dull and very heavy dark carbon slid too close to the edge of the bed of the truck. Pulling it back up, he tried again. The last thing he needed to do was bust the new converter.

"You sure you know how to use that thing?" Maxen called from a loft perched above the large hangar. Tools and parts clanged against the steel floor as the mechanic rummaged around in his stash.

Cyn ignored him and concentrated, bringing the converter down square on the bed. The antique wheeled transport groaned under the weight as it shifted and settled. Cyn doubted the old runner would still roll under the load.

"Strap it down tight," Maxen called from the balcony of the loft. He slung an enormous bag filled with heavy tools effortlessly over his back and climbed down the creaking ladder.

Sunlight broke through the overcast sky, hitting the skylights in the roof of the hangar. Light swelled in the empty space in spite of the yellowed crystal panes and the years of dust and industrial grime.

Cyn hurried to secure the converter. He had to get outside while the sun was shining. He secured the final link with a twist of his wrist then trotted to the open doors of the hangar.

Bully, Maxen's enormous guard dog, lifted his boxy head to acknowledge Cyn, then flopped back down in a patch of sunlight. Cyn closed his eyes and lifted his face to the warmth. He rolled up his sleeves and held out his hands but didn't feel like enough of his skin was exposed.

How had he ever survived the shadows?

He had to help the others still trapped there.

"Hey, I thought you were in a hurry," Maxen called as he dumped the bag in the back of the runner, making the old cargo truck sink deeper on its wheels.

"I am. Let's get going." Cyn turned to join Maxen at the runner, when a flash of green caught his eye.

Crap.

Bug flew toward him, his green aura streaking like a comet tail. He whistled in alarm.

"What happened?" Cyn nearly shouted the question as he held his palm out. Bug landed on it, barely able to perch on his wobbling legs. He wheezed a short series of low whistles.

"What do you mean, she's gone?" Cyn dropped his hand,

and Bug fell several feet before catching himself and resuming his hover.

*Damn it!*

Cyn wrenched the door of the runner open and flung himself inside. "We've got to go. Now," he insisted.

Maxen eased into the driver's seat. "Lady trouble?"

"Shut up. Just drive." Cyn scowled as Maxen placed his metal palm against the drive panel and triggered the ignition.

"You asked for it."

Cyn had to brace himself against the door as the runner leapt forward, plowing over the uneven road and turning wildly through the narrow lanes of the city.

Cyn clenched his teeth as his hands dug into the console in front of him. A man with a crate of fowl leapt out of the way while Maxen drove with mechanical indifference to his speed, or to the chaos around him.

Maxen directed the truck by the computer system integrated in his brain through the linking ports in his palm. The truck became a seamless extension of his bio-mech parts, and Maxen drove it like a madman.

The old truck roared and jumped, leaping out of the way of obstacles and dodging around the terrified men in the streets without once touching anyone or nicking anything.

"What did you do to this thing?" Cyn forced out while clinging to the monster runner.

"I fixed it," Maxen declared, spinning the back wheels of the truck so the back end of the runner swung out in a wild arc, enabling them to turn down another alley.

Cyn ducked as they punched through a closed gate, then jerked to a stop by the north gates of the docks.

Dust rose in a cloud around them as Cyn's heart pounded. "We're here." Maxen smiled.

Cyn would have decked the man, but the bastard couldn't feel it. Instead he eased out of the old runner and let the heavy door swing back before stalking forward in an attempt to get his legs back under him.

Polarx waddled up from the control array at the center of the docks. "You're back so soon! Going to get to work on that converter, ah. What a mess. It's a good thing your passenger found new transport."

Cyn had hoped Bug made some sort of mistake, but deep down he knew that was unlikely. *Shit.*

"Where did she go?"

"She was interested in the Bacarilen transport docked over in the Blackstock."

"Damn it." She'd have to pass through Aggen Street to get there. Yara wouldn't get taken without a fight, but flesh traders were masters at striking without warning. People just disappeared. Boom, gone.

If she made it through that den of shadows, then he had a new problem. If she'd signed onto a Bacarilen ship, it was a good possibility she'd be home within hours. He couldn't allow that. How would he get her off the ship? She wouldn't come willingly, and the Bacarilen would probably back her up. They were close trade allies with Azra.

"I have to stop that ship."

"I can stop it right now, no problem," Maxen admitted. "I'll just call in the circle."

Cyn didn't want to bring pirate law into this, but he didn't have any other choice. He couldn't stop the ship on his own.

"What will you hold them on?" he asked.

Maxen shrugged. "Doesn't matter, we'll think of something when we get there."

"Do it," Cyn urged, knowing Maxen only had to think to send a message to the pirate enforcers.

"Already done."

"Polarx, can we borrow a runner?" Cyn asked as Maxen stepped up next to him. He didn't want to damage the converter with more of Maxen's driving.

"Ah! My pleasure. I'll add it to your docking fees." He tossed a code key to Cyn, but Maxen snatched it out of the air with the unnatural speed of his right hand.

"I'm driving," Cyn insisted.

"You drive like an old woman." Maxen jogged over to the younger and unburdened runner and pulled himself into the driver's seat. Cyn grumbled as he took the passenger side and strapped himself in.

After a harrowing ride through the mineral markets, they arrived at the Blackstock. The Bacarilen ship still perched on the western end of the dock. Cyn felt a rush of relief burn down his back and arms. They didn't have much time.

Maxen brought the runner to a skidding stop, and Cyn leapt out as if the thing were on fire.

A small transport lifted off from the far ends of the docks. The roar of its engines sent a turbulent hot wind through the open platforms. Cyn strode with purpose and military bearing as he approached the Bacarilen ship.

Three crewmates worked on stowing the last of the shipping containers and securing the lift. One of them spared Cyn an unimpressed scowl.

"Ship's due to launch. We're closed to trade," she stated once the roar from the transport died down.

"How about stage passage?" Cyn asked. "You have anyone traveling with you?"

The girl locking the straps on a container watched him with a superior expression.

"We haven't taken on any guests this trip. Why? You looking for passage?"

*Liar.* Cyn hoped the circle arrived soon.

A fourth Bacarilen, a tall woman with a high-collar coat, stepped out of the shadows. "Is something wrong here?"

"We need to speak with the captain," Maxen demanded.

"She's busy. I'm the second in command of the ship. We're due to launch." She clasped her hands behind her back, but Cyn caught a glimpse of some deep red welts forming on her wrist. Cat scratches.

Bacarilen never kept pets.

"Have a run-in with an Azralen korcas cat?" Cyn asked.

The woman straightened her shoulders and sneered.

"Yara's on this ship," he stated.

Suddenly the docks filled with the roar of fan engines as six hoverans flew over the crowded market and floated above the docks, their pulse cannons trained on the ship. Down draft from the spinning fans that gave the circular angrav ships their propulsion threw clouds of dust into the air. It provided cover for the runners descending on the ship like wolves. Cyn shielded his eyes as the hoverans surrounded the ship and eased to the ground in a lopsided circle. The pirates poured out of the vehicles, leaving one man behind in each craft to man the guns.

"What is this about?" the scratched-up Bacarilen demanded.

"We're holding the ship," Maxen announced.

"On what charge?" Her eyes narrowed, then looked calculating as her lips turned up in a manipulative grin.

"Why don't you tell us?" Maxen stalled.

The crowd of roughly thirty pirate enforcers closed ranks. Their faces were hard, diverse, an eclectic mix of everything the human races had to offer, but their expressions were all set with the same resolve.

Maxen drew a sono. It became an integrated part of his metallic hand as he pointed it at the Bacarilen. "Bring out the Azralen, and we won't search the ship."

"What is going on out here?" a shrill voice rose above the crowd as the Bacarilen captain descended the ramp leading up into the cargo hold.

"Where's the Azralen?" Cyn stated.

"What Azralen?" she retorted. Voices rumbled, filling the docks as more merchants and traders entered the open space from the mineral markets. Everyone seemed to want a part of the spectacle.

"Commander Yara." Cyn searched the woman's hands for any scratches. Maybe he was mistaken. "Polarx said he directed her to your ship to book stage passage."

"I haven't seen any Azralen here," the captain snapped a little too quickly. She turned on her heel and strode back toward the ship with the stiff spine of someone expecting to be struck in the back.

"She's a liar," someone shouted from the back of the crowd. "I saw the Azralen pass by my stall."

The robotic voice of a trader with an old interpreter-collar added, "She boarded the ship."

"I'm inclined to believe the witnesses. What do you think, Cyrus?" Maxen asked. He lifted the sono to the captain. The crewmates that had been out on the lift jumped forward, but the second in command held them back with a single wave of her hand.

"She's on board," Cyn affirmed.

"Search the ship." As soon as Maxen gave the order, a large man with deep brown skin and a wicked-looking DEC rifle rushed up the stairs, followed by at least fifteen others.

"Care to confess now? It may lighten your sentencing," Maxen offered the captain.

"Go to Nek," she snapped at him.

"I hear it's lovely this time of year." Maxen smiled a cruel smile.

Cyn crossed his arms. He had to wait for the circle to finish the search, and it was killing him. If he stepped in and interfered, he'd have to get mixed up in the trial. Right now this was Maxen's game. He only had one concern. He needed to find Yara, throw her pretty ass over his shoulder, drag her back to his ship, and then weather the wrath of her fury.

Maxen went still for a fraction of a second. "Cyrus, they're having a problem in the corridor. They need your help."

It was all the invitation he needed. He ran up the ramp and entered the crowded cargo bay. Bug zipped up beside him and landed on his shoulder.

"Where have you been?" Cyn asked, as he passed by row after row of neatly stowed and aligned shipping containers.

Bug's aura pulsed in heavy exhausted heaves. He rattled off something about Maxen and his driving before shutting down. Cyn stashed him in his belt. A loud crash sounded in the corridor ahead of him, followed by a feline war cry and a string of foul curses.

"Tuz!" Cyn shouted.

He ran over the plush red carpeting of the opulent Bacarilen ship until he came to a jam of bodies in one of the corridors. Tuz growled, hissed, and one of the pirates came away holding a bloody hand.

"Tuz, where's Yara?" Cyn demanded.

The cat howled then darted off down another corridor. Cyn pushed through the crowd and followed, entering a richly decorated lounge.

A scrap of mismatched rug from the cargo bay lay askew by the couch. Tuz looked at it, spun and hunkered down on it, his yellow eyes slanting with feline concentration. He swished his dark tail and let out a low moan.

The Bacarilen were practically genetically programmed to be obsessively neat. Not a single line in the room was askew, and something from the cargo bay didn't belong in the captain's lounge, though it would probably just look like a throw rug to anyone who didn't know the Bacarilen as well as he did.

He lifted the rug to find a damp spot and a tiny chip of pottery, barely noticeable to his naked eyes. The Bacarilen had rushed to hide the mess before they could clean it to their stringent standards.

Cyn pulled Bug from his belt. Holding on to the bot with his left hand, he traced his finger around Bug's edge to wake him up.

Bug groaned, beeped, then rattled what could only be interpreted as mechanical snoring.

"Get up," Cyn urged. "I need to you analyze this."

Bug blinked his eye and wobbled off Cyn's hand. A green light flared out, scanned over the spot, then Bug prattled off the contents of the liquid.

One ingredient stood out among the others.

*Floran.*

The drug would have knocked the drinker out cold.

Rubbing his hand over the carpet, he inhaled deeply. The subtle scent of the kiltii extract Yara had used to bathe her wound rose into the air.

Cyn brought his knuckle to his lips, unable to breathe for a moment. What had they done to her?

Tuz rubbed his round face against Cyn's thigh.

He picked up the cat, put Bug back in his belt, and stormed out of the ship.

"What happened in there?" Maxen asked. His mechanical hand hadn't wavered at all, the sono still pointing ominously at the heart of the Bacarilen captain.

"Yara was on the ship. This is her cat." Cyn held out Tuz, but the cat refused to be dropped on the ground. Instead he dug his claws into Cyn's bracer and held on. Cyn pulled him back into his body. "She was drugged with floran."

"Where is she?" Maxen demanded of the captain as he took a step forward. Another pirate grabbed the Bacarilen from behind, pinning her arms behind her.

"You can't prove anything." The captain tried to pull out of the grip of the pirate, but he held firm.

"I can," the second in command offered.

The whole crowd turned to her.

"Melor," the captain warned. "You're my sister."

The second arched a haughty brow then turned her back on the captain as she faced Maxen.

"The Azralen tried to book passage on this ship. She was taken to the personal lounge of the captain. The captain then left the ship and met with a Kronalen man on Aggen Street. He came on board and unloaded a shipping container."

An angry rumble of male voices permeated the docks. Flesh trading was a prime offense on Gansai.

The captain tried to pull her hands free again. "That's a lie. She's after my ship."

Tuz hissed in Cyn's ear.

*His collar.*

"Maxen, check the recording systems on the cat's collar. Tuz is trained to spy," Cyn offered, pulling the collar over Tuz's thick head.

Maxen holstered his sono and took the collar. He turned it over and over in his hand before connecting to it through his fingers.

A disembodied voice rose over the crowd.

"*Another round?*" A malicious chuckle rang out. "*I think I prefer to negotiate with Palar. She's been very generous and promised me much more profitable contracts as soon as she ascends the throne of Azra.*" The unmistakable voice of the captain projected clearly from the collar. "*Did you enjoy your drink? It should make your trip to Krona more comfortable.*"

"*Tuz, run.*" Yara's voice sounded weak and panicked. Cyn felt as if he'd been punched in the gut. "*Run!*"

Disgust churned through his body while his raw rage clouded his vision. Cyn drew his sono, and it warmed in his hand. He pointed it at the captain. "I'm going to shoot her," he warned. His voice came out as a low growl.

He felt Maxen's natural hand on his shoulder. "That won't help us find her."

He tried to take a deep breath to quell his rage but it flooded his blood like a white-hot fire. The thought of Yara subjected to the cruelty of the Kronalen sickened him. He had to get her out. It was completely irrational. He knew it. But he couldn't stand the thought of her pierced by slave bands, raped and killed in the betting pits. She had never known darkness or shadows. She'd fight, but they would kill her. Physically and mentally, the slavers would destroy her. He couldn't think about what it would mean for the revolution. That thought slipped out of his mind like poisonous mercury. *She* was in danger, and he couldn't stand it.

"Where is she?" His voice boomed over the crowd, making the Bacarilen crewmates flinch.

The second answered. "The Kronalen left on a ship called *Ti Kataf.* It launched just before you arrived."

*No.* The ship would be in macrospace by now and untraceable.

How were they going to find her?

Cyn dropped Tuz to the ground and tried to focus, tried to search his mind for anything that might help him find her.

"Take this one to the pits," Maxen ordered, nodding at the captain. "We'll organize a formal court later."

His words were like a low buzzing in Cyn's ears. There had to be something. He searched the endless blur of knowledge for anything he could grasp. He had never heard of the ship. He needed more information. Where could he find it?

The pirates hauled the protesting captain to one of the hoverans as the second in command spoke to the crowd. "I'm ashamed of Brill's despicable behavior. I'll be sure to tell Azra the unfortunate circumstances of Commander Yara's loss."

*What?* If the Elite on Azra knew Yara was lost, her rivals would pounce on a chance at the throne and the Elite would be thrown into chaos before the revolution was ready to strike.

He couldn't let that happen.

"No," he shouted. Maxen looked at him, confused.

"We don't know if the second in command was in on this or not. For all we know she drugged Yara to frame the captain so she could assume control of the ship. The cat scratched her. She was there." Cyn turned his sono on her.

"He's right," another one of the circle chimed in, grabbing the second before she could pull away. "It takes more than two people to unload a shipping container."

"This is ridiculous," she protested.

Maxen smiled. "I'm afraid for a fair court, we need the testimony of all witnesses. Take her to the pits, too, and lock down the ship."

The crowd cheered as the other Bacarilen was hauled back to the holding pits. Maxen grabbed Cyn by the arm and pulled him through the crowds back toward the runner.

"How are you going to find her?" he asked. "I don't have anything in stored memory about *Ti Kataf.*"

"I don't either," Cyn admitted. "We need Xan."

8

"MAXEN, DRIVE," CYN ORDERED AS HE CLIMBED INTO THE PASSENGER SEAT
and strapped himself in. Tuz landed with a heavy thud on his
lap. Cyn snatched Maxen's dog's worn blanket from the back
and shoved it between the cat's claws and his thighs.

The engine rumbled to life, and Maxen peeled the runner
around in a circle before racing out of the docks. "Do you
know where Xan's ship is?" Cyn shouted as Tuz managed to
sink his claws through the blanket and into his jeans.

"He's on the northern outskirts of the city. I haven't seen
him around in days." The wind whipped Maxen's long bangs
away from his silver eye.

"Keep your eyes on the road!" Cyn grabbed on to Tuz with
one hand and the door frame with the other as the runner ca-
reened around a broken-down hoveran.

The crumbling ruins of the northern slums whipped past

them as the streets closed in, and more ancient stone and metalwork jutted up from the dirt streets.

Maxen managed to avoid every obstacle until the buildings finally succumbed to the natural layered rock formations to the north.

Xan's large crewship rested on the crest of one of the roundtop hills. The shadow of the city stretched toward the ship but couldn't quite grasp it.

Maxen pulled the runner to a stop near a roaring bonfire. Roughly a dozen of Xan's crew sat around rolling thupa stones and drinking.

A woman stood and lifted her thick mug to them. "Maxen!" she called with a warm smile. Cyn knew better than to let it lull him into a sense of complacency. Even though they were friends, Venet was not a woman to mess with. She was a worthy second in command to Xan and a fierce pirate. "And you," she gave him a teasing frown. "What are you calling yourself today?"

"Cyrus," he answered, before jumping out of the runner and then steadying his balance. "Where's Xan? It's urgent."

"Camping." She frowned in earnest this time. "He needs to get back. The men are getting edgy."

"How long has he been out there?" Maxen asked, stepping over a rolling thupa stone.

"Three days. He didn't take anything with him." She paused, looked at the dwindling contents of her tankard, then back up at Cyn. "He's getting worse. The headaches are more frequent."

Cyn nodded. His old friend had been withdrawing more and more. The constant battering in his mind from his psychic connection to his people was wearing on him. He could no longer block it out. There was nothing Cyn could do to help. Instead he was here to beg Xan to connect even deeper with his people, an act that would certainly cause him an even greater burden of pain.

How could he ever repay such a debt?

He couldn't think about that now. He had to get Yara back, and this was the only way he could do it.

"Which way did he go?" Maxen asked, scanning the horizon.

"Toward Vulture's Stoop." She pointed to the northeast. "It's dark enough. He should be awake by now."

"Thanks, Venet." Cyn climbed back into the runner, nudging Tuz with the toe of his boot. The cat wedged himself underneath the console and growled.

Maxen steered the runner through the camp and raced at break-neck speed down a rutted trail without the aid of lights. If his driving was bad in the day, it was ten times worse in the descending night.

"Could you turn the lights on?" Cyn ducked as a low-hanging branch whipped overhead.

"Blinding Xan as we approach is not the best way to ask him for a favor," Maxen pointed out. "Don't worry, I can see fine."

His silver eye glowed with an eerie red light.

Maxen had a point. Xan was full-blooded Hannolen. He was naturally nocturnal and his eyes were oversensitive, even for one of his kind.

Cyn wondered if it was because he was born with the rikka, streaks of white in his dark irises. They reminded Cyn of lightning and meteors, flashes of brilliance in a sea of shadow. They marked him as a true-born prince of his people. They revealed his ability to mentally connect with anyone with Hannolen blood, anywhere, in any dimension, including macrospace.

It was the reason Xan was in so much danger, and the reason he'd never agree to help.

Cyn had to try.

They turned up a path that led to the rounded peak of Vulture's Stoop. As the runner crested the top of the trail, Cyn caught sight of Xan standing in the center of the hilltop, staring in silence at the emerging stars. His eye shades hung from the slit in his shirt, while his dark blond hair looked gray in the dim light.

The rumble of the engine drowned out the delicate noises of the night and threw up a cloud of fine dust that swirled like eerie fog in the waning light. The engine let out a loud whine, then sputtered to a groaning stop.

Cyn jumped out as steam poured out from beneath four of the runner's wheels.

"I'll get on that," Maxen commented. "You deal with Xan."

Xan looked scruffier than normal, his hair longer, his face rougher. But it was more than that. He looked tired.

"There are too many clouds here," he stated without bringing his gaze down to Maxen or Cyn.

Cyn walked forward with slow, cautious steps.

"Xan, I need your help." Cyn was too used to Xan's eye shades. They made him seem hard and strong. Seeing his friend's eyes for the first time in at least a year haunted him. It made what he was about to ask that much more difficult. "I need you to contact your people."

"I told you to never ask me to do that again." Xan slowly dropped his gaze from the sky and focused on Cyn. "What mythical planet are you trying to find this time? The Hannolen people are not your personal spy network. Leave me alone."

"I'm sorry I asked you to find Byra. I shouldn't have. But now an innocent woman's life is in jeopardy. I have no other choice."

"Batshit." Xan turned away from him. Cyn reached out and grabbed his arm. Xan stopped, but his ominous silence spoke volumes.

"Her name is Yara. I need her. She was taken by a flesh trader in the Blackstock. She's on a ship called *Ti Kataf*. It's a Kronalen vessel. Chances are one of your people is on board. We need to know which slave port they're going to. A psychic connection is the only thing that can reach them between dimensions."

Xan had the power to unite all of the Hannolen, possibly lead a revolt that could single-handedly bring down the power structure of Krona. But he had never once used his gift. The Hannolen wasted away in despair, believing they had no prince, no one to lead them out of slavery. Cyn's Rebel blood couldn't understand why Xan didn't act.

What would it take to convince him to help? What could Cyn give that would be worth the risk?

Xan had said something obtuse about a prophecy. But that was the problem with the damn Hannolen. They'd been so caught up in their stars and prophecies, they failed to stand as one and fight when their planet was at stake. The swift and merciless Kronalen war fleets were upon them before they could interpret shit from the *all-knowing* stars.

"Yara," Xan mused. "Isn't that the Azralen bloodhunter who's supposed to kill you?"

Cyn stared his friend down, facing the scrutiny of the only person that knew him well. "She doesn't know who I am."

Xan shook his head. "Does anyone?"

"You do."

They fell silent for a long time. The rolling clouds above cracked open, revealing the velvet black of space sprinkled with endless stars. Cyn felt his frustration like a pounding hammer in his chest. Xan could stare at the stars and ponder his prophecies until he withered and died. They weren't going to change, damn it.

"I'm sorry." Xan looked back at the stars. "I can't."

"You need to act. It's time to do something. Connect to the river of thought," Cyn demanded.

"You know nothing about the river." Xan's voice lashed with an edge as sharp as a knife.

"I know enough." Cyn knew Xan could hear the river louder than the others. An endless song, it ran through the backs of the minds of all Hannolen, connecting them all together and recording their experiences as a people. Cyn had heard him sing parts in his sleep. If Xan wanted, he could speak out in the song, and anyone with Hannolen blood would hear his voice in their mind. Only those born with the rikka could do it, which is why any child born with the rikka was royal. The prince stood before Cyn, as lost as his people.

"I'm warning you, Cyn," Xan looked up, his dark eyes burning with anger. "Leave now."

"You know what they're going to do to her. You hear it over and over in the river. How many times do they cry for help? How many voices have suddenly cut out?" Cyn asked. "And you sit in silence and do *nothing*."

Xan swung, his fist smashing into the side of Cyn's face. The pain pounded through his head and jaw as he tasted hot blood in his mouth. He bit his lip and stood straighter.

"Please." Cyn wished his friend could see into his mind, hear his desperate thoughts. "Please."

Xan let out a long breath and shook out his hand. "You're a bastard."

"Help me." Cyn felt his throbbing flesh begin to swell. He didn't care.

"I told you, I can't. If I act before the will of God, we will be punished and spend another thousand years in slavery." He crossed his arms. "If I act too soon, the Kronalen will find me, and all hope will be lost." His tone was less lofty, more grounded in reality. Cyn understood what was at stake, but the Union forces wouldn't fight the Kronalen forever. At some point, the Hannolen would have to fight for their own survival. "According to the path of Halstos, I must stay hidden."

"Damn it, Xan. Will you forget about your high prophecies and stargazing and deal with what's happening now? Your people are out there. They're suffering. They need to know you live. It's time."

"You need to let the prophecy shit go," Maxen commented, wiping grease off his hands with an old rag. Cyn didn't have time for this. A life was at stake and they were standing around in the dark waiting for some great spirit that controlled the universe to send them a sign.

"We don't have enough strength to defeat the Kronalen. You can see it, right there on the path of Halstos." He swung his hand in an arch, tracing through the patterns of stars above. "Cryais the snake needs to move to Anarya the falcon, and

then the balance of power can shift. We will have more strength."
Xan pointed to the sky. "Faeneth has moved into its fourth
orbit. The river is so loud, I can't think anymore. My people
are crying out, and I can't answer them. It's killing me."

Cyn stood shocked. *This is the prophecy?* Fear pounded in
his veins. What if the Hannolen prophecies weren't about stars
at all?

Cyn unbuckled his bracer and ripped it off. Xan stared at
the snakes tattooed around his wrist and forearm. "She's marked
with the falcon."

Xan stared at his wrist for what seemed like an eternity.
Then he looked back up at the cloudy sky and ran a frustrated
hand through his hair. "If you're lying, toying with the hand of
God to get what you want . . ."

"What are the fucking odds, Xan?" Cyn shouted. "Her name
is Yara, of the line of Yarini the Just. What is the family symbol? Maxen, look it up."

"It's a falcon," Maxen confirmed.

"She's the falcon." Cyn rubbed his exposed tattoo. "I'm the
snake." Cyn hated this. He had no part in fate or destiny, and
if he did, his certainly wasn't tied to Yara's, was it?

Another chill ran down his back. It wasn't the first time
he'd wondered at the coincidence of her family ties. He didn't
like being bound by some cosmic dictate, but none of it mattered to him deep down. Only one thing really mattered. He had
to save Yara. "The revolution on Azra hinges on her. Once the
Grand Sister is gone, Azra will be strong again and in the debt
of Hanno."

Xan gave him a skeptical look, but his skin had paled, and
Cyn could read the indecision on his face.

"Well?" Cyn prodded. If this was a blasted sign, Xan had better listen to it, or Cyn would give him hell to pay.

Xan kicked a rock then pressed the heels of his palms into his eyes. He dropped his hands suddenly and glared at Cyn. "If I ever ask you for anything, you do it. Understand? As soon as I speak on the river, my people will know a prince exists, and it won't take long for Krona to find out. If I need your help against the Kronalen, you *will* aid me. Azra will aid my people. I hold you to that promise."

Cyn balked at the open nature of a promise like that. He could barely speak for himself. He had nothing. Now Xan wanted a promise of protection from all of Azra, not just him. How could he commit to such a promise? He didn't even know if there would be an Azra once he was done with it. He had to trust fate. He didn't even believe in fate. What would he have to do to save Yara?

What did the freedom of Azra mean to him?

What did *she* mean to him?

Xan turned from him and began to walk away.

"I'll do it," Cyn promised, even as his fear ate at his insides.

The prince turned back and gave him a single slow nod. "Then let me focus." He circled the hilltop, wandering amid the weeds and muttering to himself. Finally he stopped in a small clearing of ashen dust. Scuffing the ground with the side of his boot, he closed his dark eyes and lifted his hands to the night sky. The clouds rolled back as if Xan had unleashed some sort of impossible magic. As the stars glittered above, he began to sing.

Maxen offered Cyn the oily rag, and Cyn pressed it against the split in his lip. The sour taste of mech-grease touched his mouth, and he decided he'd rather bleed.

Xan's voice remained low, so low Cyn almost couldn't hear it. He strained to listen to the words, to gather a little piece of Hannolen history. He wanted to guard it for the lost people within his mind, the way he protected the Hannolen artifacts he'd found.

"What's he doing?" Maxen asked. "What is this river you keep talking about?"

"All the Hannolen are connected by a psychic link they call the river. At all times, they hear a collective thought. It sounds like a song in the back of their minds. When enough Hannolen think the same thing, the thought gets added to the song, and so it records a history of their ethnic experience across thousands of years," Cyn explained, handing the bloody piece of cloth back to Maxen.

"That's weird." He took the rag, looked at it, then tossed it under a bush.

"Yeah," Cyn continued. "Xan can connect deeply to the song and speak over it in his mind so all the Hannolen can hear his voice. If he wants, he can send a message to every Hannolen at once. He's never done it before."

"And they can answer?" Maxen looked concerned.

"Yeah." Cyn watched as Xan's voice dropped to silence. The prince hung his head then fell to his knees with his shoulders shaking.

"What happens when they all answer at once?" Maxen's silver eye flashed. Xan roared a terrible cry of pain.

*Shit.*

"Xan!" Cyn shouted, running to his friend. Xan collapsed, his eyes rolling back in his head.

Cyn grabbed him, lifted him up, then punched him across the face.

He didn't wake.

"Shock him!" Cyn ordered. Maxen's hand glowed white, and he touched it to Xan's chest.

Xan jolted awake and let out a hoarse shout. He clamped his hands over his ears and curled over.

Cyn grabbed his hand, squeezing his friend's fist until he thought the bones in his hand might break. "You're back here. You're with us."

Xan pulled heavy breaths into his thick chest and blinked his eyes.

"Are you with me?" Cyn shook his shoulder.

Xan swallowed then nodded.

"*Hork,*" he rasped out, and followed the peculiar curse with a string of equally colorful words.

"Need a drink?" Maxen offered him a flask from the interior pocket of his tanskin coat. Xan snatched it and took a long, heavy drink of whatever was inside without flinching.

"Did you find out where she is?" Cyn grabbed the flask, but it was empty. He tossed it back to Maxen.

Xan rolled his head back. "Sorry." His body shook with tremors as he stumbled over his words. "Too much."

*No.*

Cyn stood and paced on the hilltop. The thick clouds closed in, blocking out the light of the stars from above. What was he going to do?

So much for stars and prophecies. It was a load of crap. He had to find her. There had to be a way. There had to be. Once again he focused inward, searching the vast collection of thoughts stored away in his useless mind.

There was nothing.

There couldn't be nothing. There had to be some way to find her. They could fly to Krona and hack the arrays to listen to the com traffic. And they'd be caught. They couldn't stay linked up to the Kronalen array long enough to hope that someone would mention an Azralen slave. They'd end up slaves themselves.

They could search the pits.

No. There were fourteen active slave auctions that Cyn knew of and probably more he hadn't found yet. She could be in any one of them. She'd sell quickly, then go to any one of the numerous betting pits between Krona, Garu, and Flosch.

If he didn't find her, she'd die.

A connection in his memory snapped into place.

Damn it, he didn't need this.

He fought the rush of memory, the ripping anguish and helplessness it made him feel.

*Yarlia looks at him with such innocence, a rare and precious treasure in their dark world. He wants to kiss her so badly, his love feels like a fire within his heart. She's a shining light in his dark world. She watches him, the first bud of feminine awareness shining in her golden eyes. Cyani screams in the distance, snapping him out of his lovesick stupor. His sister's too far away to help. He tries to protect Yarlia, but the four men close in on them fast. Each blow the men rain down with their clubs, their boots, pushes his body deeper into a well of agony. He can't let them have her. He tries to reach her. She screams for him as he watches the mudrats carry her away, knowing she'll be raped and sold as a whore. Bleeding and broken, they leave him to die in the mud.*

"Cyn!" A jolt of electricity shot through his heart.

He jumped to the side, clutching his chest. "Damn it, that hurt!"

Maxen scowled at him. "Don't be a baby. What, are you lagging out or something?"

"No." He rubbed his chest, thankful to be free of the memory that had gripped him before he had to face his final memory of Yarlia. "We have to find her. I don't care what it takes."

"Yeah, well, I got nothing." Maxen shrugged. "How about you, Xan?"

Xan pressed a palm to his head. "I couldn't make out anything. They all clamored for my mind at once, shouting for me to help them."

Cyn sat down next to him; his face still throbbed and now his chest ached from the shock. "I'm sorry," he admitted.

"Yeah." Xan picked up a rock and threw it into the darkness. He jolted then furrowed his brow. "Wait."

Cyn's heart nearly jumped through his ribs. Xan closed his eyes and went very still.

The staccato screeches of a colony of bats carried over the rhythmic hum of insects in the rustling grasses. The rumble of a docking ship rolled in the distance, but Cyn knew Xan was listening to something deeper, much deeper than anything his ears could hear.

"There's a boy," Xan finally said. "Others are trying to reach me, but I can hear him now. He's strong."

The throbbing beat of Cyn's anxious heart joined the night

sounds as Cyn waited while Xan listened to the spirits of his people.

"He's with her on the ship." Xan got to his feet and jogged toward the runner. "A Rasso-Ancarlen is going to buy her at the auctions in Ungar."

Relief seemed to radiate out from the center of his gut as Cyn followed Xan. Xan jumped into the passenger seat, then shouted in pain.

He cursed as he fought to remove Tuz from his shin. Cyn had to grab the cat and haul him into the cargo bed.

"When?" he asked.

"No time. We have to leave now or we won't beat him there. Maxen, alert my crew," Xan commanded.

"Got it," Maxen affirmed as he started up the runner and launched it down the steep path.

"What, you're helping now?" Cyn couldn't hide his shock.

"I've got the fastest ship," Xan shouted as they bounced over a rut in the trail.

"You've got the only ship. His isn't going anywhere," Maxen interjected, throwing a mocking gesture back at Cyn.

"Will you keep your damn hands on the controls?" Cyn didn't want to admit he had a point.

"You're only going to have one shot at getting them out of there," Xan warned.

"Them?" Cyn asked. When was it them?

"You get the boy out, too, or I don't take you there." He didn't pause for a counter-offer. The negotiation was closed. "You speak Ankarlen?"

"Yeah, well enough to fake the accent. Do you still have an Ankarlen crewmate?" Cyn asked. If he was going to pass himself off as Ankarlen, he'd need to dress the part. "I'm going to need his clothes."

"What about their eyes?" Maxen interjected. "I've never seen an Ankarlen with dark eyes."

"Don't worry. I've got it covered." Cyn clung to Tuz as Maxen hit a bump in the road that nearly sent them flying out of the back of the runner.

Cyn focused his mind on every bit of information he knew about the Rasso-Ankarlen. Fortunately, he had dealt with them quite a bit during his stint as a Union liaison. While their physical mannerisms would be tricky, he could play the part. He couldn't give anything away. He could not fail.

"If you're not convincing, we're dead," Xan pointed out.

Cyn gripped the back of the seat harder. "I know."

# 9

YARA'S EYES FELT GRITTY AS SHE CRACKED THEM OPEN. HER HEAD THROBBED, and for a moment she couldn't concentrate on anything but the pounding in her head. She didn't have the strength to sit up, so she remained still, her skin pressed against the cold, black floor. She had to fight through this. She had to wake. Nausea ate at her insides as insistently as her fear.

She couldn't see. The dark room blurred. Rolling over on her back, she tried to focus. Chains rattled against the icy floor while she trembled, her naked skin exposed to the frigid air.

Yara eased onto her side and pulled her legs into her body. As she held her bare legs she realized fully that she was naked and chained.

Hard shackles dug into her wrists and feet, and the cold steel of slave bands circled her biceps.

Her heart raced and she couldn't breathe. Panic choked her,

squeezing her chest as tightly as the shackles. She curled into a tighter ball as a hot tear fell against her arm.

She desperately wished she could feel Tuz's warm fur brush up against her shoulders, or his hard head push insistently at her cheek.

No, she was alone, alone and enslaved.

She had to gather her strength. She needed to think clearly, take each moment as it came. Her life was at stake.

Performing a slow mental check of her body, she assessed her strength and any injuries. She felt sick. Her head pounded as if she'd been struck with a club. She couldn't see clearly yet, and it was too dark to see much anyway. The only light seeped in from a pair of vents near the ceiling.

Her skin crawled at the thought of someone stripping her while she was unconscious, but she didn't feel anything to indicate she'd been raped yet.

"Don't move." She didn't recognize the voice. It belonged to someone young. A boy. "You'll hurt yourself."

She felt a small rush of relief. The wound on her shoulder throbbed, aching. She flexed her arm and felt the hard pinch of the needles from the slave bands embedded in her muscles.

Her head spun and her mouth watered. She thought she was going to throw up, but thankfully she managed to quell the feeling.

"Stay calm," the boy urged. "Keep your heart slow, or the bands will knock you out again. Tell yourself you're sleeping."

She wished she were sleeping and this was all some terrible nightmare. Concentrating on her body again, she willed her heart to slow. She breathed deep, picturing the air like warm water rushing through her body and filling her toes. She let the slow intake of air soothe her as she tuned in to her body, focusing, calming calves, thighs, back, stomach, *heart*. The boy was right—she didn't need any more drugs in her system.

"Who are you?" she asked. She looked up just enough to see a shadow of a skinny teen boy with gangly limbs, sitting in the corner.

"I'm Hannolen," he said as if that explained everything. It explained enough. He was a slave, just like most of his people. *Just like her*.

The crush of helplessness pressed her, but she couldn't give in to it. She had to live in the moment, control what she could. She had to survive.

"Do you have a name?" If she could focus on something, she could keep her body under control. Her mind still felt sluggish, too sluggish.

"No." His young voice sounded quietly defiant. He was strong. They hadn't broken him yet, even though he'd probably been enslaved his whole life.

"Do you know where we are? Where we're going?" Yara pulled on the chain tying her foot to the floor. She had to test each of them. She couldn't take anything for granted.

"We're being sold." The boy fell quiet again.

Yara felt as if she'd been punched in the gut. Whoever had her intended to sell her. He wouldn't harm her until after the deal was done. If she was unspoiled, she'd be worth more. She had time, only a little time, but it was all she had so she clung to it.

She tested the length of the chains holding her arms. She had about double her arm span free. The chains rattled against the floor again as she scooted back to the wall. The brief exertion caused a new splitting pain to blossom in her head, so she curled back up into a ball, careful to position the chain just right in her hand.

If someone bent over to touch her, she could wrap it around their head and snap their neck before they had a chance to set off the bands. If her captors wanted, killing her would be as easy as saying the word, and the bands would inject her with poison.

She had to keep them from speaking. Her only weapons were her hands and the chains.

If only she could land a heart-strike. One blow to the chest and they'd drop dead.

Why was she even thinking about any of this? It wouldn't do any good. What was she going to do? Kill everyone one by one? They'd have to get close enough for her to strike them. One word and she'd be dead. It was impossible.

Once again, the darkness of the room seemed to press in around her. She couldn't give in to despair. So long as she was breathing, she could fight. She would fight, even if she died doing it.

She was not helpless. She'd take them down with her. If they touched her, she'd kill them.

"Who are you?" the boy asked.

The question snapped her attention back to the boy. "My name is Yara," she said. It was one thing they'd never take from her. She wouldn't let them take her name.

"That's a nice name," he commented as if nothing were wrong. The thought sickened her. Was this all he'd ever known in his life? Was this normal? Or worse, was this good?

"Why does he want you?" the boy asked.

"I don't understand." Yara felt sick again. She rested her head on the hard floor. The chill of it soothed her aching temple. She closed her throbbing eyes and continued to breathe slowly, carefully.

"The prince." The boy scooted to the right. No chains rattled as he shuffled along the floor. He was banded, but he wasn't tied.

She might be able to use that to her advantage.

"I don't know what you're talking about," she admitted.

The sounds of heavy footsteps and conversation drifted through the vents as a couple of men came closer to the solid black door.

"Pretend you're asleep," the boy whispered as he curled in a ball in the far corner of the room.

Yara did as he suggested, cracking the eye nearest the floor just enough that she could see shadows through her lashes.

"You'd better hope you're right," a man with a low voice warned in lilting Kronalen. Yara had to concentrate. She had learned Kronalen as part of her war training and had used it during the three years she'd worked in intelligence. Still, it would take all her effort to translate what they were saying.

"The Bacarilen assured me she's a trained fighter," a second man answered. He had a high and raspy voice, as if he'd spent too many days in Kronalen smokehouses.

"You know how the Rasso are. He wants a star for his betting pits."

Yara fought the urge to move as the one with the low voice stood in front of her, his pointed boot only centimeters from her eye. The edges of dark red robes trailed on the smooth floor. He was wealthy and dictating the conversation while the other answered to him.

He was the leader.

Smoker laughed. "I do know how the Rasso are. He's probably looking for a star in his bed as well."

The leader pushed his boot forward, digging the hard point under Yara's jaw. She stayed limp and kept her eyes shut as he lifted her face with the toe of his boot.

"She's fair enough." He let her head drop back to the floor. Yara forced herself to go even more limp. "But she's scarred." The point nudged her tender shoulder. She had to fight to keep from jumping up and breaking his neck. She couldn't move. Not until her life was at stake.

*Be careful.*

*Patience.*

She tried to remind herself not to feel fear, but the thought was ridiculous. Fear ate at her insides, clawing at her thoughts and ripping through her heart. She could taste it in her mouth and smell it on her skin.

"That proves she's a fighter," Smoker insisted.

"A bad one."

Yara clenched the chain tighter.

The leader walked toward the door. "The Rasso will try to use the scar to bring down her price. We'll just have to tempt him with some of her *finer* assets."

Smoker laughed as they turned to the boy. "What about this one?"

Yara heard a boot connect with flesh, but the boy didn't cry out.

"Get up," Smoker insisted. Another loud thump made her stomach turn over. She heard a shuffle and cracked open her eye enough to watch the boy stand.

With light spilling in through the open door, she could see well enough to get a look at the boy. Filthy blond hair stuck to his scalp as his protruding ribs pushed in and out with each breath.

Tears streamed out of his shut eyes, but his thin lips remained stoic and defiant. The tears were probably from the light, not his fear.

"He's not worth what we feed him," the leader lamented. "I'm afraid he's developing a tolerance for the bands. The pain reprimand isn't working the way it should."

"Should I test it?" Smoker suggested with a cruel humor in his voice.

"Not now. I'm hoping to pawn him off as pit fodder. If the Rasso doesn't want him, go ahead and put him down."

Yara trembled with her rage and disgust. If they activated the bands, she couldn't stop them. They were out of the reach of the chains.

If they killed him, there was nothing she could do.

Again she felt the hot rush down her back as her mouth watered again. She was going to be sick.

"Let's go. It smells in here," the leader suggested. They turned and walked out of the cell. The heavy black door slid shut behind them with an ominous boom.

Yara opened her eyes wide, trying to adjust to the dim light.

"You okay?" she whispered.

The boy didn't answer. He had huddled into a ball once again, his skinny arms wrapped around his bony legs.

Yara wanted to reach out, to comfort him. She had never done such a thing in her life, but the instinct to comfort the boy was nearly overwhelming.

"Are you injured?" she asked again.

He sighed.

"If you come over here, I might be able to help stop the bruising from getting worse," she suggested. She had enough battle-med to know how to apply pressure to a contusion.

"No," he insisted.

Yara tingled with relief. His voice sounded strong. His injuries couldn't be too severe. Still, he barely had any resources left in his emaciated body. How would he heal?

"Are you really a fighter?" he asked.

"Yes," she admitted, sitting up and pulling her own legs in close to shield her body. "I was a commander for the Union. I've fought to stop the slave trade."

The boy didn't say anything, and Yara realized the irony of what she'd just said. She obviously didn't fight hard enough. She saw her assignment as a mission, one more thing she had to complete for her ascension. It hadn't been personal, not until now.

"I want to fight," the boy said, his voice soft and hollow. "I don't know how."

"You are fighting," Yara assured him. "You were very brave just now."

His breath hitched. She couldn't see his face, but the soft intake of air was unmistakable.

"They're going to kill me."

"They won't," she promised. "I won't let them kill you." She didn't know how she'd do it. It was a futile and foolish thing to promise, but she felt like she had to. She'd protect him or she'd die trying. At least they wouldn't die alone.

"They'll probably make you kill me," he whispered.

Yara nearly vomited on the floor. They had just said as much. "I won't kill you, I won't."

"What can you do?" the boy snapped with the hard edge of anger. "They'll make you want to die. You won't last with the pain. I'll be nothing to you. Watch, you'll see."

"That's not true," she promised. "I'll die first. I promise."

They both fell into an ugly silence.

"You need a name," Yara insisted. She didn't want to call him "the boy" any longer. He wasn't an object. She refused to use a label for him.

"I don't have one." His voice sounded very soft, so very alone.

"Then take one," she urged. He needed to take this one bit of control. "What is your name?"

The boy fell silent for a long time. Yara waited in the darkness. She thought about her own name, the simplest and purest name of the line of Yarini. As she grew and fought through the ranks of the Elite, she always turned to the solid strength of her name and the honor there.

Her name marked her as the blood of the Just.

*Justice.*

She had taken pride in it. Now she realized she hadn't fought hard enough for it. In tactics meetings, delays were accepted, casualties reduced to numbers, slaves thought of as a commodity.

It wasn't right. It wasn't *just.*

She should have done more.

Yara thought about the statue of Yarini in the Halls of

Honor. It towered over the shining white floor, her strength and pride radiating out over the Hall, but her eyes were closed.

She should have opened her eyes.

"I don't know a good name," the boy said, breaking Yara's thoughts. "What does your name mean?"

"On my planet, we pass down the start of our names if we are part of the family of one of our great leaders. Each family is known for a different trait." She rubbed her wrists. The cold metal was digging into her skin just below the bones.

"What is your trait?"

"Justice." Yara watched him. His pale face looked ghostly in the dim light.

"What do you name people who are brave?" he asked.

"The bloodline of Isa the Bold are known for their bravery." She waited as he stared up at the ceiling, deep in thought.

"Call me Ishan." His words were so soft Yara almost couldn't hear them.

"It suits you, Ishan." She smiled at him, and the boy looked away, but the corner of his thin mouth twisted up just slightly.

In the silence of the cell, she heard him whisper his name over and over, as if reassuring himself that it was real.

The room jolted. Were they still on the Kronalen ship? They must be coming out of macrospace. It wouldn't be long before they'd be sold.

She shuddered as the chill of the cell sank deep into her bones.

How was she going to make it out of this?

# 10

"WHAT DO WE DO?" ISHAN ASKED AS THE JOLTS FROM THE DOCKING PROCESS shuddered through the ship.

"Stay calm," Yara advised. For the first time, the boy sounded like the frightened child he was. Her hands shook as she gathered the chain, her only weapon.

Minutes stretched into hours, or maybe they were hours. She didn't know how long she remained shackled in the dark, waiting.

Ishan crawled across the compartment and hunkered down by her side. She grasped the boy's hand and held it hard, hoping the strength of that connection could somehow give them power.

Dark thoughts circled in her mind like carrion birds: rape, pain, humiliation, helplessness, and death. They were coming for her. She tried to fight the terror but couldn't. It overwhelmed her. She had to gain control of herself. She wouldn't let them break her. Stinging tears began to form in her eyes, but she couldn't stop them.

Ishan squeezed tighter.

Footsteps echoed in the hall.

"I'm with you, Ishan," Yara whispered. The words seemed like such an empty comfort. She couldn't save him. Still, she wouldn't let him feel alone any longer. "Whatever happens, I'm with you."

Bright lights blazed to life, turning the near darkness to searing white. Ishan screamed in pain and jerked his hand away from her.

"Ishan," she called in desperation. She couldn't see him. She couldn't open her eyes. Her heart stabbed at her chest with each frantic beat while the room filled with his agonized cries. She tried to reach out when the chains around her arms yanked straight up, pulling her to her feet.

Hanging from the chains, she tried to support her weight but could barely scratch at the floor with her toes. She grasped the chains, so she could hold her weight with her hands instead of letting the cuffs dig into her tender wrists. Her arms felt like they had been ripped from their sockets, and she had to fight for each panicked breath.

She tried to kick, but the shackles at her feet pulled down as tightly as the ones on her wrists pulled up. She was helpless, strung out like a snared bird. The promise of death whispered in the air around them.

"Yara?" Ishan whimpered.

"Stay down," she warned.

*Great merciful Matriarchs, protect the boy.*

Her prayer was all she had left to save him. She tried to crack open an eye, but the light was too bright. Still, she forced herself to open one eye as she heard footsteps enter the compartment. The stinging light burned her as she fought to keep her eye open long enough to see through her tears.

She wriggled in her chains. She couldn't just give up. She would never give up, no matter what happened.

*Survive.*

The tears burned down her cheeks as she held tighter to the chains.

*By the Mercy of Ona the Pure, help me!*

"Speak or strike out in any way, and I'll kill the boy," the deep-voiced Kronalen warned. "I'll turn down the lights enough for you to watch."

He didn't value the boy at all. If she could keep his attention on her, maybe he'd leave Ishan alone. Her compliance was the only thing buying him time.

Her stomach churned as she heard more men enter the room. With each new male presence, the lancing fear in her gut dug deeper. She tried to crack open her eye again. One was tall, with a mass of snarl-braids. She couldn't see him clearly, only enough to get a hint at his height and coloring.

Another man stood behind him while the Kronalen in his blurry red robes blocked the door to the left. Analyzing their position came as second nature, but it wouldn't do her any good. She couldn't break the chains.

"As you can see she's in her prime, young, strong, agile." The Kronalen's voice sounded too cold. How could such a creature be human? It was as if she wasn't a living, thinking thing at all, but an animal. "She's marked with tattoos, and the

Bacarilen that sold her to me assured that she's been trained to fight."

"She skinny, too much so," the buyer grumbled. The lilt of his accent made his words sound like the hissing of a snake. Yara's heart dropped down into her gut. "And wounded," he added.

"It's hardly a scratch," the Kronalen dismissed. "She's healthy and ready to fight. She'll pull in good money in the pits."

"She tamed?"

Yara willed him to come closer so she could show him how tame she was. She'd bite him if she had to. Then she thought of Ishan, whose life hung in her hands. The cold-blooded slavers in the room wouldn't think anything of killing him right there in front of everyone.

"Go ahead and pet her," the Kronalen suggested with an oily tone to his voice.

Yara's body tensed as a raging war cry drowned out any thought in her mind. She couldn't let it out.

Ishan made a strangled sound. Yara fought to open her eyes. The brute of a man standing behind the Ankarlen grabbed the boy by the neck.

"Don't," Yara shouted. Great Matriarchs, what would she do if they killed him?

"Quiet," the Kronalen demanded. Yara felt a burning sting in her arms, and then weakness stole through her body. She fought to maintain her grip on the chains and her fragile hold on consciousness.

"I apologize for the boy," the Kronalen continued. "He's a distraction. I'll put him down."

"No," the Ankarlen stated. Yara's eyelids felt so heavy. She couldn't keep them open. Staying awake felt like a struggle against a mounting tide, but her life depended on it. "For now, leave him. You ask for how much?"

"Eighty thousand bars of conductive trillide." The Kronalen moved to block the door. Yara couldn't keep her eyes open anymore. Her arms stretched above her head, tingling from lack of blood flow. She wouldn't be able to hold on much longer.

"YOU SPEND TOO MUCH TIME IN SMOKEHOUSES," CYN COUNTERED, IMITATING the odd speech patterns of the Rasso-Ankarlen. So far, his disguise was flawless. Now he just had to play the part. "You can have forty for her and the boy."

Cyn spared a glance back at Yara, even though he couldn't let his worry show on his face. He was losing her to the tranquilizers. The Kronalen bastard that took her was the lowest kind of scum. If the man hadn't insisted on showing his *wares* inside the security of his own ship, Cyn would have slit his throat, stolen Yara, and been done with the leech.

He let his glance drift down the long, smooth lines of her athletic body, and his stomach churned in protest. She was too beautiful to suffer this way. He had to get her out of there. Immediately.

Then again, he had to be careful, or he'd end up chained beside her.

Xan had his back and thankfully subdued the Hannolen youth. Cyn didn't want to see the boy killed either. He looked at the boy and saw himself, years ago. The pain of it burned like a fresh wound in his mind. As it was, he was fighting with all his concentration just to keep old visions from distracting him.

"Forty, don't insult me," the Kronalen complained. "She has not been off this ship and is untouched. That alone is worth at least an extra twenty."

Cyn wanted to agree to whatever terms the Kronalen offered just to get her out of there, but he knew it would be an immediate red flag. Ankarlen were nasty negotiators.

"Forty-five. She shows no proof she is worth any more than that." Cyn tried to maintain an aloof expression, but the subdermal pinchers he'd inserted to shape his eyes and cheeks hurt like a bitch. He just hoped his grimace looked somewhat like a superior sneer. He didn't have that much trillide. He only had one thing of worth, his ship.

"Why don't you feel her out?" the Kronalen suggested. "She's quality."

The chains rattled as Yara flinched and tried to pull away. Her fear was so stark and clear on her face, it broke him. He felt his stomach clench. He couldn't touch her like this. It went against everything he believed in. He held himself to a strict code of honor, and this would be the deepest, most terrible violation of that.

"No need, her condition is evident." Cyn brushed off the Kronalen who circled around and eyed Yara with a hungry look on his ratlike face.

"What kind of a Rasso are you?" he asked, raising one dark eyebrow. "Your people love their bed pets. Perhaps you prefer the boy?"

"Pit fighters are needed stock for the pits. New bed sports

hold no interest now." Cyn risked a sidelong glance at Xan. Though he was dressed in a simple slave tunic as part of the ruse, the pirate was armed to the teeth. They both figured no one would check a slave for a small arsenal of weapons.

"*I* could demonstrate her fitness," the Kronalen leech suggested with an evil grin on his face. "If you're not interested in keeping her clean, I might as well try her out. I'm not selling her for less than sixty." He moved up behind her, and again Yara pulled on her chains as a helpless gasp escaped her beautiful lips.

He had to stop this.

"Don't touch her," he growled.

The Kronalen laughed. "Feel her out if you're interested. Then we'll discuss price."

Cyn closed his eyes behind the shades protecting him from the blinding lights.

He had no choice.

"TOUCH ME AND I'LL BITE YOU UNTIL YOU BLEED," YARA PROMISED.

The Kronalen flesh trader laughed his low, sickening laugh. "See? Fierce."

What was she going to do?

She couldn't defend herself. She couldn't defend Ishan. She didn't even know if the boy was still alive.

Her heart thundered an erratic, painful rhythm in her chest. She could barely feel her arms, the only sensations in them a deep, numb ache and the sting of the cuffs digging into her wrists.

She felt the Ankarlen's presence as he drew closer to her.

The drugs swam in her mind, but the sharp sting of her terror gave her clarity.

Somehow, she'd kill him. She swore it to herself.

Her body tensed, waiting for hot, ugly hands to grope her body, but they didn't come. She could feel the heat of him in the cold compartment. It enveloped her, making her feel less exposed, but he did not touch her.

*What is going on?*

She tried to open her eyes again but couldn't.

The tickle of breath caressed her neck. "Forgive me, Pix," he whispered, so low she almost didn't hear him.

*Oh sweet merciful Matriarchs!* Her heart pounded harder as she almost collapsed with dizzy relief.

*Cyrus.*

How did he find her?

The tips of his fingers barely touched her jaw, trickling over her sensitive skin as a sudden rush of adrenaline coursed through her blood. She turned her head away from his touch.

She had to think. This was all a ruse. He was pretending to be her buyer. She had to play along, or they'd all be dead.

Why did he come for her?

Jerking her face away from his touch, she tried to muster the strength to pretend to resist him. His fingers burrowed into the hair just behind her ears, while his rough thumbs smoothed over her cheekbones. He turned her head one way, then the other. She pushed into the touch, wanting it to look like he had to force her, but the stronger contact with his warm hands felt safe as he cradled her face.

He brushed at a cold trail of her tears with his gentle touch, and a hot, stinging tear spilled out of her eye to re-form the damp trail.

His warm palm circled one of her wrists. He gave her a light, reassuring squeeze, then let his hand slide slowly down her forearm and the backs of her tired arms. He massaged the ache in the muscles of her back and neck, his hands strong and forceful in the touch. It was part of the act, a pit-master feeling a fighter's potential strength, but he managed to relieve her pain with it instead of harm her. The rush of relief that followed in the wake of his touch made her dizzy mind swim and her heart stumble.

*Dear sweet Creator, I am going to die.*

She let her head fall forward, pretending to faint, even though it wasn't too far off the mark. Every cell in her body screamed as it came alive for him.

He brought his hands lower around the backs of her shoulders and kneaded her weary muscles. She fought to breathe as the comforting touch drove her mad with relief.

His hands skimmed over the bare skin of her collar bone, tracing along the edge of her wound.

She preferred the hard touch. Force was something she was used to while sparring. Touch was a means of control, of power. The light touch was something different, something she could barely understand.

She had no control here. Her life was in his skilled hands, and his touch tortured her. It teased her and awoke something powerful and primal.

She felt caged, trapped, but so damn alive she had to fight not to roar like some wild cat in heat.

What was wrong with her? She shouldn't be thinking like this. She should not be turned on by this. It was so wrong.

His fingers danced along the sides of her breasts, and she moaned low in her throat. His warm palms slid over her nipples in a soft and modest caress.

By Fima the Merciless, he was killing her.

And it felt so good.

It had to be the drugs. She'd gone completely out of her mind. She shouldn't want his touch. It should repulse her.

*Forgive me.* His whispered words echoed in the deep parts of her mind.

A shiver raced down the backs of her legs as his gentle hands drifted over her stomach.

His intentions became suddenly clear.

He had tried to get out of touching her, he was doing everything in his power to keep his touch light, and he wanted her forgiveness for touching her at all.

He respected her.

*Shakt.*

And what was worse?

She trusted him.

Great Ona, if this was a test of her will, she was failing miserably.

His hands sank lower, until the tips of his fingers brushed the top of her thigh and drifted toward the juncture of her legs. Her body responded with a blaze of damp heat. The pulse of her need thrummed in her head, her heart. She was no virgin. In her youth, bold and secure in her place among the Elite, she had commanded a lover. But the rules had been different. She had control. She touched him. He did as he was told.

Now helpless and in the hands of a man who ignited everything in her, her body recognized what it wanted, what it needed.

Her heart stopped. She inhaled but couldn't exhale as his powerful fingers pushed between her legs.

*Ona, forgive me.* It was her turn to beg.

Her mouth dropped open as his fingers remained still. She still couldn't push the air out of her lungs. She expected his thick fingers to work into her, feel her, but he remained so still. She realized he wouldn't do such a thing, and instead of being relieved she wanted to throw him on the floor and take her pleasure from him as if he were a simple object for her lust, but deep in her heart, she knew that wasn't possible.

She pulled against her chains.

*Shakt!*

She gasped and tried to pull away from him. She couldn't take the stillness in his hand another moment. She wanted far more. She had never wanted anything like this.

She felt her pulse deep in that place as it throbbed against his hand. She dangled from her chains, limp and weak as he pulled his hand away. He reached behind her and slid his hands from her lower back, over her buttocks and down the backs of her thighs and calves, bringing him down on one knee before her.

Her ecstasy tore through her like beautiful torture, and she let out her breath in a hard rush of air. She could feel the heat of his breath on her stomach, then lower as he touched his forehead for only an instant to the soft swell of her lower abdomen.

His position reminded her of a pilgrim before a holy shrine, seeking forgiveness. There was nothing to forgive. She didn't want him like this. She wanted him fierce, raw. She wanted him over her, in her, never beneath her.

If he ever chose to worship her, she'd be a sacrifice screaming beneath him, not a shrine.

She had been a shrine too long.

"What do you think?" the Kronalen asked. "Does she smell good enough to taste?" Cyrus stood and pulled away from her but not before her imagination placed his mouth on her most intimate place. She fought back a low groan as she hung in the chains.

The icy air of the compartment closed in around her, filling the void where his body heat had soaked into her skin. She could still smell the rich, dusky scent that had clung to his bed. She tried to hold on to that as tightly as she held her breath.

"She is acceptable, but there is no way to prove she is untouched as you say," Cyrus answered.

"You're just trying to talk her down. You know she is quality. I won't take less than sixty," the Kronalen insisted. Yara cracked open her eyes, needing to see him, though she couldn't recognize him.

Cyrus paced with slow, deliberate steps across the room. "You'll accept a macro-capable I.S. Cruiser modified for smuggling for the Azralen and the boy."

Yara's gut dropped to the floor as she hung limply from her chains.

*His ship?*

He would trade his ship?

What was he thinking?

"Does it fly?" The Kronalen sounded skeptical.

"Don't insult, trader, or your head will feed my bears." Cyrus sounded cool, in control, not like he was trading away his home for a woman he barely knew.

Something wasn't right.

Why had he gone after her?

It didn't make any sense.

"I want another ten for the boy," the Kronalen pushed.

"He's worthless. You would dispose of him. However, he might be useful as bait and practice for the Azralen. You will give me the boy as a tribute to my patience." Cyrus's voice gave her chills as he spoke about both of them as if they weren't human. The Ankarlen manner of speaking without ever referring to oneself to foreigners only made the cold denial of their humanity more distressing.

She knew it was an act, but the thought that anyone could actually dehumanize another in such a way terrified her.

She tried to stay calm. Yarini, her ancestor and the guardian of justice, would protect them. They had to make it out of this.

"I could still sell the boy on the blocks," the Kronalen insisted.

"The crowd will laugh. He barely lives," Cyrus insisted. "His price wouldn't cover the auction fees."

"Fine," the Kronalen acquiesced. "Transfer the command codes to this ship. I'll confirm its condition with my man there and pick it up on my way back through Gansai."

Yara's relief almost made her faint as she hung from the shackles. She watched the Kronalen hand over the control pin for the slave bands to Cyrus.

She was safe.

The men exited the room, and the lights finally turned out, plunging them into near darkness. The chains went slack, and Yara collapsed to the floor.

She opened her eyes wide, but drifting pink and blue spots from her burned retinas dominated her blurry field of vision.

"Are you okay?" Ishan asked.

"I'm fine," she answered, which was far from the truth. She'd never been so tormented in all her life. But she wasn't about to share that with the boy. She was unharmed, but she had a lot of questions.

And she was going to get some answers as soon as they were safe. She wouldn't let Cyrus back away.

"I'm sorry they touched you. I couldn't help," he mumbled.

"It's okay, Ishan," she soothed. "We're free."

# 11

THE DOOR HISSED OPEN, SLICING THE NEAR DARK WITH THE LIGHT FROM THE corridor. Ishan scurried away, hiding deeper in the shadows of the dim room. "Carry her," Cyrus ordered to the other man posing as a slave. "Boy, you follow quick."

Yara felt the burn of embarrassment as the heavy-chested Hannolen man wrapped her quickly in a thin bit of cloth, then lifted her into his burly arms. Cyrus removed her chains, leaving the cuffs on her wrists and ankles locked together. They had to maintain the slave deception until they were safely out of this proverbial mud pit.

Yara closed her eyes and tried to fight off the lingering dizziness from the tranquilizers. As they left the Kronalen ship, a crush of noise rose up and swallowed them. Yara tried to stay conscious as they left the shipping docks and entered the auctions.

Yara opened her stinging eyes. Fires burned on long posts, casting the thick fog in a creeping orange glow.

People, naked and starving, huddled together in cages, the adults shielding children in the centers of the groups like wild sheep at the slaughter.

Voices of hawkers and hungry crowds carried over the muffled cries from the cages, while the sickly sweet odor of filth and humanity clung to the blanketing fog.

Yara had never seen actual slaves in her time during the war, and the sight made her gut clench.

The man holding her stiffened. With her head resting on his chest, she could hear his heart beating with a sharp, erratic rhythm. He was Hannolen, and these were mostly his people.

By the swift blade of Yarini, she would help fight this. When she ascended to the throne, Azra would fully join the war, not for their own gains and experience. They would not hold back. They would help end this depravity.

She swore it.

Cyrus and his friend picked up their pace as they crossed over the wide wooden bridge that spanned the pits. Mud from years of foul feet caked the span, muffling footsteps as the misery from the auctions below rose up like a tormenting specter. They moved swift and steady as if their fear would betray them and chain them to the nearest hawking block. As soon as the sounds of the auctions faded, and the fog around them thickened, Cyrus stopped and yanked the wig from his head. He tucked it in his belt, hastily rubbed his head, then turned and pulled out a cutter from the bracers he still wore beneath the Ankarlen robes.

The cutter made short work of the cuffs binding her wrists and ankles together. Yara almost cried in relief as Cyrus pulled their heavy weight away from her raw wounds. As soon as the slave bands circling her biceps were off, she'd be free.

"Give her to me," he ordered as he held out his arms to her. "Take the boy. He's exhausted."

Yara gratefully circled his warm neck with her arms. "Thank you, Cyrus," she whispered, but stopped short as she looked him in the eye.

Even in the dim light, they shone pale and gloriously green, like the leaves in the canopy of Azra. She had never seen such green eyes on an Earthlen. His skin had been stained darker, and his face reshaped. It all looked odd on him, except for his eyes. Somehow, they seemed natural and suited to him.

"Thank you," she murmured again and let her head rest against his shoulder.

"Let's get out of here, Pix."

He pressed his cheek against the top of her head, then strode with purpose toward a pale glow and looming shadow in the fog. He had her. As soon as they got the bands off her, she'd be safe, and he could finally rest his weary conscience.

Crewmates filed out from the ship, carrying blankets and steaming mugs. Cyn waved them off as he ascended the cargo ramp.

"Whose ship is this?" Yara asked as Cyn gently placed her on her feet. His hands shook with relief as he steadied her. She looked around the cargo bay.

"Xan's the captain here. I never would have been able to find you without him or the boy enslaved with you. They saved your life."

Her expression softened as she looked toward Venet, who fussed over the Hannolen youth like a mother tiger. Xan remained close at the boy's back, leaving Cyn to deal with Yara.

He took a deep breath as the rending pain in his heart lessened. The visions of Yarlia screaming as the mudrats carried her away slowly pushed back into the recesses of his mind. He hadn't been able to save his first love, but he had saved Yara from the same fate. Now he had work to do.

Those slave bands had to come off before they poisoned her any further.

"Take them up to Med," Xan ordered, pulling off the tunic. He threw a long overcoat on his bare shoulders and replaced his eye shades, immediately transforming his appearance from a slave guard to a pirate captain.

"Are you strong enough to walk?" Cyn asked Yara as he took her hand. It felt cold in his palm. She clutched a thin blanket wrapped under her arms and over her breasts.

Damn his memory. Now that he knew exactly what her breasts looked like, he'd never forget a single detail about them. They had the power to taunt him now, even when he couldn't see them.

He could barely process what had happened. It was almost too much sensation. His shame and guilt ate at him. But he couldn't deny the power of the feel of his hands smoothing over her soft skin.

It was wrong. He had no choice. He did everything in his power to keep from touching her shamefully.

Insecurity pecked at his mind like a vengeful imp. Did she blame him for what he'd had to do?

She looked up at him and squeezed his hand. He had to look away as they boarded a lift.

"Cyrus?" She leaned to the side, so she could meet his gaze. She shifted her fingers so the slender digits wove together with his. "Let's get these things off me."

The lift slowed to a stop. He nodded and led her the rest of the way to Med.

Xan's medical bay may not have looked like much, with the worn beds and the industrial racks holding supplies and medical equipment, but it was certainly clean and functional. Xan's crew had seen their fair share of war wounds and spilled enough blood on this floor.

The lights had been dimmed to the faintest glow, while Venet ran a diagnostic tool over Ishan's eyes.

"How does he look?" Xan asked, keeping his shades on even in the near darkness. Venet pinched her lips together, not a good sign.

"We'll fix him up," she assured in a way that left Cyn with a bad feeling about the boy's prognosis. But there was little he could do to help. Maybe if he brewed more kiltii water, it could help heal the boy's eyes. It wouldn't hurt to try, but there was nothing he could do about it now. His only kiltii vine was back on his ship. No, it wasn't his ship anymore.

He just hoped Maxen had enough proof to arrest the Kronalen bastard for flesh trading as soon as he entered Gansai's atmosphere. Once the bastard was arrested, his property would be "salvaged" and taken by the circle, including Cyn's ship. He'd been able to send Maxen a quick message to strip the ship and store his possessions until he returned, but he'd never see the Black Serpent again. It was pirate law.

"Have a seat." Cyn returned his attention to Yara as he helped her up onto one of the beds. He pulled the control pin for the slave bands out of his pocket.

"No," Yara insisted as she placed her hand over his. "Get them off Ishan first."

"Yara . . ."

"Please." She gathered the thin blankets tighter around her chest as the lights in the sickening bands flickered.

Cyn sighed and handed the control pin to Xan. "Who knows how long he's had those on. Be careful," Cyn warned. "We can't exactly go back for another one or our cover's blown." He grabbed a programmer for the pinchers in his face and flicked it on. Slowly he dragged the glowing yellow bar over his cheeks and eyes. The pressure released from the pinchers, but the relief was tempered by the stinging pain of the needles pushing back out through his skin. He carefully pulled each bloody spine out and dropped it in a shallow dish.

Yara offered him a bit of cloth, and he pressed it to the miniscule puncture wounds dotting his cheeks and brow.

"You look better," she admitted.

"Thanks." He dabbed at the wounds, then let the cloth drop. "I just hope the skin dye wears off."

"How did you change your eyes?"

He looked up at her, confused. "Huh?"

"How did you turn your eyes green?"

Shit, he had forgotten about that. He hadn't gone without his contacts in over a decade. For a second he had forgotten that his eyes were naturally green and not black. "Contacts. Ancient Earthlen tech. I should take them out."

"I like them," she admitted, "even if they aren't real."

He brought his gaze to hers, unsure of how to respond.

"We've got a problem over here," Xan called. Cyn turned away from Yara to help with the boy. Venet carefully extracted the needles from one open band while Xan leaned over the other.

"These bands are so old, the connector to the release key on the command pin is corroded. The bastards hardly ever take these damn things off people. The first one was nasty, and this one is worse." Xan moved to the side so Cyn could take a look. The boy stared at him, not saying anything, but his fear shone clearly on his face. It didn't take much to set off a slave band to kill.

Venet smoothed a hand over the boy's greasy hair while maintaining pressure on the raw wounds of the boy's upper arm. Cyn carefully took up the command pin, lodged in a small port just beneath one of the injector lights of the band on his other arm.

Cyn tried to activate the connection enough to give the voice command to release, but no matter how he worked the pin, it wouldn't connect.

"Xan, do you have a nanoscope?"

"Yeah." Xan handed him the palm-sized viewer and a syringe. The boy flinched.

"Don't worry. I won't hurt you." Cyn inspected the syringe. Once he injected the gel into the port, the nano components would automatically arrange their projection structure, sending images to the viewer of the interior of the slave band. He injected a tiny amount into the port, conscious of the risk of setting off the band.

The screen on the viewer glowed, giving him a good look

at the broken connector. If he came at the connector from a slightly skewed angle, he might be able to make enough of a connection to get the thing off.

With steady hands, he made the connection and issued a sharp command to release. The band opened with a hiss, and the boy exhaled loudly as Xan pulled the terrible needles out of his arm.

"Thank you," he whispered with a hoarse voice. "What happens now?"

"What do you mean?" Cyn asked.

"You bought me." The boy looked at him with a sad resignation in his dark eyes.

"You're free. You don't belong to me."

"Where do I go?"

Cyn looked at Xan, who had busied himself trying to remove the command pin from the band. "Stay here with Xan. He's a good captain. He'll teach you well."

Cyn heard a snap. "What?" Xan grumbled.

He shot his friend a quick glare. "I no longer have a ship. I can't take him on. You have plenty of room. He's Hannolen." Cyn pushed the viewer into Xan's hand. "He needs *you*."

"*Hork*," he cursed.

"Damn it, Xan, you can't hide forever."

"It's not that." Xan handed him the band and the viewer. "I think the command pin is broken."

"Shit." Cyn examined the viewer and tried to dislodge the pin, but it was hopelessly stuck in the corroded band. He looked over at Yara. Her brow creased.

"You can't get the bands off?" Her eyes widened.

"You have any microbes?" he asked Xan.

The pirate shook his head. "We used the last of them when we overtook a large transport."

Cyn ran a weary hand over his sore face. "I'll have to pick them."

"Can't you get another key?" Yara's voice pitched higher.

"The key was coded to the trigger programming in the bands for the two of you. Usually these pins are only used to transfer the codes to a master control. But we don't have any other slaves, so we don't have a master control, and we can't go back to the Kronalen and ask for another copy of the code. The only way to get them off now is to pick them."

"Can you do that?" Yara kept her expression very still, but Cyn caught the slight tremble in her voice.

"Yes." He tried to answer with as much confidence as he could give her.

"Are you any good?"

At any other time, he would have teased her. Perhaps he should have, to ease her fear, but he knew just how serious this was. One slip and he'd kill her. This would take all his concentration. "I can do this."

She pinched her beautiful lips into a tight line. "Okay."

"We'll take the boy up to quarters to clean him up and find him some clothes," Xan stated as he pulled the boy to his feet.

"His name is Ishan," Yara snapped.

Ishan looked up at her and blinked his clouded eyes.

"That's not a Hannolen name," Xan commented as one of his brows arched above the rim of his shades.

"He is the blood of Isa the Bold." She gave Ishan a slow nod then turned her glare back to Xan.

"It's a good name. Come Ishan." Xan looked as impassive

as ever, but his stance shifted. "Good luck. I'll leave the med alert on."

Cyn picked up a charge probe and the nanoscope. He'd need luck. Taking a deep breath, he focused on retrieving the information he needed from his mind. He'd have to delve into his muscle memory, something he didn't like to do very often. It took him so deep in his mind, he'd be less able to block out old memories.

The stillness overtook him. He reached a state of concentration so complete he could no longer feel sensation. "I'm going to disable the poison injector first, since it's the most dangerous, but as soon as the poison one is disabled, the rest get really tricky. You might get injected with a behavior modifier as we do this," he warned.

"Okay." She swallowed.

"If you get injected, don't panic. Try to stay calm." He sat on the bed next to her and lifted her arm as he injected the nanos into the port.

Her skin blanched. "That's easy for you to say."

She was strong. He knew she could control her fear. "Just stay still and quiet. We can't afford any distractions. If anything goes off on this band, we'll have to work quick to get the one on your other arm off before it cycles." Cyn took a deep breath. "If the injector signals don't match when it cycles, we're in trouble."

He focused to the point where the only thing in his awareness was the small screen of the viewer. He felt connected to his hands as he fed them direct signals from his memory. He'd only done this three times before, but each was successful, and his hands already knew the path they had to take. He just had to guide them.

Each careful move of his hands seemed to last an hour as he severed the command paths to the injector. The light within the injector slowly faded, rendering it harmless. He broke his concentration and the rush of pain stabbed through his body from his aching back to his stiff neck.

"Well, this one won't kill you." He wiped his brow with the back of his wrist and stretched his shoulders. "Hopefully the other one will go as easily."

"Thank the Matriarchs," Yara sighed. "How many more injectors are there?"

"Three in this band. I'm not sure what's in them. Usually they're loaded with a tranquilizer, some sort of stimulant, a pain inducer, and lately they've incorporated a truth serum. Once we're done here, we get to start all over again with the other arm." While the poison was the most dangerous, it was fortunately the least tricky. He still had to be careful.

"Why do they need a truth serum?" Yara asked as he bent over the slave band once more.

"The Kronalen are starting to have trouble. I think they're trying to find a way to root out the slaves helping the Union forces." Cyn carefully extracted the probe from the poison injector and moved on to the next in line.

Cyn quickly disabled the second injector. He didn't want to waste time or energy, so he maintained his focus and continued.

A loud yowl reverberated through the surgery, followed by the frantic screech of cat claws dragging over the door.

"Tuz!" Yara sat up straighter, and Cyn's hand slipped.

"Damn it." The probe pushed too far into the injector and the light started blinking.

"I'm sorry," Yara offered. "*Shakt,* what is that?"

"I don't know." He grabbed her arm and held it still as he tried to repair the damage. Eventually, he got the light to fade out. "Are you groggy?"

"No." She dragged out the word, as if she had had too many cups of nilo.

"How about jittery?"

"I feel strange. Why did you trade your ship for me?"

"What?" Crap. They set off the truth serum. Yara swayed on the table, her expression puzzled.

"Your ship. Why did you trade it for me? Why did you come?" She shook her head, then rubbed her eyes. "I can't focus on anything. I want to see Tuz. Is he okay?"

"We set off the truth serum," he stated, while trying to keep his exasperation at bay. "I need you to try to stay quiet. The serum inhibits your ability to hold back what you're thinking." They didn't have time for this. At least he hadn't set off the stimulant. Chatty was better than convulsing.

"I'll try." She took a deep breath and closed her eyes.

Cyn focused again, even with Tuz growling on the other side of the door. He had to get both bands off immediately.

He had the last injector's pins immobilized when Yara started back up again. "Thank you for saving me."

He had to ignore her. Responding to her would only keep her talking.

"There's nothing to forgive," she continued.

A chill ran down his back. There was plenty to forgive. She

had no idea what he was involved in. He was her enemy. He couldn't ever forget that. Why did she have to look so much like Yarlia?

*Focus.*

"You're sexy," she whispered.

"Crap." He made the final cut and the last light died. "You need to stay quiet, Yara."

He cracked open the slave band and pulled out the needles.

"Why did you come after me?" she asked again. "You barely know me."

He couldn't take it anymore. Every time he looked at her, he saw a reflection of Yarlia, her terror as she was taken away from him, her broken spirit when he finally freed her, and her despair as she died in his arms after delivering her stillborn child. "I had to, okay? I couldn't just leave you to them. They'd destroy you." He threw the band toward the shelves. "I'm not going to be responsible for that again."

"Again?"

*Aw, shit.* "Look, Yara. I have to disable that other band. As soon as the band cycles, it will take a bio reading and realize that you have serum in your system that isn't in its programming. That will set off the tampering mechanism, and it will inject you with poison." He cupped her face in his hands and forced her to look at him. "You have to stay quiet. You have to."

Her wide, golden eyes searched his. She swallowed and nodded.

He moved to her other side. Time was running out. He didn't have the luxury of coaxing his memory. He had to move quickly. He injected the nanos then set to work.

He had the probe locked into the injector. Just a slight turn, and she'd be safe.

"You lost someone to slavers, didn't you?" Her words were barely a whisper, but Cyn felt like he'd been punched in the gut. He tried to keep his hand still but felt the trembling race through his whole body.

"You lost someone you loved." Her voice sounded even quieter this time, but it rang in the empty room.

"Yes," he whispered back. He kept his hand still while he tried to steady his racing heart. He was almost there. One more turn.

*Carefully.*

*Yarlia's screams rip through the still air. She reaches out for him as they carry her away. The pain of each blow to his head, his ribs, courses through his body.*

*The hot, ripping pain of the blade cuts into his chest above his heart as he makes his first kill. He bleeds as he watches the life fade from her flesh-master. He'd freed her, but he can't save her. The damage has been done.*

A sharp steady beep broke into the fog of his memories.

"Cyrus?" Yarlia's eyes were so wide, so afraid. No, not Yarlia. Yara.

What was happening?

The lights on the band began to blink.

*Shakt!*

Cyn's panic grabbed his throat and stole the strength from his hands. He grabbed a med strip and firmly tied it around her arm above the band.

"Xan! Launch! Set coordinates for Oriana. We need the Touscari now!" The race of healers on Oriana were the only ones capable of neutralizing the poison.

"Cyrus?" Yara grasped his hand as the med-alert sirens blared through the ship. He laid her back on the table and smoothed a shaking hand over her hair as she looked at him with panic in her bright gold eyes.

"Stay calm." His heart raced, wild and frantic, as his blood rushed like a flooded river in his veins.

"I don't want to die." She grasped his hand tighter as Tuz yowled and screeched on the other side of the door.

"I won't let you," he promised, squeezing her hand. The ship rumbled to life as he heard Xan's crew racing through the corridors. "Don't you dare give in."

# 12

"WHAT HAPPENED?" XAN DEMANDED. THE SHIP LURCHED, SENDING AN UNSE-
cured instrument tray clattering to the floor. Cyn braced himself against the bed even as he helped Yara lay her head down.
She closed her eyes and moaned.

"It hurts." She coughed.

"Pain?" Xan grabbed her wrist, feeling for a pulse, gave up
and put his hand to her neck, cursed, then grabbed heart-
charges.

"Poison." Cyn could barely force the word out. His mind
was spinning in dark memories. He could barely see, barely
think. He tried so hard not to lose himself in the hard fist
of terror that had clenched around his heart. "Are there any
Touscari-Orianalen on board?" The healers had the rare ability to heal through powerful psychic powers and special glands
in the skin of their hands.

They also had a strange culture based entirely on a barter system, and he had nothing left to trade for her life.

"I don't have any Touscari on board." Xan slapped a reader on Yara's chest. "We'll get her to Oriana as fast as we can."

"Bug, medical emergency," Cyn barked at him. His aura flared as he zoomed over Yara. "Contact the Touscari-Orianalen as soon as we are out of macrospace and negotiate with the healing sanctuary at Rastos for a purging on my behalf."

Bug squeaked a series of questions.

"I don't care what parameters you use. Get creative. We no longer have the ship."

Bug let out a shrill alarm.

"I'll explain later. Just do it." Cyn snatched the viewer. He still had to get the band off. Yara started to shiver. She wouldn't open her eyes, and she had pulled her legs up into the fetal position. They didn't have much time.

Bug shot out of the room as Tuz and one of the ship's medics charged in through the door.

"Javin," Xan commanded. "She's been injected. Get over here now."

"Do whatever you can to keep the poison from the heart and brain. Anything will help," Cyn stated.

The petite medic took a place at the head of the table as Tuz jumped on Yara's chest and yowled.

"Get that cat out of here!" Xan demanded.

Cyn ignored him as the ship shook and yawed to the right. They seemed to push through the launch for an eternity before the ship finally settled into macrospace.

Each second ticked by with the oppressive weight of an

eon. Cyn watched the beads of sweat form on Yara's forehead, dampening her short hair. He wiped her sallow brow, trying to comfort her as he waged a painful war with his own mind. For years he had immersed himself in learning and pleasure, trying to drown his mind in information and pleasant stimulation to keep the terrible horrors of his life from overwhelming him.

Now none of it mattered. His agony was driving him mad. The medic tried to say something to him, but he didn't hear it. All he could hear was Yarlia's screams. All he could see was her pale face, her life gone. Her eyes were closed, so peaceful, so much like Yara's. Yara's skin paled further, her life ebbing.

*No!*

Cyn shook with agony as he tried to swallow the lump in his throat. He shut his eyes against the pain, trying to stay in the present. He felt himself slipping. He'd pass out cold if he wasn't careful and end up in a coma in the healing sanctuary for the next couple of days. Then he'd be no good to her.

He wouldn't fail again.

Cyn clenched her hand tight then picked up the tools. He had to get the band off her, before it did any more damage.

Immersing himself in his task, he ignored the medic's movements, ignored Tuz pushing his hard face up against his shoulder. His whole world became the tiny screen and his hands. He eliminated the last of the lights and pulled the band out of her arm. The thick needles slid out of her flesh, leaving welling pools of blood on her bicep. One of the needles still dripped poison as he tossed it back toward a deep basin.

Yara's skin felt so cold, not like the hot fire that had burned beneath his hands not even an hour earlier.

He couldn't lose her.

Tuz mewed at him, a soft plaintive sound so at odds with the cat's personality.

"I'm doing all I can," he offered as he rubbed one of Tuz's thick ears. He purred and pushed into Cyn's hand.

The ship slowed. They'd be docking soon. Xan stood. "Hang on." He left the room, jogging out the door and down the corridor.

Bug bulleted into the room, pinging off a wall before flying into the center of Cyn's chest.

Bug rattled off a long string of his click code so fast Cyn could barely process it. He said something about living kiltii vines and Tola.

Cyn's gut felt like it hit the floor.

"Tola is here?" He hadn't spoken to the Union medic since the man served as his sister's second in command. This could get nasty. According to Tola, they had an unfinished debt.

Xan's medic looked up. "Tola Pinaro-Trabal? He's got the best hands on Oriana. The man can work miracles. I didn't know he was back from his tour with the Union forces."

"I didn't either." He'd worry about how to get back into the healer's good graces later. Yara's life was on the line.

The ship shuddered as it came to a rest on the docking platforms. Cyn lifted Yara in his arms as he ran down the corridor to the lift platform. Once on the base level, he ran toward the crew ramp. The light from Oriana's tropical sun burned through the dim interior, searing his eyes.

The great estuaries and wetlands of Oriana stretched out before him like a quilt of light and bright green life.

Giant flocks of white-winged birds took flight over the

city of Rastos as a herd of stacarns lifted their crested heads and watched him run down the ramp onto the docks.

The relatives of Earth's long-extinct corythosaurus chewed thoughtfully on reeds as the hot wind from the engines whipped the dripping branches of the cypress trees.

Two women with the thick black hair, dark skin, and sharp expression of the Touscari marched toward him without so much as a hello. Cyn didn't worry about niceties. During an emergency, he knew the Touscari were all business. One of the women removed her gloves and placed her deep bronze hand on Yara's pale shoulder.

"She's bad. Alert the sanctuary," the healer told the other girl. "You"—the healer's slanted eyes narrowed as she pointed at Cyn—"follow me."

Yara's head lolled against his shoulder as her hair tickled his neck just beneath his ear. With his heart pounding, he prayed that this time it would be different, that this time he wouldn't lose her.

With the strength of a full-grown man, but the fear of the lost young boy he'd been, he carried her out of the docks. As soon as he set foot in the marketplace, a Touscari man took her from him and placed her on a stretcher carried by four others. He didn't have time to think as he watched them hurry her away.

Tuz jumped out of the ship, followed by Bug.

Cyn broke into a run, chasing the Touscari down the wood-planked street with Tuz at his heels. He'd been here many times before to trade in crocodile leather, spices, and stacarn oil. This time, the crowded marketplace only got in his way.

People parted for the healers but closed in on him again.

He ducked to the side to avoid getting clocked by a man carrying long wooden pikes on his shoulder, only to fall dangerously close to the jaws of a monster crocodile skull. The two boys playing hop-stones inside the jaws looked at him with disapproving glares as he accidentally kicked one of their stones into the street.

He had to keep moving.

The wide arch entrance of the healing sanctuary loomed over him as he ran into the central courtyard. Great oval pools burst with flowering lilies and swamp irises while an enormous black egret watched him as it waded near a waterfall.

*Damn it.* The peace and beauty of the Rastos sanctuary was meant to calm the sick that came from all over the universe for help from the Touscari, but it did nothing for him. He began to pace, and Tuz followed in step. He took a swipe at Cyn's calf.

"I don't know where she is, so don't ask," Cyn snapped.

One of the women that met him at the ship turned the corner from a shaded walkway and nodded to him.

"Follow me," she stated with a distinct lack of panic in the low timber of her voice. "Tola wishes to speak with you while he heals the patient."

Cyn cursed under his breath. He followed her down the walkway, around a corner, and entered a small room with a single bed.

Yara remained unconscious, wrapped in clean white linens and nothing else. His eyes immediately fixed on her chest, watching for the soft rise and fall.

"Cyrus Smith," Tola stated from the doorway. Cyn didn't bother to turn around. "I'm surprised to see you here, consid-

ering your ship was attacked and destroyed by rogues somewhere near the Farlan cluster. Wasn't that the official report
filed on your death records?"

To protect his sister, Cyn had faked their deaths to the
Union. After that, he'd disappeared back to Gansai, bought
fake identification codes for himself and his ship, then enjoyed
toying with the Union by continuing to use his Earthlen alias
as a trader instead of a cultural liaison. It amazed him how
well the bureaucratic jungle of information protected him.

"Yeah, well, you know how rumors get started," Cyn hedged
as Tuz jumped up on the corner of the bed. Tola crossed too
closely behind him. The healer glared at him through dark,
slanted eyes as his hawklike features seemed to harden even
more with disapproval. The swirling white patterns painted on
his temples and winging just above his brow stood out in sharp
contrast to his dark skin. "She's been injected with the latest
Kronalen culler, the truth serum, and probably still has kiltii
extract in her system if you can channel it."

The healer didn't move.

"What are you waiting for?" Cyn demanded, his voice sound-
ing like a panicked roar.

"We haven't settled our debt." Tola's calm voice sounded
sharp with accusation.

"You've got to be shitting me. Bug negotiated . . ."

"You negotiated with the sanctuary, but you haven't settled
your debt with me." Tola jerked off his gloves but still didn't
lay a hand on Yara. "I spied on Cyani for you. Sent messages
detailing information about our positions while on the front.
It was treason, yet I trusted you. You told me you were facilitating information for Azra, but that was a lie, and now the

Union thinks Cyani's dead. I want the truth." Tola clenched his jaw and fist. "You were the last person to see her alive."

"*She's* going to die if you don't help her, now," Cyn protested, holding his hand out toward Yara.

"Then do something." Tola crossed his long arms.

"What?" Cyn shouted, as panic nearly choked him. "What do you want from me? I've already lost everything."

"What happened to Cyani?" It was Tola's turn to shout while a look of intense pain creased his painted brow. Had Tola been in love with his sister?

Cyn reached up and ripped open the clasps of his shirt, letting the material fall open, exposing his scar. Tola could read and interpret every chemical signature of his body down to his DNA through the glands in his hands.

"You want answers?" Cyn dropped his gaze to his chest. "Take them. Just save her." One touch. That's all it would take to have his entire physical history laid bare for the intelligent healer. His life story, no lies, no hiding, no disguises. He'd know his connection to Cyani. He'd see the signature of every lover, every intoxicant. He'd feel the mark of every scar and even the chemical echoes of his deepest emotions.

Tola reached out and placed his hand over Cyn's heart. The skin of the healer's palm burned as the glands established a chemical connection to his bloodstream through his skin. The healer's dark eyes met his, wide with shock.

"Well? You get it now?" Cyn demanded.

Slowly Tola laid his other hand on Yara's chest. Cyn felt the cool rush of relief pour through his body as the healer established a connection with Yara. *Finally.*

"Why didn't you tell me you were Cyani's brother?" Tola whispered.

"It would have meant my life if I did. I'm wanted on Azra. I didn't know if Cyani was brainwashed," Cyn admitted. "Hell, even this one's on a bloodhunt for me."

"You're kidding," Tola huffed. "You have strange taste in women."

Cyn shrugged. "Can you neutralize the poison?"

"Cyani?" Tola prodded.

"She's alive and hidden. I can't tell you where. Her safety is at stake."

The healer slowly closed his eyes, took a deep breath, then released it. "Thank the Maker. Is she happy?"

"Yes." Cyn smiled.

Tola nodded, but there was no mistaking the shadow of sadness over his deep eyes. "Good."

Cyn shifted, feeling uneasy as Tola's hand grew even hotter. "Uh, you can take your hand off now."

"I'm reading the chemical structures of the antibodies in your immune system and transferring them into her while I neutralize the poison," Tola explained. "Unless you want me to stop."

"Whatever it takes." Cyn was willing to do it. He just didn't like the feeling of being so exposed.

"Your immune system is remarkable," Tola commented. "Hers is terribly weak. She's been very sheltered, hardly even a head cold in here."

"I guess being raised in filth has one advantage." Cyn took a deep breath.

He tried to hold still, feeling more raw and open than he ever had as the hours slowly ticked by. Tola hardly moved, his face a hard mask of stark concentration. Yara didn't move at all. Though she'd stopped sweating, and her face didn't seem as pale, Cyn couldn't shake the sick dread in his heart.

With the sheer force of his thoughts, he tried to will his own powerful immune system to somehow heal her through Tola. It all seemed futile.

He couldn't shake the terrible gripping dread that he was going to lose her.

Slowly Tola withdrew his touch.

"Will she make it?" Cyn dared to ask.

"I don't know, but the poison is neutralized. If she has the will to live, she has a chance." Tola stood and stretched, then pulled his gloves back on. "Get some rest. We'll try again in the morning."

Cyn gathered her hand in his. He wouldn't leave her side. She sighed and rolled toward him, her bright hair sticking out in crazy wisps around her face.

Tola retreated from the room as the chorus of insects rose with the light of the twin moons.

A stacarn let out a mournful cry in the distance, answered by his herd.

For nearly fifteen years, Cyn had kept his restless mind immersed in learning to keep his terrible memories at bay. Now alone in the dark, he had nothing to protect himself except the lingering hope that this time, it would be different.

This time, he wouldn't lose her.

# 13

YARA FELT THE PULL OF AIR WITH EACH BREATH, AN EASY IN-OUT RHYTHM that reassured her she was alive. Her ears rang, and she didn't want to open her eyes.

Her whole body ached and felt hot and cold at the same time. She didn't want to move. She didn't ever want to move again.

*She was alive.*

She felt her heart thud with long, heavy beats in her chest. Thank the merciful Matriarchs and the Creator in all his glory she'd survived.

As the soft ringing in her ears died down, music swelled to take its place. An intricate and exotic melody danced around her. It was as if a chorus of hundreds sang in strange harmony, each tone ringing with an individual voice. But it didn't sound like bells. It didn't sound like anything she had ever known.

Maybe she hadn't survived.

Yara cracked open her eyes. Curtains of sheer, loosely woven white cloth hung around her like spiderwebs. They surrounded her soft bed, keeping her in a shimmering cocoon.

Where was she?

Through the veil, she saw him. Dressed in the dark blue Earthlen pants, and a simple black long sleeved shirt that clung to his chest and long arms, Cyrus reclined in a wooden chair, caressing a strange instrument as he played the haunting melody filling the room.

He cradled the voluptuous form of the instrument, her golden curves reclining in his lap like a familiar lover. His fingers fluttered over her long neck as he stroked the tender cords over her entrance.

And she sang for him.

Passion, longing, terrible, terrible pain. The music poured out of him like a confession.

A look of deep concentration etched his handsome features as his fingers continued their work with blinding speed and surreal beauty. His inky hair fell in haphazard locks across the intense furrows of concentration in his brow.

Yara swallowed the dry lump in her throat as her body burned with a new fever.

Her imagination began to roam as she watched his hands. She could still feel them fluttering over her skin, toying with her nerves.

She closed her eyes.

She could feel his warmth, his strength as his body pressed so near hers. His silky voice had sounded so pained as he whispered reassurance and salvation into her ear. He had saved her life.

He had burned her with his hands.

She shivered as she drew a hand up to her bicep. No bands. He had saved her. At what cost? *Why?*

The music swelled once more, so filled with pain. This was not the man she thought she knew. The man playing this music was no pirate, no criminal. The thought unnerved her.

Who was he?

And what had scarred his soul so deeply that his pain could transform into music that nearly broke her heart?

"Where are we?" she whispered, suddenly aware that her only clothing consisted of a very loose shift and a cool clean sheet. She turned her head and glanced at the wound on her shoulder.

A pale pink scar that looked like the corona of an eclipsed sun blossomed over her skin. She tried to lift her hand but let it fall back onto the sheet. She felt so weak. "Where's Tuz?"

"He's hunting stilt rats," Cyrus stated as he gently leaned his curvy instrument against the wall and pulled a chair near the side of the bed, just on the other side of the netting. "We are on Oriana, guests of the Touscari."

"Can you open the veil? I want to see you." She shifted, trying to lift herself up some.

"Right now, there is a Tici swarm in the city. Until it passes, you have to stay in this net to keep you safe. They're nasty little bloodsuckers. You don't need another fever. Your immune system is very weak right now."

Yara groaned as she let her head flop back onto the soft pillow. "Where's Ishan? Is he okay?"

"He's with Xan. They had to return to Gansai to recharge his converter and testify against the Bacarilen that sold you." Cyrus's voice sharpened with an angry edge.

Yara felt the burn of betrayal in her gut. "Good." If Brill survived pirate law, she could look forward to dealing with Azralen law as soon as Yara took the throne. *If* she took the throne.

"How long have I been here?" Worry gnawed at her mind. What if she was already too late and Palar was on the throne? She had to communicate with Azra.

"You've been healing for about thirty-two standard hours. And the Grand Sister still sits on the throne." He smiled. "She's getting anxious for you to find this *mudrat traitor*, I think it was."

She sank back into her pillow. *Thank Ona the Pure.*

"You intercepted my messages?" Yara didn't hide her irritation. She had come to terms with the fact he was a pirate, but a snoop was a different story.

He shrugged. "You have time to heal. By the time Xan gets back, the swarm will have moved on, and you will be strong enough to return home and teach your rivals a thing or two."

"How do you know all of this?" She still couldn't believe he'd be brazen enough to read her private messages.

"Maxen, the leader of the Circle on Gansai, got some interesting information about Azralen's political situation out of his *guests*. Don't worry, Yara. Your planet hasn't fallen apart yet." He chuckled. She wasn't sure she understood the joke so she huffed at him.

"Oriana's pretty diverse. I've met a couple of Lilkia-Orianalen, but I don't think I've ever met a Touscari-Orianalen." Yara shivered. The deep feeling of cold seemed to clench around her ribs and hold her in a terrible grip. She had never been so sick or wounded in her life. It shocked and frightened her. She didn't know what to do to feel better.

Cyrus strolled to the far side of the room and lifted a thick blanket off a rack of reedy sticks tied together with twine. He carried it back to her bed, carefully inspected the outside of the net, then unzipped a long seam and stepped within it before closing it behind him.

Yara scooted backward on the bed, feeling very vulnerable. The world closed in around her until it was just her, him, and the soft bed between them.

He spread out the blanket and tucked it in around her feet. The secure pressure of the blanket helped infuse her body with warmth. She clung to the edge of it as he reached for the seam to let himself out.

"Wait."

He paused and looked down at her. His eyes still shone bright green. A shiver ran down her spine and a different kind of warmth spread into a sweet throb.

"I don't want to be in here by myself. I feel like I'm in a cage."

He smiled and sat at the foot of the bed. "In that case, I should've grabbed my guitar, too."

"The instrument you were playing?"

"Yeah, I needed something to pass the time. I'm always surprised by what I find in the marketplace here." He lifted one shoulder in a lazy sort of shrug. Yara felt her skin warm.

"You play beautifully. I've never heard anything like it. How long did it take you to learn?"

"I learned on Earth when I was young." He shifted, as if he wasn't sure what to do with himself. The gauzy, white walls of their tiny room seemed to press in. She felt it, too, the growing sense that they were too close, too confined for comfort. She just couldn't bear to be alone in her pure white cage.

"And you're already a master," she teased.

The skin at the edges of his jewel-like eyes crinkled slightly as he chuckled. She was glad he'd kept the green contacts. They fit him. "I like a challenge."

"The music suits you," she offered. "It's very passionate." As soon as she said the word she felt her face flush hot. Instinctively she grasped the sheet and pulled it higher on her chest to shield herself from his amused smile.

"I relate to it." Again he half shrugged, letting her off the hook.

"You saved my life," she mumbled. "I guess I should thank you."

"Yeah." He smoothed the blanket near her hip. The gentle tug of the fabric on her skin sent a shiver of pleasure down the backs of her legs. "Are you okay?"

"I don't know," she admitted. With the still silence and the protective shelter of the clean white cloth all around her, she couldn't shake the images of the slaves out of her head. Their eyes, she couldn't erase them from her thoughts. They chilled her. "I can't stop thinking."

"I know how that feels." Cyrus reached for her hand, and gently lifted it. With skillful hands, he massaged her palm, then stroked her fingers. The tender touch brought all her focus to him, and the horrors she'd witnessed receded into her mind, while something else came to the forefront.

"Why are you still wearing your contacts?" She had to stop thinking about him. Every time she looked into those green eyes, she remembered how it felt to have her body exposed to him. She trusted him. He took that trust and saved her life.

"What?" A strange expression flashed across his face.

"Your eyes are still green. Why are you wearing the contacts that made you look Ankarlen?"

He seemed confused, like he was searching for an answer.

"You said you liked them," he murmured, then stroked the back of her hand again.

She felt a soft melting somewhere deep in her chest.

"Will you be able to get your ship back?" her voice sounded deeper, husky. She tried to clear her throat, but couldn't.

"No." He looked out the window for a moment, his expression unreadable.

"Why not? Aren't the pirates going to arrest that Kronalen mudsucker?"

"They'll execute him."

Yara felt like his words punched her in the chest. She shuddered as she thought about the stark terror the slaver had inflicted on her. He deserved to die, but Cyrus's certainty felt so hard, so final. "So what happens to your ship?"

"Since it's the property of a pirate criminal, as soon as he's dead, it will become salvage for the Circle. Those in rotation will bid on it."

Yara remained silent for a long time.

*By Yarini the Just, it wasn't fair.*

She didn't invoke her own bloodline often, but nothing else seemed to fit. "I'm sorry," she finally admitted.

He squeezed her hand. He couldn't just brush this off as nothing.

"It was your home." She thought about the quilts, the broken-in warmth and comfort there.

"I sent Bug with Xan to help strip the ship of my things. I'm not sorry, Yara. It's just a ship. I'm just thankful you survived." He reached up and brushed his fingertips over the sensitive skin of her cheek. She turned toward his touch as if pulled to it. Her eyes drifted closed for a moment and she sighed.

"It wasn't just a ship. It was more than that." She pulled her face away from his touch and leaned back on the pillow. It reminded her of her one treasured childhood possession—the gift from a friend she wasn't allowed to keep. "I should know. I haven't exactly had a home."

"What about Azra?"

She looked him in the eye. With his eyes green, his whole face seemed more Azralen to her. "Azra isn't a place to me, it's a purpose."

"I'm not sure what you mean by that," he admitted.

"I look back on my time on Azra, and my only memories are of instruction. Someone was always there to tell me what to do, where to go, what to be." She shivered. "No laughter. No—I don't know. I don't even know."

He placed a hand on her knee. "Home is more than a place."

Damn it, she knew that. That was the point. She had a place. She didn't have anything else.

"You must feel very lost." No, *she* felt lost. The truth hit her hard. In one week, his ship had been more of a home to her than she had ever had. Now it was gone.

"I don't get lost easily." He smiled at her, but it didn't seem to lighten her mood. She stared at the light pouring in through the open window.

"I'm lost," she whispered. She felt as if everything that was certain in her life had been turned upside down.

In the dark moments on the Kronalen ship, she had gone from a woman of comfort and security to an object, a thing, hopeless and scratching for any means of survival. Before this journey, she had been so certain of who she was. After all, she'd been told who she was, what she should be, from the time she was a small child. But on that Kronalen ship, she felt like she had been honest with herself for the first time in her life. Naked and tied in the dark, helpless, she discovered the depth of her strength. She had trusted another with her life and her body.

*Cyrus.*

She blinked at him, her eyes stinging.

"I'm sorry for what happened on the Kronalen ship," Cyrus admitted, as if the incident had been playing through his thoughts as well. "I had no choice."

"Don't apologize. Please." By Ona, she didn't want to hear his regrets.

"You were ... I shouldn't have touched ..." He paused as his jaw tightened. "I shouldn't have felt ..."

He shouldn't have felt what? Desire? *Shakt!* She was the one who shouldn't have felt like her whole body burned for him. She had no control, she had put her trust in him, and he had woken something in her.

"I'm a hypocrite," she admitted.

His burning gaze met hers.

He shouldn't feel like he compromised anything. She compromised her own beliefs long ago trying to find something she could cling to as her own.

"No, you're not," Cyrus stated with a conviction she couldn't feel.

"Yes, I am." She tried to keep her voice from cracking as she crossed her arms over the blanket. "I'm no saint for the temple. I took my vows for granted."

She looked at him, searching for his understanding. She didn't want to state the depth of her recklessness out loud. It hurt her. But he didn't say anything. He just waited.

"I took my body for granted." She couldn't look at him. Instead she stared at her knees. "I'm no virgin."

"You think I am?" Even though his eyes were green, they still looked dark, hidden beneath the thick fringe of his lashes.

Her mouth went dry.

She huffed at him. "I'm trying to be serious. You didn't do anything to be sorry for."

"I've done plenty to be sorry for," he countered.

She touched her hand to the center of her chest. It felt so hollow, it hurt. "Everything I've done, I've done to make my family proud, the Elite proud, and it's all so empty. I feel nothing."

"You feel guilty." His words came out as a statement, but not an accusation. He just watched her, patient and still.

She did feel guilty, guilty and vulnerable. It was so hard to admit she had failed herself. "I was only three years into the training in that stupid time when nothing could touch me and

I was so reckless. A group of the other girls in training became obsessed with the old ritual of the Alkar and arranged a mock-up of it for us. I didn't know his name, it didn't matter. He was just a submissive thing in a girl's twisted game. He wasn't allowed to move, just lay there, willing, beneath us."

Cyrus's mouth pinched into a tight line. She shouldn't have told him.

"So you used him."

Yara's eyes stung. "And I hated it." She looked away from him. "I hated it."

His fingers touched her chin. With gentle pressure, he lifted her face.

"We all do things we regret," he admitted.

"I just want to be true to my blood. I want to be worthy of it." She leaned forward and drew her knees up to her chest and wrapped her arms around them. He let his hand drift to her knee, and then his palm slid down the length of her shin.

Even through the thick blanket, she could feel the burn of his touch.

"Be fair, be wise, help the innocent, and you will honor your blood." He leaned closer to her, tilting his head so he could look her in the eye. "Forget the Elite and their rules. Whether or not you're a virgin doesn't change the fact that you are an intelligent, strong, and *just* woman."

Why did he always have to be right?

Her heart thundered in her chest as she slowly leaned forward. She felt a dizzy rush, heard the roar of blood in her ears as she held her breath and closed the distance between them.

She let her eyes drift shut, and in the dark, alone with herself and her terrible longing, she waited.

Finally, the warm brush of his lips met hers. So soft, she didn't think it would be so soft. How could something so soft make her feel so much.

She caressed his lips with hers, then exhaled, shaking as she blinked. She couldn't focus.

He brought his hand to her cheek, gently holding her face as his warm lips pressed against her forehead.

Then he stood and exited the net, leaving her alone with her torturous thoughts.

# 14

*DAMN IT.*

Cyn rubbed the back of his neck as he paced outside of her room. He could still taste the warm skin of her lips.

He'd always be able to taste her now.

How had he forgotten to replace his contacts? They were second nature. When did he have the opportunity? The only thing he had thought about for the last two and a half days was whether or not Yara would survive.

He'd have to be careful with his bracers. If he let those slip, there really would be no hiding from her.

He ignored a nagging feeling somewhere near his heart. Hiding was becoming a very tedious exercise. If she found out who he really was, she'd kill him without question.

He thought about all the things she had revealed to him. She was no cold and hardened Elite warrior. She was a real woman, with a real human heart, capable of empathy, capable of mercy.

What would Azra be like with her on the throne?

"I'm such an idiot," he grumbled to himself. He couldn't even let himself think such things. His course was set.

"I'm not going to argue that."

Cyn lifted his head as Tola stepped up next to him. He wore the light-colored, loose-woven clothing of a master healer on duty for the Sanctuary. Tola's talent level was rare among his people. While they could all heal to a certain extent, Tola had a reputation for being able to correct extremely complex disorders of the blood, including genetic disorders and cancer. He hardly seemed like the hardened soldier Cyn knew lurked inside the man. Only his short hair revealed his position with the Union.

"When do you head back to your assignment?" Cyn asked. He hoped Tola remained around long enough for Yara to get back on her feet. He didn't want to negotiate with another healer, and to be honest, he didn't want anyone but the best working on her.

Tola shrugged. "I have another month." The lazy ease of his expression didn't quite reach his hawklike eyes.

"So you're taking a working vacation?" He hoped Tola hadn't just been called to the Sanctuary for Yara's emergency.

"When you have nine siblings, you do what you can to support the family when you're home." He smiled, then his expression cooled once more to his standard piercing seriousness. "How is she?"

Cyn wasn't sure how to respond, considering the chaste kiss they had just shared had him out in the hall walking off a shaky feeling in his legs. "She's finally awake."

"Good. I want to talk to her." He reached out toward the door.

"Tola, she thinks I'm from Earth." Cyn swallowed, his throat constricting. He couldn't let her discover the truth now.

Tola watched him, his dark brown eyes cautious and assessing. "You *are* from Earth, Cyrus."

"Thank you." Cyn let out the breath he was holding.

"We'll negotiate that point later." Tola entered the room before Cyn could call him a scheming bastard.

He felt a sting on his neck and slapped one of the Ticis. "Damn the swamps," he grumbled. He glanced over at the door. "And the creatures that live in them."


AFTER TWO DAYS OF HELPING TOLA FINISH THE ROOF ON AN ADDITION TO HIS family's home, Cyn was ready to leave the planet. While he could always count on finding a way to survive in Rastos by bartering his knowledge and skill, not being able to just click over funds got really tedious after a while. No wonder Rastos wasn't much of a draw for tourists. The Touscari considered all forms of representative currency evil. You could live happily on Rastos so long as you were willing to work or trade for everything you needed. It was exhausting, but convenient considering his current financial situation.

Cyn wiped his sweaty brow, trying to clean up as he entered the Sanctuary. At least he'd gotten his fill of light exposure working without his shirt on the roof, and he hadn't been bitten by a single fly. It looked like most of the swarm had died off or moved on.

Unfortunately, Yara was still trapped in her nets. Cyn felt

terrible for her. He knew she needed more direct light exposure than the little bit that filtered through the window and netting. When he had visited the night before, she was going crazy.

He took a fortifying breath as he entered the room.

"Tuz!" Yara scolded as she jumped on the bed trying to knock her cat down from the top of the netting. Cyn stayed in the doorway a minute watching her soft breasts in the skin-fitting top he had gotten her. It was a good choice. The vibrant blue with swirling white patterns around her neck complemented her skin, and the short cut showed off her luscious abdomen. He shifted as he felt the now-familiar rush of arousal that tormented him every time he was near her. "Tuz, get down! You're going to shred it."

Cyn laughed.

Yara went still, then squeaked as she dropped onto the bed, wrapping her hands around her waist to hide her bare midriff. She tucked her long legs beneath her. The shorts he had bought didn't cover enough for her modesty either. Perfect.

Her yellow eyes darkened to rich honey as her gaze drifted over his bare chest. She bit her lip.

"You could put a shirt on," she suggested, grabbing a pillow and hugging it to her midsection. Cyn enjoyed the flush of pink in her cheeks as she looked at him.

"I don't have any clean ones left, and I refuse to negotiate with Tola for the use of his laundry. The man's a menace." He ambled over to the bed and unhooked Tuz from the netting. The cat perched on his shoulder and affectionately chewed his hair. Sometime after saving Yara's life, Tuz had decided he was acceptable.

"I've got to get out of here," Yara admitted. "I can't take it anymore." She eased off the bed, let the pillow drop and grabbed the netting in her fists.

"Then come on."

"What?" She took a step back. He gently placed Tuz on the floor.

"Let's go. We can spend the day in the marketplace. It'll be fun." He stepped forward and reached for the seam, but she held it closed from the other side.

"I shouldn't be having fun at the expense of my health. I was just venting."

"I haven't seen a fly all day." He closed his hands over hers. "Come out, Yara. I know there's a rebel in you somewhere."

"Don't insult me."

He peeled apart the seam, opening the veil. "I meant it as a compliment."

Yara's heart thundered in her chest as she took a tentative step through the nets. She looked down at herself and almost ran back in. This wasn't like her. First of all, she couldn't be seen like this in public. The shirt and cutoff pants Cyrus had managed to find revealed far too much skin. She didn't complain at the time, because she needed the light, but she couldn't go out in them. And the blue color on the top wasn't even real. She had never seen a color more vibrant. Everyone would stare at her.

She'd be completely exposed.

Cyrus took her hand and pulled her a step closer to him. His naked skin glowed with a fine sheen from working bare out in the sun.

*Ona, forgive me.* She'd been thinking that a lot lately. As soon as she reached Azra she'd have to do penance to Ona forty times over.

He leaned in close to her ear, and as the heat from his skin reached out to her, her stomach tightened with sweet anticipation.

"Let's have some fun," he whispered.

Before she could say no, he had pulled her out of the room, and she matched his strides as they ran like disobedient children down the hall and out of the Sanctuary.

*Yes!*

The sun washed over her, bathing her in heat and light. She closed her eyes and held out her bare arms. She wanted to pretend she was alone, that no one could see her, but the noise from the streets overtook her.

She felt Cyrus's hand on the small of her back. The skin of his palm felt rough and hot against her bare skin as he led her away.

"We need to get lost in the crowd before Tola finds us," he said in a conspiratorial hush.

"Yeah, in case you hadn't noticed, I have green hair."

She opened her eyes and was nearly overcome with the sight before her.

"The color." Her words came out because she simply didn't have the power to keep them in her head. The crowd blazed with vibrancy, a rainbow of swirling colors as hundreds of people walked through the wooden streets, haggling with vendors and laughing with friends.

Their clothing sparkled with vivid dyes. Suddenly Yara didn't feel as if she could stand out amid the bright yellows, pinks, and purples. It was almost garish, but at the same time it complemented the Touscari's dark skin and hair. The elegant swirls of white painted just above people's brows and across their temples drew Yara's eyes to faces alight with good humor while they argued to negotiate fair trades.

Everything seemed to move at once, while the wooden streets rumbled under the crowd. And the smell, it overwhelmed her. The scent of heat and wet wood wove in and under the pungent odor of exotic spices and loam.

Yara glanced through a gap in the buildings at the shimmering wetlands beyond. Drawn to the light, she absentmindedly pulled Cyrus with her until she reached a railing at the edge of a dead end.

The sunlight glittered on the twisting waterways with surreal beauty as birds by the millions flew across a sweeping horizon.

Enormous reptilian beasts lifted their crested heads and thoughtfully chewed swamp grasses with wide, flat mouths. Striking black markings across their faces accented the bright yellow skin covering their blade-shaped crest. Yara had never seen anything like them.

One leaned forward and lowed, the deep sound resonating out over the wetlands with such power it made the water ripple around the great beast's feet.

"This is a swamp?" She took a deep breath, trying to take it all in.

"It's beautiful, isn't it?" Cyrus commented, with his gaze fixed on her.

She gave him a sidelong glance. "It's very beautiful. Is the whole city built on stilts?"

"Yes. The water's low right now, but during the floods, the

city almost looks as if it's floating on a river." Cyrus reached out, and one of the gigantic reptiles pushed a wet nose toward his hand.

She turned her back to the rail and rested her forearms on it as she studied him. "You like it here, don't you?"

He smiled. "Come on. There's a lot to see in the marketplace."

Yara felt giddy and light. Even her clothing didn't bother her once she realized that the tight and supportive top was a fashion staple for the Touscari women. Only healers from the Sanctuary wore muted or bleached-out robes. The majority of the women seemed comfortable in their skin and the rich colors of the marketplace.

Her body rushed with adrenaline as she shocked Cyrus by haggling for a meal for them both, then daring the vendor to add extra spice. After Yara spent about five minutes showing the vendor a faster way to sharpen his knives, he handed her a heaping oblong bowl filled with a hearty fish stew. The vendor laughed as Cyn choked on it, but Yara loved it. She enjoyed the rich burn of flavor as the spicy fish melted in her mouth.

By the Beauty and Honor of Isa, she felt alive.

"You'd better take it easy," Cyrus said as he pounded his chest and coughed to hide the tears of pain in his eyes. "You're still sick, remember?"

"I guess Tola will know what I've been eating," she said then took another bite. "Hopefully it will fry his hands. Then we won't get in trouble."

"Yeah, that'll work." Cyrus laughed his deep laugh.

Yara stopped, and watched him. She wanted to join him, to

laugh, too. It should have been natural, shouldn't it? Why didn't she?

Was she that broken?

She turned away from him, and a crowd near an open pier caught her eye. "What's going on over there?"

"Looks like a round of terc." Cyrus straightened, peering toward the end of the pier. A loud crack whipped over the crowd, followed by a splash. The mass of bodies erupted in shouts and cheers.

"Is it a game?"

He looked at her with a wicked gleam in his eyes. "Why? You want to play?"

An electric tingle raced down her spine as she thought about sparring with him on his ship.

"Yeah," she said, turning back to him. "I'll play."

Cyrus took her hand and pulled her through the crowd until they reached the edge of an open lattice of springy poles built over a large hole in the pier. It was a good five-meter drop to the river below.

Cyrus spoke with a man holding two wooden staffs. Each had a blunted hook on the end, just large enough to catch an arm or a leg. The man smiled, shouted at the crowd behind him, and tossed Cyrus the hooks.

Yara looked up at him as he kicked off his shoes and climbed onto one of the thin logs. He tossed a staff down to her.

"Well?" he invited.

She jumped onto the lattice with the grace of the Elite and stood on the unsteady pole with sure feet. With a flourish, she spun the staff around her back. It felt so good to stretch out her arms, and feel strength in her muscles, like she had control of her body for the first time in a long time. The crowd sent up a roar of approval, shaking their hands in the air. The colorful fingerless gloves that covered their palms flashed in the sunlight like confetti. She turned her attention back to Cyrus, determined to block out the visual distraction. "What are the rules?"

"Simple, first one in the river loses." Cyrus walked backward on his log while keeping his gaze locked with hers.

A thrill of awareness surged in her gut. He had good balance.

*Impressive.*

Too bad he was hopelessly outmatched at this game. "Any other rules?" she asked, stalking forward.

"Nope, that's it."

"This should be fun," she admitted. She leapt forward, landing hard on a pole near him. The lattice bounced, but Yara flexed through the surge in the wood, keeping her balance. She wasn't as strong as she'd like, but it was enough. It felt so good to move.

Cyrus bent his knees, maintaining his balance as he hunched forward. The sun gleamed on his bare back. She had to strike.

Sweeping the hook toward his ankles, she thought she'd catch him, but he jumped at the last second, letting her hook pass beneath him as he landed with un-Earthlen grace.

Her momentum turned her balance to the side. He struck forward with the curve of the hook and pushed her side just enough to set her center off balance.

She jumped and vaulted on one hand, turning an elegant flip before landing on another part of the lattice.

The noise from the crowd deafened her as the motion of their hands pumping and waving in the air distracted her for an instant.

It was all Cyrus needed to jump from his pole to the one nearest her. The bounce in the wood caught her off guard and she tried to plant her foot but didn't have time. Cyrus's hook shot at her ankle.

She had to leap again, this time cartwheeling along one of the thin poles before finding her feet. She gripped the bending wood with her long toes, finding her balance as she watched him.

How did he learn to balance? Earthlen were notoriously clumsy. Was that just a stereotype? She watched his feet as he ran toward her. His arches seemed to flex around the poles while his gangly toes gripped the wood, much like hers had.

Ducking down, she prepared for his attack. At the last minute she dove down and to the side, catching a pole with one of her hands and swinging herself back up and around.

He smiled at her and straightened, as if he were standing on solid ground. With a lazy arrogance, he placed the butt of his hook in front of him, and crossed his hands over the arc of the hook.

"Give up yet?" he asked.

The crowd laughed. She smiled at him. "Not on your life."

"You know, you should take it easy," he suggested. "You're still sick. Honestly, how long should it take an Elite Azralen warrior to hook a man?"

"That depends," she shouted over the taunting *oooh* of the crowd, "on what we intend to do with him."

She sprang, flipped, landed in the center of a springy pole, and used the momentum to launch herself into the air. She twisted as she flew, reaching her hook out and catching his shoulder. She pulled it in, twisting him off balance as she landed.

She let go of the hook and concentrated on her landing as he fell through the lattice.

The crowd erupted in a deafening cheer.

Yara lifted her arms in victory, her heart pounding with exertion and the thrill of winning.

A strong hand grasped her ankle from below and yanked her down.

Yara's heart flew into her throat as she fell through the lattice and into the arms of Cyrus. Together they dropped until the river crashed around them.

Cool water engulfed her, and Yara pushed away from Cyrus, fighting to the surface. She erupted from the water, gasping for air. She thrashed her arms. "I can't swim!"

Immediately Cyrus's warm arm wrapped around her. She held on to his neck as his limbs surged through the chilly water.

"You cheated," she accused, as she relaxed and let him carry her.

"No," his voice sounded husky, so close to her ear. "I won."

Yara felt a tightening in her chest. She coughed, and Cyrus supported her, his warm arm pulled her tighter to his chest as he swam both of them to the ladder attached to one of the pier stilts.

He pulled her to it and let her climb up until she could perch on the cross support beams. Her cough turned into a chuckle.

"We tied," she protested as she tried to breathe.

"If you say so," he insisted, pulling himself up next to her so he could rub her back. "But I saw your toe hit first."

She looked at him, and a limp piece of river grass hung in the soaking wet hair plastered to his handsome forehead.

She couldn't stop it as the chuckle turned into a laugh.

The laugh blossomed, something she couldn't control even if she wanted to. She laughed so hard it hurt her ribs. She had to hold them, fight for breath. She could feel droplets of water clinging to her cheeks and wasn't sure if they were tears as her laughter poured from her.

He laughed, too, leaning against her arm.

By the Mercy of the Matriarchs, it felt so good to let go.

Yara took a short, shaky breath as her overwhelming mirth stabbed at her. It turned into something more poignant, more painful with each choking breath.

She felt her tears spill over her cheeks, burning hot trails through the cool water.

"Hey," Cyrus wrapped his strong arm around her. "You okay?"

"I'm fine," she sniffed.

He rubbed her back, and it helped her draw a shaking breath. She expected him to try to say something smart about how she couldn't stand being beaten by a man, but he didn't.

He just reached out and wiped away her tears.

His fingers lingered on her chin, tipping her face toward his.

She took a deep breath and sniffed.

He smiled at her, and she smiled back.

In a rush, he surged forward, capturing her mouth in a searing kiss.

# 15

YARA DROWNED IN THE HEADY PLEASURE OF CYRUS'S KISS. SHE LET GO COM-
pletely and felt like she was falling. A deep pulse of pleasure
thrummed within her, stealing her breath.

She felt so hot, so open. One arm wrapped around her,
pulling her into the strength of his body, while he held on to
the stilt with the other. The heat of his skin seeped into her
damp clothing as his lips slid over hers.

They commanded her pleasure, demanded her submission
to the exquisite torture. And she succumbed. She let herself be
pliant even as she reached out to taste him, savoring the feeling of being hot and wet and completely out of control.

She gasped as his hand fisted in the damp strands of her
hair and pulled her head back so he could slide aching kisses
down her throat and over her bare collarbone.

She closed her eyes and shivered. She'd never felt this awake, this alive.

"Ona help me," she gasped as his teeth nipped her skin just above her heart.

"Don't pray to her," he growled against her throat.

What did he know about the Matriarchs?

In his defense, her thoughts had nothing to do with being pure.

He kissed her hard on the neck, the intense shot of swirling pressure overloading her nerves. Ecstasy, so intense it hurt, coursed through her body.

She reached up around his neck, twining her fingers in his cool hair. She had to hold him, just to hang on to something. She didn't want him to stop.

She tipped her head down and kissed him, a light nip on his lips. He answered by taking her mouth again, his rough skin burning her cheeks as his tongue slid into her.

*Sweet Creator.*

She was on fire. All awareness left her until the whole world became his touch.

"I want you," she confessed as his teeth nipped her ear. He stilled. It took her a moment to focus as she looked up into his deep green eyes. "I want you."

Something buzzed near her ear, and Cyrus's hand jabbed out with a sharp strike. He took a deep breath as he looked down at the crushed fly in his hand.

"Damn it." He wiped his palm on his jeans and shifted so he could stand on the cross beam. The dizzying letdown left her wobbly as she took the hand he offered her and stood on the beam as well. "We have to get you back."

*Shakt!*

Damn flies. She tried to push aside the sting of rejection as he helped her up to the ladder.

She climbed the rungs of the ladder with her frustration clawing at her. He was right. She had almost gotten bitten, and she couldn't afford any more delays.

It was just . . .

It felt so good to laugh, and kissing him felt even better.

She pulled herself back up onto the wooden walkways of the marketplace. The crowd cheered and laughed, but she no longer cared about the game.

Her insecurity needled her.

What was Cyrus thinking?

Did he regret the kiss? She knew nothing could come of a love affair with him, but he didn't seem the type to deny himself a willing partner. Why had he pulled away from her? It wasn't just the fly.

She watched him carefully as he emerged from the pit, holding up their hooks and handing them back to one of the Touscari.

It wasn't her imagination—lines of tension etched in his brow. She tried to slow her racing heart as she watched him rub his scar, then press his hand to the small of her back to lead her out of the crowd.

They walked in silence back to the Sanctuary. Yara was aware of the crowd around her, but the noise and smell of the marketplace seemed muted as she watched board after board cross under her purpose-driven feet. Even as her heart raced with adrenaline, her thoughts tore around in her mind like a sea-driven storm.

When they reached her room, she looked up. Like an angry command sergeant with a gaggle of untrained troops, Tola stood with his arms crossed. His dark eyes blazed with disapproval.

"Commander," he stated with a hard tone in his voice.

"I needed to get out, Captain." She lifted her chin and stared him down, but he met her gaze. What was with these men? His eyes challenged her as he stepped closer to her and closed his hot palm around her bare forearm.

"You are my patient." He gave her arm a slight squeeze as he turned his slicing gaze to Cyrus. Yara watched as Cyrus offered the healer a half shrug and a scowl.

Tola huffed and led her back to the bed, where he gently placed her within the nets. "I'm sorry, Commander, but your immune system is still vulnerable to illness. You have to stay within the nets until your ship arrives."

Yara sat on the edge of the bed, wrapped once again in her frustrating cocoon. Through the netting, she watched Tola turn on Cyrus.

"What in your hell were you thinking?" the healer scolded as if she weren't in the room. "And for Honor, put a shirt on. You have no shame."

"I was thinking she needed the light, and she's in the care of the best hands in Rastos." Cyrus scratched at the welt of a fly bite on his neck. "And if you're tired of seeing me without a shirt, let's deal. Give me a shirt, and I'll wear one."

Tola placed his hand on Cyrus's shoulder and forced him down into a seat. "You were out eating spicy kitarc and playing terc. I'm surprised both of you aren't passed out in your recuperation, and if I hadn't infused her immune system with your biomarkers, she'd be getting sick right now."

"What?" Yara grabbed a fistful of the netting and watched as Tola slowly turned to her. Cyrus glared at him. What was he talking about? He was Earthlen, not Azralen. They didn't have a close enough genetic code to transfer immunity, did they?

He looked abashed. "I'm sorry. Never mind. You need to rest," he said to her. Then he turned to Cyrus. "You need to behave. I'll check on you in the morning."

Tola left the room, with the authoritative air of a military commander.

"You think he's going to bring me a shirt?" Cyrus asked, his tone teasing.

Yara chuckled, then crossed her arms and rubbed her biceps. The shaded interior of the Sanctuary cooled her wet skin, and she didn't like the feel of her damp clothes. "I need to get out of these clothes."

Cyrus's bright gaze slowly traveled the length of her body and he inhaled a slow, controlled breath. He didn't say anything as he turned his back to her.

She peeled off her wet clothes, then tucked herself under the blankets of the bed. The soft sheets warmed her chilled skin as she sank deeper into the mattress, pulling the covers over her naked body.

Cyrus crossed the room without looking back at her and picked up his guitar from the corner.

"May I turn around?" he asked.

Yara shivered. "Yes."

He moved toward her with the grace of a cat. She found her attention drawn to his scar. It cut across his chest like a shining brand, unobstructed by any hair. She had been captivated by his chest all day, and couldn't help staring at it now. For an Earthlen, he didn't bronze in the sun like so many of that species. He had a fairer complexion that had glowed with the kiss of the light. Her eyes followed the path of the scar for the hundredth time, starting over his heart, and trailing down just above his flat nipple, until it graced the top of his sculpted abs.

She tucked the blankets up higher on her breasts as he opened the net and slid inside. He sat in the chair near the head of the bed and settled his guitar in his damp lap. His wet jeans had to chafe, but she couldn't bring herself to suggest he strip as well.

His long fingers slid over the strings, pulling a sweet and quiet melody out of the beautiful instrument. The Orianalen sun touched the far horizon, and the golden red light of dusk painted the small room in a warm hue.

"I had fun today," she offered. "Probably more fun than I've ever had in my life."

He smiled as he looked up at her with his wicked green eyes. "You should get out more."

She laughed. "Isn't that the truth." She listened to his song, enjoying the way the melody added a layer of complexity each time he repeated it. Eventually he brought it back down to its most simple, and somehow most potent, phrase. "Thank you," she said as his fingers stilled on the strings.

"My pleasure." Their gazes locked for an instant. She had said that more than once, and he seemed genuine in his answer.

"How did you get your scar?"

He dropped his gaze to the instrument in his lap. He once again caressed the strings. This time the song was sad and full of longing.

"Knife wound." He continued to play, though his fingers seemed hesitant, as if his mind weren't focused on the melody.

"Who was he?"

Cyrus looked up at her. "How do you know it wasn't a she?"

She shrugged. "I can't see you really fighting a woman. We've sparred, and I could tell you held back blows."

"Maybe I just didn't want to hurt you."

Yara chuckled again. "As if you could. Who was he?"

"A pimp," he answered with a sharp edge to his voice. "A master of a brood of enslaved whores." He paused, repeating the last phrase of the music and stumbling on the notes. "My first kill."

Yara felt as if she'd been punched in the side. Earth was chaotic, but the planet adhered to the rule of law. She didn't understand. "Was this on Earth?"

He looked up at her with those eerie green eyes. "No," he admitted. "It was a much darker world."

She shivered. How many worlds out there abandoned reason and the rule of law? Unfortunately, it could have been any number of places, Krona, Ankara, Garu, they were obvious, but there were other worlds out there. Ones no one cared about. "What happened?"

"I was out gathering food for my family with my sister and my best friend." He paused. "She was my first love," he admitted with a note of hesitation in his voice. "My only love," he mumbled.

He shook his head as if to clear it. "My sister wandered off to check a trap, and we were alone for a bit . . ."

"Did you kiss her?" She couldn't help it. She wasn't jealous, just intrigued by him.

"I didn't have the chance. We were attacked. I was beaten. I watched them carry her away. She screamed for me, but I couldn't protect her." He inhaled and held his breath, his face tight with pain as he continued to stare at the still guitar. Yara reached out and touched his shoulder. He breathed again, but he looked as if a heavy weight still rested in his heart.

"And your sister? What happened to her?"

"She was taken from me."

Yara felt tears prick the backs of her eyes. "I'm sorry, Cyrus."

"Yeah." He tuned the guitar, tapping the strings so they rang with soft bell-like tones. "They were gone, and I couldn't think. I just . . . I had to do something. It took months, but I found the rat that attacked us and killed him."

Yara couldn't speak. She had a hard time rectifying everything he had told her in her mind. The part of her ruled by justice supported his actions, but this was vengeance, not law, and it was dark, ugly.

"What happened to them?"

"My friend was already pregnant when I found her. She'd been forced by men willing to pay for the privilege. She died in childbirth." His voice sounded hollow and so filled with pain. "I couldn't reach my sister."

Yara felt a tear spill over her cheek as her stomach turned in her disgust and rage. "I'm sorry."

He looked at her. "You remind me of her—my friend."

"What was she like?"

He smiled a sad smile as he leaned the guitar up against the side of the bed. His gaze dipped down, then he slowly drew it back up to hers. "Her eyes were shaped like yours, and your smile reminds me of hers. She was driven and focused like you, but she wasn't as funny."

Yara laughed softly. "You've got to be kidding."

"I'm serious." Cyrus admitted. "We had a very hard childhood. There wasn't much to laugh about. I just wanted to hear her laugh. I never did."

"Is this why you came after me?"

He swallowed and looked around, not focusing on anything. Eventually, he just closed his eyes. "I knew what they did to her. I could see it in my mind, and I couldn't stop it. I still see it."

Yara took his hand. He squeezed it so tight, but she bore the pain of it without flinching. His dark green eyes teemed with emotion as he stared at her. "I could *not* leave you to that fate. Stranger or no, I knew what you would suffer. I can't bear that weight again."

Yara leaned forward and caressed his lips in a soft, soothing kiss. He stayed still, allowing her to take the initiative and comfort him for a moment before he reached up and cupped her face with both his hands.

"I should go," he whispered against her lips.

"No, you shouldn't." She reached out and ran the tips of her fingers over the raised edge of his scar. "Stay with me."

He kissed her. It was a hungry kiss, full of longing and sadness. He pulled back just enough to break it and lean his forehead against hers. "God, Yara, I can't. I'm going to hurt you."

She kissed him.

"Now you're going to be noble?" she asked, after breaking the kiss. She knew this would never work out, and she didn't care. She had never cared about anyone in her life, except for him. She wanted him. Yes, there would be consequences, and she'd deal with that. She just wanted him.

She let the blanket slide from her naked breasts. A tingle of nerves and anticipation slid through her as she reached out and caressed the short curls just behind his ears. His gaze drifted down to her breasts, and she felt him tremble.

"Please," she murmured, leaning close to his ear. "I need you, and I know you need me, too."

# 16

CYN HUNG HIS HEAD AS HER DEWY LIPS TEASED, CARESSED, SEDUCED. WITH such a simple thing as a kiss, she drew him in.

What was he going to do?

He felt so tight, each of his muscles humming with an unseen energy, writhing in the desire to touch her skin and feel her soft and willing beneath him.

He couldn't let himself cross the line.

But he burned.

God, he burned.

For once he didn't want to think. He was so tired of his incessant memory—of the constant strings of information that flowed through his head. He had even studied the ancient art of Tanro in a futile attempt to quiet his mind. He was done with thinking. He was tired of darkness and pain, of war and death. He just wanted to feel.

Only seeing his sister happy and in love had given him any sense of peace.

Until now.

Yara trailed her kisses over his bare shoulder, then nipped him with sharp and playful teeth.

"*Shakt*," he whispered under his breath. He was falling. He was falling hard and it would kill him.

He didn't care.

He caressed Yara's damp hair as he rose to his feet. Yara kissed his bare chest. With her tongue she teased his nipple. He drew in a sharp breath as he felt like he'd just stepped out onto a very thin limb. She kissed his scar, then let her fingers delicately brush over the skin of his abdomen as she reached for the waist of his jeans.

The last light of the sun died, casting the room in the dim shadows of dusk. He stroked her shoulders as she knelt on the bed. His damn mind remembered the feel of her skin beneath his hands, but this was so much softer, so much sweeter without the pain and fear. He could let himself really touch her without his mind screaming that he was violating her somehow. The blanket slid from the pale skin of her naked hips. Her toned muscles looked so sleek and smooth in the dim light. Now his mind screamed for a different reason.

She was glorious, absolutely glorious, and he wanted her.

He needed her.

She unfastened his jeans, her long fingers manipulating the classic buttons, and then she slid the damp cotton down his thighs. Her full lower lip dropped open just slightly as she looked at him. He let her look, enjoying the peaceful yet hungry expression on her beautiful face.

She trailed the tips of her fingers down his abdomen, and he felt the light touch deep in his body.

He slid his hand over the back of her head to her neck and tipped her face up so he could kiss her. He needed her. He needed to taste her, to feel her. He needed it like sunlight.

He surged forward into the bed, covering her naked body with his own. The last of the light died, enveloping them in darkness.

It didn't matter. He could feel her body, and his memory would never forget the beauty of it. He kissed her, hard, commanding. She was his.

She reached up to touch him and he caught her wrist, pinning it into the soft pillows near her ear.

"Mercy," she gasped as she fisted her hand and slid her thigh along his. "Please," she begged.

She needed him; by Ona, she was on fire. Her body thrummed beneath him as she pulled against his firm grip on her wrist, testing his strength. He mastered her with such a simple touch, and the pleasure of it was killing her.

She did everything she could to touch him, to coax him to end this exquisite torture, but he held firm. He was in control. All she could do was open herself to him, in all ways.

He kissed her, stroking, soothing, even as he kept his weight propped up on one elbow. She felt the cool leather of his bracer near the side of her face, the sensation heady and erotic.

She opened herself, inviting him in. She wanted his warm weight pressing into her. Sweet Creator, she was on fire.

He settled his weight on her, and she almost cried with the pleasure of it, yet he didn't let go of her wrist. With his free hand, he traced patterns, gently stroking her face, her neck, her chest.

Each stroke he followed with soft kisses, sometimes nips, as he played her body like his precious guitar. Her nerves came alive, until she felt a vibrant energy building within her, tuning itself to his touch.

"You know Tanro?" she breathed. She'd only ever heard tantalizing rumors of the spiritual practice and the ability of Tanro masters to tune and manipulate a body's energy. Healing through sex.

"I know a lot of things," he whispered back.

The pleasure was so intense, she pulled in earnest against his firm grip, but it was useless. He wouldn't let go. He was in control.

She felt something gathering within her, an energy deep in her core. It pulsed out, reaching toward him. She tried to fight the flood of pleasure as he kissed her breasts. It was all so intense. She just couldn't let herself give in to it. But he didn't let her shy away, didn't let her distance herself.

She could feel his hard body poised at her entrance.

She didn't want to escape.

She let her fist fall open.

He kissed her, and with a surge of his body, sank deep into her, filling her, claiming her.

She cried out as his palm released her wrist and slid into hers. His fingers twined between hers, and she gripped him tight, even as he started to move within her.

Her pleasure was so raw, so intense as he slid into her over and over. Every time he pulled back, she felt the pang of loss until he surged forward again, pushing her closer to the exquisite tension building within. She matched the rhythm of his hips. She clung to his back, feeling the tension building in his powerful muscles.

"Yara," he gasped as he gripped her hand tighter. He relaxed, settling more of his weight on her willing body. And she took him, all of him, driven by the madness that demanded more pressure, more friction, just more.

"Yara," he whispered again before capturing her in a stunning kiss. It was too much, she couldn't take it. It was too much.

She reached up with her free hand and grasped the back of his neck. His soft hair tickled her palm as he kissed her neck while his body drove into her over and over.

By Ona, she'd never felt anything like this. Sliding her hand over his strong shoulder, she met him with her hips, even as a deeper, more elemental feeling began to grow in her heart.

"Yara," he begged, kissing her forehead.

"Take me," she demanded.

He squeezed her hand as he let out a hard breath, then thrust into her with a fast and relentless passion.

Yara lost herself in the building pressure. It swelled, filling her, until the pleasure rushing through her body seemed to push out of her and flow through her to him.

They were one, so completely one. He drove her to the edge of something she had never understood, and with a coarse shout of passion, pushed her to a place she didn't know existed.

When the release came, it consumed her with a deeper potency than the rush of any fight. She let herself go, and in that moment she no longer felt the sting of loneliness.

Cyrus collapsed on top of her, his hot body trembling, even

as hers couldn't stop shaking. She welcomed his warm weight as she fought to breathe. The thrumming pulse of their joining echoed through her body.

By the Creator, she felt alive.

Cyrus kissed her, and she kissed him back without reservation. Their hands remained linked as he eased to her side and pulled the blankets over them.

His fevered lips caressed the backs of her knuckles as he squeezed her hand, refusing to let go.

"Cyrus," she began, but didn't know what to say.

He brushed the hair off her temple and leaned forward to kiss her forehead, then her lips.

She sighed, as the lingering warmth of his love pulsed within her. Relaxed and sated, she curled into the security of his body. She felt both exhausted and energized—completely overcome.

"Rest, Yara," he whispered as he kissed her one last time. "We'll talk in the morning."

THE NEW LIGHT OF DAWN CREPT INTO THE ROOM AS YARA SLOWLY OPENED her eyes. A light breeze made the gossamer netting around her flutter. She blinked, trying to process everything that had just happened.

She stretched her back, then noticed Cyrus's fingers still twined with hers.

She smiled.

Sweet Creator, it felt good.

She was surprised he was still with her. A part of her had

expected him to leave the bed. But no, he lay beside her, sleeping as deeply and as still as any Azralen.

She brushed a lock of hair off his forehead.

He was so beautiful. She brushed the backs of her fingers over his cheek then let her fingertips trail along the edge of his jaw.

For the first time, he really seemed at peace. She chuckled. Maybe he should sleep more.

She relaxed on the pillows as she watched him. He bore so much pain. What he had told her about his sister and his young love had hit her so deeply in her heart, she still felt the sting of it.

She had a hard time believing that such depravity could go unchecked. What sort of society just didn't care about the fate of its children? How had justice become so broken that the disgusting rats that perpetrated such violence would have to be stopped by a young boy?

She stroked his face again. He was strong, and he was a good and noble man.

When had she ever felt this close to anyone? She looked at him, and it triggered an ache deep within her. It was as if everything about her just needed to be with him. She wanted to stand beside him, spar with him, challenge him, meet his constant challenges.

A bird sang from somewhere outside while the low moan of one of the great reptilian beasts rumbled over the wetlands. Again, the breeze from the window caressed the nets. The movement was ethereal and hypnotic.

This was a place of beauty.

She finally felt at peace.

"What am I going to do?" she whispered to herself as she pulled the sheet over her naked breasts. The hollow feeling inside her chest had dissipated.

She had felt the ache there for so long. In her whole life, she had never mattered to anyone. Her bloodline had mattered. Her talent had mattered. Her position mattered. But *she* had not mattered. If she'd been kicked out of the Elite, shamed or rejected in any way, no one, not even her parents, would have stood up for her. They would have rejected her and cast her off.

No one would support her no matter what.

But here was a man who had given everything to save her life, and hadn't ever asked for anything in return. He just wanted to know she was safe.

They were connected.

She couldn't deny it. And she didn't want to.

She mattered to him.

And he mattered to her.

She smiled. Her body tingled as she clasped his hand tighter. How was she going to give this up?

Would knowing that she had mattered to someone be enough to carry her with strength and conviction as she led her people? The thought of trying to be strong daunted her. She couldn't be herself. She didn't want to be hard, untrusting, but the truth was, any one of her *sisters* would stab her in the back to secure their own political fortunes.

She was expected to be disconnected from everyone and everything. Impossible. Eventually, isolation would drive her mad.

How could she give herself to her people and understand them if she became a lone figure on a lofty throne, disconnected from them?

Too many questions. They tormented her.

She just wanted to enjoy the peace of feeling like she belonged with him, even if it was only for a moment.

Yara continued to stroke his hand, then touched the edge of his bracers. He hadn't taken them off. The knives they held seemed so much a part of him.

She wished he would find peace in his life, a time when he wouldn't need weapons.

She drew her fingertips over one of the hilts when her attention fixed on the edge of the bracer.

What was on his skin?

She looked closer, black and red surrounded his wrist just beneath the edge of the leather. Did he have a tattoo?

Glancing at the falcons circling her own wrist, she felt a heavy weight on her chest. His eyes, they didn't look like Earthlen eyes. His balance was too good.

All the little details she had been ignoring cut through her mind like the knives in his bracers. His mental abilities, his gift with languages, his long toes.

Her heart raced with fear.

*Fima be Merciful, it can't be.*

She turned the hooks locking the bracer on his forearm. He stirred, turning his face away from hers. Her fingers paused on the hook. She had to wait for the right moment to slide it out of the circle of metal that held it. It wouldn't be long before he woke up.

His breathing hitched.

Yara bit her lip and unfastened the three hooks in quick succession and pulled the bracer away from his arm.

She couldn't breathe as she stared in shock at the pale blue-tinged skin of his forearm. Around his wrist and elbow, the red and black snakes of Cyrila the Rebel peered up at her, their mouths agape baring their deadly fangs.

Searing pain tore at her heart. No one bore the mark of the Rebel. Only one man in the entire universe would have the guts to mark himself with the snakes.

He clenched her hand as he woke.

Yara's heart pounded out of her chest as she brought her gaze up to his Azralen eyes.

"You're Cyn."

# 17

YARA'S AGONY GRIPPED HER. IT COULDN'T BE TRUE. THE PROOF LAY RIGHT
there before her, angry serpents on his wrists. He was Cyn?
How did he escape the shadows? It didn't make any sense. She
couldn't breathe as she stared at him. She had been tricked,
manipulated. Her heart faltered.

He'd lied to her.

And she had fallen for it. He had pushed her, challenged
her, teased her, played with her, bled for her, healed her, res-
cued her, and sacrificed for her. With him, she had become
more than a thing, more than just an Elite warrior. For the
first time in her life, she felt like a whole person. He'd given
that to her and in an instant ripped it away.

Her pain sliced at her head. Why? If he was out of the
ground shadows, why would he seek her out? It would have

taken a lifetime to find him if he had just disappeared into the vastness of the galaxy. Did he think if he seduced her she wouldn't bring him back to the Grand Sister? He'd broken her down and made her feel. Then he manipulated those new emotions so he could save his own hide.

Was it all just a twisted game?

"Yara?" His musical voice sounded low, uncertain.

She could barely hear it through the cacophony of noise in her head. Fear, uncertainty, confusion gave way as her body ignited. The disarray of her thoughts found their focus in clear, burning rage. The pain still gripping her chest fueled the fire as her thoughts homed in on one thing.

She gripped the hilt of the dagger from the bracer, and in one smooth motion she rolled on top of him and pushed the blade against his throat.

His Azralen eyes went wide with shock as she felt his breathing hitch beneath her bare thighs. He pulled his hands up near his sex-tousled hair and left his palms open in surrender.

She tried to breathe. Her hand shook as she watched a slow drop of blood slide down his neck from the nick of the blade. It wouldn't take much, and he'd be gone, one less festering rat. Her stomach twisted again as she looked at the face of the man she'd trusted. He'd fought beside her, bled with her.

Now she bled him.

A new pain stabbed her in the gut.

By Fima, she wished she could just kill him.

She gripped the blade tighter but couldn't move. Her arm seized even as the rest of her exposed body shook. Through the haze of her tears, she looked down at his naked body lying still beneath her.

*By the Creator.*

What was she thinking? She couldn't kill him. She felt like she had the knife pressed to her own throat.

Hot tears slid over her cheeks. She couldn't stop them as they flowed out of her. They couldn't release the pain. It constricted her chest. She tried to draw a breath, but it entered her as a choked sob.

Her hand shook on the cold hilt of the knife, even as she watched her tears fall on the scar over his heart. Through bleary eyes, she tried to look at him.

He remained still, braced for her decision. His life was in her hands.

The initial shock in his expression softened to deep sadness.

*No.*

Her soul screamed, over and over. She couldn't think through the pain. She couldn't kill him, but she couldn't let him go either.

"Yara," he croaked. "Listen to me."

*No. He'll lie again. He's the snake. He's a traitor and a liar.*

With her hand shaking, she eased the knife away from his throat.

"Drop it, Yara," Xan's deep voice rumbled from right behind her.

"Fall to filth, Xan," she shouted. The searing pain of a sono blast burned through her back.

She cried out in agony and shock just before her strength

fled from her muscles and spots of white light overcame her vision. She couldn't hold on to consciousness any longer.

Cyn launched himself forward, wrapping her in his arms as his hand cradled her head. Her soft hair tickled his palm as he pressed his face to her shoulder.

God, he was sorry. He was so sorry. What was he going to do now? The knife fell limp on the bed. He eased her down onto the pillow, then grabbed the hilt and flung it back at Xan.

The knife knocked the sono out of his hand and both weapons skidded to the far side of the room. "You didn't have to shoot her!" he roared.

"She was about to kill you."

He pressed the back of his hand to the cut, but the bleeding had already lessened. "I've bled more playing ralok with you." He checked her pulse and pressed his lips to her forehead, then brushed a lingering tear away from her swollen red cheek. She looked so damn human, so terribly heartbroken. Even unconscious, her pain was etched into her fine brow. He stroked the tip of his finger over her temple. He loved her smile, and he feared he'd never see it again. He didn't have time to wallow in his guilt. A sono blast wouldn't keep her out for long. What would he do when she came around?

"Now what?" Xan tossed him his jeans, then took up a guarding position at the door.

"I don't know. I have to keep her someplace where she won't kill me."

"Yeah, good luck with that," Xan offered.

"*Shakt.*" He wrapped her carefully in the blanket, and slipped on his jeans before picking her up in his arms, the way he had when he'd freed her. Damn it. They'd been so close. She trusted him. She might have even fallen in love with him.

He didn't want to think about that.

*Shakt!*

She was so much more than he had ever expected. She was so strong, had so much heart. The depth of her dedication and her conviction could be powerful enough to save them all if he could have convinced her to join him. Now it would never happen.

He ruined it. If he could've just gotten through and shown her the real Azra, they would have changed the world together. Not now. She'd never trust him again. Now she was his enemy, and she would destroy him. Or he'd destroy her.

"This was not supposed to happen this way," he whispered as he pressed his cheek to her soft hair. Somehow he had to make her understand. His heart pounded with his surging adrenaline. He was familiar with fear. The stark terror that gripped him was a hundred times more powerful than any he had ever felt before. She had to understand.

*What? That you're going to destroy her way of life and everything she stands for? That you're going to hand her over to a bunch of rebels who want her dead? That you will throw innocent people into lawlessness and chaos with no clear leader?*

God. What was he supposed to do? He had to think of something. He couldn't focus, all he could think about was the heart-wrenching betrayal he saw in her beautiful eyes.

He never meant to hurt her.

*Damn it to the filth and darkness.*

He knew one thing for sure, he had to get her out of the Sanctuary before anyone came looking for them, especially Tola.

"Come on," he urged. Tuz jumped up on the windowsill, his paws damp from whatever he had been doing outside. The war cat pushed his ears flat on his head and hissed.

"I'm not going to hurt her," Cyn stated. *Yeah right.* He was going to hurt her and he knew it. He already had. The cat growled at him and bared his fangs. So much for the brief truce.

Cyn kissed the top of her head and carried her out of the Sanctuary.

Xan had his back as they ran through the empty marketplace. The young light of early dawn barely broke the horizon. An idle vendor put out ragtag wares as a fisherman or two walked toward the end piers. Other than that, the city still slept. The air around Xan's ship curled with heat from the trip here.

As soon as they reached Azra, the revolution would begin.

He felt sick to his stomach as he held Yara closer.

He didn't want to spill the blood of Azra; he just wanted change. Azra needed to change.

He marched up the crew ramp into the ship. Tuz had caught up with him and was taking nasty swipes at his bare ankles with his sharp claws. Venet raised a hand in greeting, then quickly let it fall. Ishan stood next to her, his eyes covered in bandages. She took the boy by the shoulders and led him away.

Cyn hoped she could keep him out of the way. He didn't want to betray the kid, too.

Bug rocketed into the ramp platform, chirping wildly. Cyn shrugged him off.

He pushed past curious crew as he entered the secondary cargo bay that also served as the brig. Deep in the belly of Xan's ship within the smaller of the two bays, a lonely pair of prisoner cells pressed against a thick bulkhead. The crates of weapons he'd smuggled loomed in the cramped cargo bay, dark sentinels of a darker purpose.

Cyn felt his heart shred as he placed Yara on the cold metal shelf attached to the bulkhead that served as a prisoner bed. He tucked the blanket around her and bunched it under her head. Tuz leapt on her and hissed at him, baring his sharp fangs. He had to let her go.

Cyn stepped back and activated the force shield, locking Yara in.

He paced in front of the cell, trying to alleviate the wrenching pain, but nothing he said to himself could ease his terrible guilt.

*What have I done?*

He kicked a crate, then pulled it forward and sat on the edge, letting his face fall into his hands. Beaten and raw, he felt like his scar had ripped open and his heart lay bare in his chest for the world to see.

He had intended a lot of things when he had manipulated her into boarding his ship. He did not intend this.

YARA GROANED AS SHE WOKE. HER HEAD POUNDED AND HER HEART ACHED. She felt Tuz's hard skull press against her shoulder, and she opened her eyes. By Fima, she hurt. Her heart *hurt*. She had heard about heartache, but she had never believed it was an actual physical pain strong enough to double her over and make her feel sick.

Her eyes stung with raw tears as she stubbornly blinked to try to clear them.

The light from the edge of a clear prison energy shield illuminated the small brig cell and the rest of a crowded, but neatly organized, cargo bay. Tuz batted at the shield, his paws leaving energy trails as he furiously worked at the invisible wall. It was a standard Union brig lock. People could pass things in from the outside, but she couldn't get out. There was no use trying.

At least it was clean. A chill seeped through her, intensifying the painful ache in her chest. The air even smelled cold.

Her gaze drifted over the stacks and stacks of projectile weapons, an ominous reminder of the threat to her planet. *He* sat on the edge of a crate, twisting a knife so it slowly bored a small hole. She clutched the blanket around her body. Only hours earlier it had embraced them as they made love. Now it weighed on her.

"There are some clothes in the corner," he said, his voice cool and emotionless. How could he not feel anything? Had that all been an act, too? He stood and turned his back to her. She glanced at the clothes, then tested her strength as she stood and slowly pulled the black shirt and pants over her naked skin. She sat again as she put on the boots and leaned back against the hard bulkhead.

Her fear and rage blossomed, spreading through her blood and blocking out all other thoughts.

He turned back around and crossed his bare arms. The

blue tinge of the skin on his forearms tormented her. How could she have been so stupid? Not only was he Azralen, he was probably catgar, too. She had noticed it from the beginning, his flawless memory, that machinelike mind. Why didn't she see through it?

"Look, Yara," he began.

"At what?" Yara glanced around the dark bay. All she could see were the crates of weapons that had been hidden on Cyrus—no, Cyn's—ship. "At these?" She pointed to the crates.

"These are for Azra, aren't they?" she stated, recalling his admission that the projectiles were for a revolution. No wonder the Grand Sister had urged her to find him quickly. She must have known that the mudrats in the shadows were about to stage a revolt. She had wanted Yara to stop it by capturing Cyn. Instead, Yara had complained that the bloodhunt was beneath her, fell into the traitor's snare, then slept with him. "You are Cyn, aren't you?" she demanded.

He stalked toward her. "Yes."

A filthy mudrat. She had let him touch her.

She felt the heat of her anger and shame in her face.

By Ona, the knot in her stomach slowly tightened. "I guess you're living up to your family name," she sneered.

"Cyrila's name is honored for a reason," he defended.

"Oh, don't," she shouted, shaking her head. She pounded against the shield, the sparks of energy radiating out in a web from her fists. The shock of it stung but not nearly as bad as his words. "Don't you dare preach the Matriarchs to me, *Cyn*, you bastard. You're going to destroy everything they stand for, and you used me to do it." Her heart beat faster. He had wanted her on his ship, and now she knew why.

"At first," he admitted. His voice sounded rough, raw. He rubbed his bare wrist. "I was supposed to delay your return to Azra long enough for the last of the weapons to be delivered. As soon as Palar lit the fires in your absence, we were going to strike."

Yara couldn't fight back her tears as she let her head fall back. She blinked up at the ceiling. "Strike when we're divided."

"I didn't intend for this to happen, Yara."

Her fury roared to life, feeding off her stark pain.

"You're a liar," she shouted. She rose to her feet and marched toward the shield. "Traitor." She felt her tears slip down her cheeks, and she didn't bother to brush them away.

He let out a ragged breath and rubbed the back of his neck.

"You don't understand." He stepped forward and touched the shield, his fingers pushing through the energy lock. The bastard actually had the gall to look tormented.

"Understand what? That you manipulated me into getting on your ship?" She felt her emotion clawing at her throat, and her voice rose. "Am I supposed to understand why you kidnapped me?"

"I know I tricked you into getting on my ship, but—"

"Don't make excuses now," she snapped. "There are no excuses. You're smuggling projectiles and putting them in the hands of criminals."

His expression hardened, and he smacked his fists against the shield before lowering them stiffly to his side. "Criminals. Damn it. This is exactly what I'm talking about. Azra is suffering. Your people are dying and you are blind!"

"Maybe I was blind. I certainly didn't see this coming. You

seduced me for your own sick purposes, just so you could use my emotions against me." Fresh tears rolled down her cheek as she crossed her arms and hugged them to her chest. She had trusted him. She thought he had given everything for her. She thought she had finally found someone who had her back; instead he stabbed her in it. "By Ona, the Elite were right. They've always been right."

"I didn't seduce you." His voice sounded low, angry. "You seduced me, Yara. God, I tried to resist you."

"Well you didn't try hard enough, did you?"

"Yara, I'm a lot of things, but I'm no saint."

"No. You're a filthy mudrat who can't keep his pants on." She bit out each word, feeling the sting of it in her heart.

"You're the one who took my pants off, Pix."

"How dare you call me that," she shouted. "How dare you ever call me that again. I trusted you, I trusted you with everything, and it was all a lie."

"Only my name was a lie," he insisted. "We fought together, we bled together, Yara. Everything else was real. You know me."

"I know you're a rebel and a traitor."

"Damn it, I'm trying to bring justice to our people. You should understand that!"

"You're trying to kill the innocent, Cyn. How could you do such a thing? Spilling the blood of Azra is not justice. It's murder."

"The innocent are dying every day, Yara. You don't bother to see it. Babies are being beaten, girls raped, people die of starvation and infection every day." His voice took on a strange tone, a deep growl of fury.

"The shadows are punishment."

"The shadows are a living hell, and there are innocent people down there." He crossed his arms again. "They need to be saved."

"Are they all innocent like you? Killer, smuggler. Look at what the shadows turned you into. You don't deserve to live." Yara felt the punch of her words deep in her soul. As soon as she said them, she knew she didn't mean them.

"Maybe I don't." He turned away from her. Her eyes burned. Her heart thudded, stabbing into her chest with each aching thud. This was all so wrong.

She walked away from the shield but could only walk a couple of steps before she reached the shelf once again. Tuz paced along the edge, the rhythmic back and forth of his movements like a strange metronome in the silence.

"Why did you come after me?" she asked as she closed her eyes. She opened them again and turned to face him. "If you wanted to destroy me, why didn't you just let them have me?" He accused her of not understanding, but she understood plenty. The one thing she couldn't understand was why he had given up so much to save her life, only to turn around and betray her.

He sighed and picked up the knife off the crate. "I told you, not everything was a lie." He didn't look back as he left the room.

# 18

YARA SETTLED ON THE EDGE OF THE METAL SHELF, WITH HER WEIGHT RESTING on the heels of her palms. She hung her head, overwhelmed by the emotional battlefield she'd just crossed. She didn't have the luxury to wallow in her own pain or guilt. Azra needed her now, and for the Glory of Esana she would not crumble and leave Azra to those who would destroy her.

She took a ragged breath, the pain in her chest still choked her, but her mind began to clear. Fear overrode her betrayal and grief. Her thoughts came quickly, pushing aside her emotion.

Her whole life she had thought the training to expunge her emotion had been a waste. She needed to rely on that training now.

Azra needed her.

Cyn. Her thoughts lingered on his name for only a moment. It almost surprised her how quickly he became the rebel traitor in her mind. It was as if Cyrus, the man she had known, evaporated, leaving a gaping wound in her chest. The void she had known her whole life grew deeper, like a vicious and unforgiving black hole.

Oh yes, she was alone. As the Grand Sister of Azra, she always would be. She could never trust anyone. Friends would only try to manipulate her, and lovers would have the power to destroy her.

*Cyn.*

He wasn't going to kill her, not directly. She had that going for her. They were also traveling back to Azra, which meant at some point he'd probably turn her over as a hostage to the mudrats staging this uprising.

She didn't have any weapons.

She was an Elite warrior, bred and trained for one purpose.

She didn't *need* any weapons.

If she could stay calm and purge her heartache, she would be the perfect spy. She didn't know how much the Grand Sister knew about this uprising. Details were essential, and she had been trained by the Union army in intelligence.

She also had Tuz. Her cat rubbed up against her arm, his rough purr filling the compartment while his thick tail lashed at her back. She sat up and stroked him, thankful that she wasn't completely alone.

Why did she feel so alone? Deep in her heart, she mourned the man she thought she knew. But she did know him. He couldn't lie about the love and care he showed his ship. He couldn't lie about his bravery in the face of battle or his self-lessness in the face of evil.

*Not everything was a lie.*

His words tormented her.

The story of his scar was real, she knew that for certain. The girl didn't die on some backward planet—it was Azra. Did she deserve it? What was her crime? Being born in the wrong place? He was right, that wasn't justice.

But it wasn't possible for everyone on the ground to rise to the cities. There were dangerous criminals there. Absolution for all of them wasn't justice, either. Giving the true criminals projectile weapons and having them unleash generations of resentment against the peaceful inhabitants of the high cities was out of the question.

Once she became Grand Sister, she'd consider ways to help those on the ground and bring it up for debate with the rest of the Elite. Maybe if she spoke with Cyn and promised things would change, he'd call off the attack.

She wanted to believe it. She needed to believe that the man she had surrendered herself to was noble. The crates of the projectiles stood like silent prison guards, shackling her to the truth.

The ship shuddered as they came out of macrospace. Yara's heart pounded as her adrenaline made her limbs feel weak.

A light cracked the shadows as Yara looked up at Cyn's silhouette. A shadow himself, he exuded raw power, grace, and the chilling resolve of a soldier.

"Put these on," he commanded as he slid a set of arm shackles and a lock belt through the shield. The transparent barrier sparked with shots of yellow discharge, then returned to normal.

"Why should I?" She didn't bother to look at him. She couldn't.

"If you do as I say, I'll take you with me. If you refuse, I'll leave you here." His voice sounded as calm and sure as she'd ever heard it.

*Damn him to the filth.* He could have threatened her with death, come in with some sort of weapon aimed at her, he could have promised to beat or torture her, but no. He knew the one thing that would get her.

"Bastard," she whispered as she picked up the cuffs, secured them to her wrists, and tied on the belt. Her wrists came together then, magnetically locked to the plate on the belt, rendering her arms useless.

"Now, give the voice commands for Tuz's collar exactly as I give them to you." He slowly stated a string of commands. The first set forced Tuz to remain within close range of her, the second shut down his ability to record intelligence, and the third was a locking password so she couldn't change the commands. The password he had created was at least seventy characters long. There was no way she could remember it to unlock the collar. *Shakt.* No one could remember a code like that except a filthy catgar.

Once satisfied that they were secure, he let down the shield. Yara stepped through. She fought the surge of emotion as she walked directly toward him and looked him in the eye.

"How do you live with yourself?" Her heart raced as his gaze slowly wandered over her face. He blinked once, a slow, sad motion that almost seemed tired.

"I manage."

The cargo ramp opened with the deafening squeal of metal grinding on metal. Hard light poured into the bay with a gust of damp, salty air. Yara had expected to see the green of the jungles of Azra. Instead, she looked out at a vast and endless ocean. The wind whipped distant frothy crests of water as the occasional sea bird circled overhead.

This was one of the landing platforms for the Nudari miners. They came to Azra seeking refuge from a plague of oxygen-leeching bacteria that had destroyed the oceans of their home world. For over a thousand years, they'd lived beneath the waves, mining ores that the Azralen traded on the intergalactic market. Their mutually beneficial relationship had always been peaceful. The Nudari knew their place and never stepped out of it.

The miners couldn't be a part of the revolt. It would ruin their livelihood. It would take a truly vile act of corruption to turn the Nudari against the Elite. Yara's unease twisted through her gut as she stepped out on the bleak platform. A hexagonal panel split into triangular sections and disappeared into the platform as a lift emerged from beneath the deck.

Cyn took her arm and pulled her forward. His hand was gentle and firm, but his expression was unreadable. At least twenty of Xan's crew efficiently unloaded the stacks of crates, turning into a surge of coordinated motion, as pile upon pile of boxed weaponry formed a long wall on the barren platform.

A Nudari man with smooth skin, shining blue black hair, and hooded eyes stepped out of the lift and greeted Cyn.

"Welcome, Cobra." He noticed Yara for the first time and his eyes narrowed. "What is this?"

"A witness. Don't mind her. Have your people found a way around the communications barrier?"

The Nudari's grim expression remained fixed on her. "Was she a witness to the poisoning?"

"What?" Yara turned to Cyn, hating that he was her only source of any information.

He grasped her arm tighter and pulled her back behind him, just enough to put himself between her and the Nudari. "I told you, very few of the Elite were involved in that," he stated. "Only the Grand Sister and two others."

"What poisoning?" She leaned to the side so she could make eye contact with the Nudari man. Some of the Elite negotiators believed the Nudari had mind powers, but she knew it was nothing more than a culture-wide attention to the most miniscule facial expressions. She wasn't lying about her shock, and he'd know it.

He assessed her. She didn't have to struggle to see the pain in his face. "It was your leader's generous way of renegotiating our contracts. She contaminated the air supply to the fourth sector of the Skeal complex." He swallowed, as if he found it hard to speak, while his hands clenched into tight fists. "It was our residential sector. Two hundred thirty-seven. Dead." His voice shook, even as Yara tried to think through her shock and horror. It couldn't be true. The Grand Sister wouldn't do such a thing. "We will be paid back in the blood of those responsible."

"Dalan," Cyn warned. "I promised that those responsible would be delivered to you to face the justice of your people. A thousand years of peace and prosperity remains between our two cultures. Let's not abandon it for revenge."

The Nudari straightened and glared at her. "Change will come," he promised with bitter sincerity. "We are ready to rise. We follow you, Cobra."

Cyn nodded as Xan's crew unloaded the last of the projectiles. A small black canopy cruiser glided swiftly over the horizon, its triangular body cutting through the powerful wind. It hovered with the grace of a sea bird before perching on the far side of the platform. The overhead shield dissolved and an Enforcer with a scarred cheek stepped off the low open platform behind one of the short wings.

*An Enforcer is a part of this?* Yara's feeling left her hands as she felt her shock steal through her body, leaving behind a terrifying numbness.

How deep did this revolution go? If those tasked with keeping order in the mid cities were on Cyn's side, the Elite were in real danger. Without the Enforcers on their side, they didn't have the numbers to quell an uprising.

Yara's fear gripped her. This was much bigger, much more organized than she ever could have imagined. It wasn't just criminals on the ground. All of Azra was about to take up arms. Why hadn't anyone seen this coming?

Cyn stashed Bug in his belt and led Yara toward the canopy cruiser. "We need a way around the Elite communications array. The Nudari have developed angrav tech and have modified ships ready to rise. But they can't enter the high cities until we disable the com system, or the cannons will take them out."

Why was he telling her this? He just gave away their greatest weakness, communication.

"Cobra," the Enforcer greeted. "You brought a guest, I see. Welcome back, Yara."

Cyn looked at the woman as if he had known her for years, another of his trusted soldiers. "Just take us down. I need to meet with Ceer."

Cyn helped Yara up onto the step of the cruiser and seated her on one of the bank seats along the side. They lifted off without another word. Yara watched the turbulent waters of the ocean fly beneath them. Occasionally, the form of a large felam beast stalking schools of fish would darken the clear waters.

As they reached the sea cliffs of her home, instead of rising to the canopy of the dense forest, they cut through it. Yara had to hold on as the cruiser darted with precise agility through the thick foliage of the outer forests. As they came under the shadow of the canopy, the smell of rot and decay choked her. She fought the urge to vomit as the putrid air stung her eyes.

Daylight faded into shadow, lit only by fires burning in pockets of darkness. A city formed beneath them, bits of light Yara could barely make out through her stinging eyes. *City* was a generous term. It was as if people had desperately tied together decades of refuse to create shelter, resulting in a tangled maze of jagged garbage and dreck.

Nothing could shelter her from the smell of sickness and death. Black mud clung to everything, painting it in sludge and stealing what little light remained in this depraved darkness.

Mercy of the Matriarchs, it was worse than anything Yara had ever imagined. There were children here?

She looked over at Cyn; his expression seemed as hard and calculating as the moniker he had adopted, Cobra, the snake of Cyrila, but in his eyes she caught something else, a lingering sadness.

He had been a child here. This sickness was his home. This was *his* Azra.

The ship slowed, and the air seemed to thicken around her. She fought the urge to cough as she inhaled slowly through her mouth. She could taste the filth. How would she ever get the smell off her skin? This was a place of disease.

Did the Grand Sister know what she was sentencing people to?

She didn't know what was worse, the slow fall to the ground for those sentenced to live in this cesspool or the quick one for those condemned to death.

She managed to breathe without choking, but her eyes still streamed.

Tuz sneezed and vigorously rubbed his face with his paw.

The weight of gravity pressed down on her as the glider slowed to a stop on a crooked platform, spliced together from two different pieces of cracked metal.

Yara blinked through her burning eyes long enough to gaze out on a towering pile of garbage. That is what it looked like, anyway. Bits of old ships, great fallen limbs, and jutting pieces of discarded metal and wood formed a maze of leaning shacks covered with a thick black mud.

The humid air buzzed with insects, but Yara couldn't see them in the dim light of small fires burning here and there throughout the maze of debris. The entire slum seemed abandoned. The heavy choking air didn't move at all.

"Welcome to Ahul. It's relatively safe here," Cyn stated as he leapt down off the platform onto a street of packed mud. "This section of the city is protected by the Cyri."

As if on cue, two young women carrying torches marched

toward them. The younger girl, no more than sixteen, wore flimsy scraps of rags tied over her young breasts and around her too-thin waist. The older of the two wore what remained of a low-cut smock, its sleeves and skirt hacked back to reveal long, jagged, and rusted blades tied to her arms, legs, and shoulders. Each one brandished a staff with a rough-cut metal spike protruding from the end.

Yara found herself staring at the starlike scars arching across the chest of the younger girl. Were they brands? Had she done that to herself? Somehow, she didn't think so, and the thought made her sick. The other guard bore the telltale puckering on the skin of her abdomen. She had borne a child here.

Yet in their eyes, she saw strength and resolve. Yara felt like she was looking into the faces of any of the Elite. There was power here in the shadows.

Cyn helped her down, and the two guards watched her with suspicious eyes. Suddenly she felt ashamed. She'd never thought of the people down here as people. In all honesty, she hadn't given them much thought at all. They'd been an abstraction.

This was too real, and her guilt ate at her.

"Come with me," Cyn murmured in her ear.

They passed down narrow alleys of packed dirt.

"Outside of the gates of Ahul, the mud is looser, filled with insects that will strip your flesh if you step in the wrong place," Cyn stated. Yara immediately picked up her feet, treading gingerly on the ground.

Cyn watched her awkward hop but didn't acknowledge it as he continued. "The whore-masters build houses up some of the larger trunks where they hold the girls prisoner. Higher up the trunks, out of the stench, they build clean and decent *houses* just below the mid-cities. They take their enslaved whores and bring them up to the higher brothels to work so the high-hawks don't have to get dirty."

He kept his hand on her, but his eyes remained wary, and he held one of his knives in his hand. Yara barely had time to process the systematic exploitation of the women before he stilled, listening to the sounds around him like a stealthy beast of the forest.

"I thought you said it was safe here." She stared into the shadows, suddenly aware of the feeling of being watched.

"No place is really safe down here. My mother did her best to create law and security out of the chaos, but sometimes the mad ones get in." He looked back over his shoulder, then continued at the same careful and steady pace. "The Cyri are in a constant battle with the whore-masters. The attacks never stop." He brought her to a hollow trunk of a long dead eldar tree. The center had been carved out by rot, and the interior bustled with activity.

In front of the strange dwelling, a woman with shaved hair, a heavily scarred face, and a missing eye crossed her arms and glared at them.

"You bring pretty presents, boy." The woman scowled, then spared a glance to Tuz, who had a similar expression on his face.

Suddenly a little boy wearing no more than a rotting sack for clothing ran out of the tavern and threw himself on Cyn's leg. The boy bore the same scars across his neck and arms that the younger guard had.

Cyn smoothed his hand over the boy's hair and gently pushed him toward one of the guards.

"The Nudari are ready. Have you heard from the other is-lands?" Cyn asked the one-eyed woman.

The other islands? Yara closed her burning eyes as she real-ized all of Azra was involved. The high cities would turn into a slaughterhouse. Forty Elite warriors, the guardians of the temple, and maybe a thousand Enforcers couldn't take on ground dwellers and all of the Nudari, especially if the Enforcers were in on the conspiracy.

The one-eyed woman wiped her hands on a ragged bit of cloth. "We have a total force of over one thousand three hun-dred from the ground."

Yara saw the unfolding disaster in her mind, and each time seemed more bloody and hopeless. There had to be a way to stop this.

Before she realized what she was doing, she glanced up at Cyn. What was she thinking? He was the one behind this. He wasn't going to help stop it.

He met her gaze, the fires reflecting in his eyes.

"I need a place to interrogate the prisoner," he said, with-out taking his eyes off her. There was no malice in his voice, no threat. But she still felt paralyzed by the horror around her.

The woman slapped the bit of cloth over her shoulder, as if they were discussing ordering a drink at some Scum bar. "Take her to the storehouse around back."

Cyn took her away from the light of the doorway. In the near darkness, she had to depend on him to lead her. He moved slowly, keeping a hand on the rotting trunk of the dead eldar as they climbed over large coiling roots and ducked under haphazard and threadbare awnings with support poles thrust into the decaying tree.

They tucked themselves under a hanging bit of cloth that served as a door, and Yara froze as she found herself in pitch darkness.

Cyn moved with ease and lit a single taper that smelled pungent but offered the small shack a little light.

Cyn placed the tiny light on an overturned bucket between them. "It's past time we had our talk."

# 19

"SO TALK," YARA STATED AS TUZ PERCHED ON A HALF-BROKEN CRATE AND
sniffed at the mud on his paw. The flickering light from their
small fire cast her face in a wavering light. Cyn didn't know
where to begin. He only knew he had to tell her everything.
He had to somehow convince her to join his side.

It was now or never.

"I know you're mad," he began.

"Mad?" She half laughed.

"We're going to argue here, now?" He didn't want things to
erupt between them the way they had in the brig. He needed
her. He needed her to see all that he was and to understand.

Yara frowned but let him continue.

"I'm sorry I lied about my name, but what was I supposed
to do? Shake your hand and introduce myself as Cyn? That
would have gone over well." He crossed his arms. If he had

admitted his name from the start, he'd be in a cell in the high cities right now waiting for the Grand Sister to use him for her own sick schemes.

Yara looked down at a half-rotted casing for an old environmental control system. The tension fell out of her shoulders. "I know why you hid your name. I can't blame you . . . for that."

"If you need more to blame me for, I've got a running list."

Yara sat back on a heap of junk and looked up at him from under an arched brow.

The blackness of the small room closed in until all he could see was her face. He couldn't joke anymore. She had to understand. Time was running out for them. "My name is dangerous," he admitted, feeling the truth of his words. Even here, his real identity could kill him. "You're one of a handful of people who know it." He tightened a buckle on his bracers. His identity had to remain secret. He couldn't lead his people and fight off bloodhunters and the assassins of the whoremasters at the same time.

"Would these people still follow you if they knew who you were?" she asked.

To her, his name was synonymous with disgrace. Her Elite world was so small, could she see the pain of all of Azra? Azra needed a hero. The name didn't matter.

"The Nudari would follow me no matter what my name. They would follow anyone willing to offer them justice for the deaths of their children." He paused.

Yara could appease them. He knew it. Dalan had seen her face and knew the truth. All the Nudari wanted was retribution and security. If she offered them justice from the throne, his Pix could prevent this war. He lingered on that thought. She couldn't prevent it alone. She needed the loyalty of all of Azra, and Azra was deeply divided in so many ways.

Yara let out a long, slow breath, making the flame of the candle dodge the shifting air. "The Nudari are patriarchal. What about the Canopy-Azralen? The women of the mid- and high cities aren't going to follow a man into war," she dismissed.

"Are you sure about that?" He crossed his arms as the flame flickered and dimmed. The quiet isolation of the darkness forced him to see her and only her. "What about the men?"

"The men aren't going to fight."

His expression hardened. "I fight."

She huffed, "You aren't—" Her eyes went wide as she clearly realized she was heading into a stupid mistake. He could see it in her abashed look.

"From Azra?" He glared at her.

"Damn it, Cyrus." She shifted, twisting her body, but there was no room to move.

"My name is Cyn." He lowered himself onto a broken stool, feeling like a cat about to pounce on unsuspecting prey. "Where have you been the last ten years? When was the last time you spoke with one of the male artisans of the mid-cities?" He pounded his fist on the bucket, nearly overturning the candle. "Oh, that's right. The men from the mid-cities aren't allowed to sell their own work. They have to be gouged by an approved, which means female, dealer from the high cities, so the women don't have to debase themselves."

"You're being dramatic," she defended.

He shook his head in disbelief. "Have you spoken with any of the scientists? No. Why? They aren't allowed to keep or represent their work. It is stolen from them by the government. You haven't noticed, because the high cities don't bother to look down, but the economy of the mid-cities is crumbling. Even the women of the mid-cities are frustrated and ready for change."

Yara took a deep breath and twisted her fingers together. She looked afraid and so very alone. Her humility cooled his anger. He wanted to reach out and touch her, convince her that the problems of Azra could be solved, but at this point, he couldn't see how.

"And the ground?" she whispered. "Why do you hide who you are from them?"

"Because I'm the son of Cyori," he huffed as he scratched the place above his scar. "That's one thing the Elite and the shadows have in common."

"I don't understand." Yara's bright gold eyes met his. His heart hammered in his chest, just three beats out of rhythm, but the open and curious expression in her face made him feel connected to her again.

His mother's eyes were also yellow, but fear had hardened them, fear and the deadly resolve of a mother protecting her young. "My mother brought order and law to this place. She ripped apart anyone that threatened our family. Eventually, that family grew as she took in the innocent and defenseless. The beaters, the bleeders—she saved them, she taught them to fight, and she made a lot of enemies in the process."

Yara leaned forward. "Is she dead?"

"She escaped to Earth to protect me," he explained, grateful that she seemed to be listening. He was glad that their escape to Earth had saved her as well. She was happy, though driven to protect the Earthlen victims of abuse as fiercely as she had defended the Azralen.

But that wasn't the point. After they lost Cyani, his mother could not lose him, too. "I'm the living blood, the last of my line." Cyn looked her in the eye. "She knew one day the Grand Sister would want me. She tried to protect me. My name is dangerous, because my enemies are everywhere."

Was one of them sitting across from him? He couldn't tell, and it drove him mad.

"So you call yourself Cobra, and they follow you." She seemed so still, the fire in her subdued. He thought he knew the woman inside, but so far, she hadn't reacted to all that he'd shown her. It made him uneasy. Perhaps he was mistaken. Maybe he couldn't trust her to help him lead Azra into a new age. His determination didn't waver. He had to let her into his world. But would this world ever trust her? She was Elite, the enemy. This was one divide that couldn't be bridged with policy, only loyalty and action. What would it take for the ground to follow her?

Cyn noticed a bit of sticky mud on the side of his finger and rubbed it with his thumb. "They follow me because I've fought for them. I've bled for them. They trust me to lead them, and I will protect those who deserve it. I kick the shit out of the ones that piss me off." He thought about the whore-masters, the endless battles. Cobra had as many enemies as Cyn in the shadows. He kept his new name because the Cobra had earned their fear and respect through his actions alone.

"Everyone is scarred here," she mused, as her gaze turned to his chest. "Even the little boy. Those scars on his chest . . ."

"They're brands." A muscle in Cyn's jaw began to tic, but he ignored it. "A whore-master tortured him to keep his mother submissive."

Yara's eyes widened, just a flash of expression. His hope surged. "I've spent the last seven years trying to protect the children here. That's why the people here will follow me to the death."

She swallowed.

They fell silent. The fickle light faded and surged as it waged its tiny war against the darkness. He watched her, watched the subtle changes in expression in her beautiful face. He'd see moments of hard determination followed by confusion and sadness. Eventually the sadness lingered as her posture closed in. Her fingertips absently stroked her stomach.

Cyn watched the self-soothing gesture. This conversation was about to get personal. His guilt flared. He couldn't let himself feel remorse for fighting for what was right for Azra, but he did feel deep remorse when it came to how he had treated her.

"You manipulated me. You tricked me into getting on your ship, and you used me." She brought her hot-honey gaze to his again. In the depths of her cool expression he could see her deep hurt.

"I'm sorry." He sighed, not knowing what to say. "I thought I'd be taking a brainwashed mercenary on my ship, a woman who only cared about her power and position." He swiped the dark stain on his hand against his jeans. How could he explain?

"I was willing to use that woman, because I hated her," he

admitted. "The Grand Sister is a liar, a master deceiver, so I fought back with my own deception."

Yara blinked rapidly and looked down. The light caught in the single tear that fell from her eye. He reached out and lifted her chin.

"So you used me, and you were going to hand me over to people who would kill me," she stated with a cool, detached voice, as if they weren't talking about her life.

"No."

She looked up at him.

It was the truth. He couldn't have let her die.

"Who will lead Azra once everything was destroyed? You?" She pinched her mouth into a tight line. "Did you even think that far ahead?"

"Not until recently," he admitted. He had been ready to let Azra decide her own fate, but that was no longer good enough.

"When I found you, I didn't find a power-hungry mercenary," he offered. "I found a woman of strength and conviction. I found a woman who is brave, compassionate, and driven by a pure heart. You are noble, you are just. I believe if you sat on the throne of Azra, you would try to change things for your people because you . . . love them."

Yara's breathing hitched as Cyn stumbled over the last two words. He wanted to say so much more, admit so much more, but couldn't.

"You captivated me," he whispered.

Yara let the words sink deep into her battered heart.

"I don't know what to do next," he confessed. "Everyone is looking to me to start this war, but . . ." He hesitated. "We need a way into the high cities. Someone has to access the Elite com array to bypass the block on the Nudari systems. We can't wait. The Grand Sister will never willingly step down. She'll destroy even more if we let her. Change can't wait."

"What was her name?" Yara interrupted. She needed to know.

"What are you talking about?" He stopped cold and stared at her with confusion crinkling his brow.

"The girl you loved, what was her name?"

Cyn looked down, his face a mask of deep sadness.

"Yarlia."

Yara felt the impact of the name deep in her gut. Her kin. Another bearing the name of Yarini had suffered and died in this place.

Mercy, she couldn't believe it was possible. How had her kin ended up in this place?

"What was her crime?"

"*Shakt*, what crime? There was no crime. Her mother, Yarin, discovered tampering in the archives. Someone had modified the writings of Yarini the Just. When she alerted the Grand Sister, she was banished here. Yarin was raped, gave birth to Yarlia, then succumbed to an infection when her daughter was barely six."

Yara remembered the name Yarin. She had been her mother's cousin. She'd been near the end of her trials when she suddenly disappeared. The family assumed she'd killed herself after failing her training. They had used her dishonor to push Yara even harder.

The truth dawned on her. In a way it freed her. It was as if Cyn had turned the last piece of a puzzle around so it could finally fit. The Grand Sister had disbanded the old jury-based judicial system, the Council of Reckoning, and convinced the high cities that the justice system would be more efficient if she were the sole hand of the law. She used the writings of Yarini to justify it. False writings.

By the Mercy, if what Cyn was saying was true, the woman stopped at nothing to solidify her power, not fraud, not murder. She had defiled the sacred trust of Yara's line. No one dared question it, and now she knew why. The Grand Sister had eliminated her opposition.

What had she done?

*Great Creator.*

Someone had to stop the Grand Sister before she destroyed any more lives. But it was impossible. What he was asking was impossible. "What do you want me to do, Cyn?" she said, her voice shaking. She didn't have the power to challenge the Grand Sister alone. Only a revolution could rip the old woman from her throne, but at what cost? "You want me to start a war?"

He stood. "No, prevent one."

Yara felt dizzy with the rush of her terrifying thoughts as she listened to Cyn rattle off the password that unlocked Tuz's collar. What was he doing? Why would he release her scout? He turned and placed the key to her cuffs on the bucket by the candle. His fingers lingered over it as his dark gaze burned her.

His stunning face looked so open, so honest. She knew this man. "I want to trust you, Yara."

Without another word, he turned and left her in the dark.

Yara remained still, staring at the key resting beside the candle. A chunk of burnt wick fell off, renewing the flame.

She felt the weight of her thoughts like a tangible thing as she contemplated the key.

What was she going to do?

She had no idea any of this existed. In her mind, the ground was filled with criminals fighting with one another over food, not this rot. Not this depravity.

He was right. She couldn't let the innocent people here suffer. When she took the throne, she'd bring the innocent up, she'd listen to every crime, and she'd dispense fair justice along with a panel of her peers. She wouldn't leave criminals alone, and she wouldn't excuse the criminals in the high cities either.

She'd find a way, but it would take time, and the rage she could feel here was like a fire that could consume all of the jungle if given the chance.

Then there were the Nudari. She needed to know the truth of what happened there. It made her sick in her heart to know how easily she believed their story.

The Grand Sister ruled Azra with an iron fist. Yara had always believed it had been the fair hand of law, but now she doubted it.

The Grand Sister had become more and more irrational as her condition deteriorated. Yara never doubted the strength of the woman's conviction, but something in her leader's eyes made her uneasy.

Her name was Fira, last of the line of the great Fima the Merciless. She had no heirs. At one point, Yara thought she'd had a brother, younger than her by a decade, but he had disappeared.

There were no children. She had no living legacy. All she had was her power, and she clung to it with all her strength.

Yara's heart pounded with fear as she thought about what she needed to do. There was only one way to prevent this revolution.

Did she have the strength to see it through?

Her decision could destroy her.

She had to do it. She was prepared, her training had taught her well. She had the support of enough of the Elite. All her life had been moving toward this moment. Now she had to take it.

"Tuz, open com link to Onali," she stated.

Static buzzed from Tuz's collar. "Yara?" Her friend and closest ally's voice broke through. She let out a breath of relief; it hadn't been long, but it seemed like she'd been cut off from the other Elite forever. Onali and Esalin were her closest supporters. She needed them now.

"I'm here on Azra, Nali," she answered.

"What?" the Elite warrior squeaked like an unschooled girl. "Thank the Matriarchs. Where are you?"

"I'm on the ground. I need your help. Find Esalin and bring a judgment lift to the coordinates Tuz gives you from his collar. I've found my mark."

Yara grasped the key from the bucket, then unlocked her wrists and removed the belt. She glanced around, her mind filtering out all distractions as she prepared for battle. After grabbing a crude, rusted blade, she snuffed the small flame and left the shack.

The foulness of the ground city choked her. The great trunks of the eldar trees rooted in this festering soil. If she didn't do something about this place, the eldars would die and the high cities would topple.

She couldn't let that happen.

Her lingering doubt ate at her with the persistence of the bugs feeding on the rot all around her.

This had to be the right choice. It was the only way.

With furtive steps, she stalked through the slum. Occasionally she could feel a wary stare fix on her, but like an animal, the watcher remained hidden amid the decay.

"Tuz, track Cyn." Tuz dropped his head low and ran through the streets. She had to find him before the other Elite arrived.

Yara did her best to follow, heeding Cyn's earlier warning. This place was not safe. She kept the rusted blade at the ready as she used her training to block out the vestiges of her emotions.

She had a mission. She would do it with precision and control.

She found Cyn in a clearing near a wall of jagged metal. It gaped up toward the canopy like the jaws of some voracious shark.

He stood alone, staring up at the underside of the layers of civilization above them.

"Tuz, scan area," she whispered. The lights on his collar blinked the all-clear signal.

Cyn turned his gaze to her, his strong arms crossed over his chest.

Yara felt a stabbing pain in her heart. He looked at her with such trust. She knew he was a man who did not trust easily, but his loyalty was absolute.

He'd never forgive her for this.

"Tuz, send coordinates," she stated.

His brow lowered as his open gaze turned to one of suspicion.

"What are you doing, Yara?" he asked.

"I'm sorry," she answered.

He rushed to her, crossing the clearing in a few urgent steps. He grabbed her by both arms and looked her in the eye. She took a step back to brace herself, but he didn't let her back away. The feel of his body pressed to hers woke her memories, and she felt torn. Her decision could destroy him.

"What did you do?" He held her close, wrapping his arms around her. She felt the rush of longing in her heart. She couldn't give in now. She was out on a very thin limb.

She pushed out of his embrace and held up her blade.

"I'm sorry."

The roar of engines filled the area as a foul wind buffeted them from all sides. The small craft landed in the clearing. Onali and Esalin fixed their weapons on Cyn.

The shock on his face slowly faded to contempt as he turned his green eyes to her.

"How could you?" he growled. "You will kill us all."

Like rats crawling out of their nests, a crowd of people peered out from the rubble, cautious and fearful. The Elite lift had the capability of releasing a sonic discharge that could make all of their ears bleed. Usually it was enough to keep them away from Elite business, but Yara was taking their hero, their leader. As soon as they realized what was going on, they wouldn't stand for it without a fight.

She had to get out of there.

Grabbing Cyn by the arm, she pushed him forward. Tuz leapt into the lift.

"Move," she commanded.

He stiffened and stopped. The voices of the crowd rose as

they filtered out of the heaps of refuse and into the streets. They pointed, savage expressions of rage and confusion on their muddy faces.

"Damn it, Cyn. Move." He was her prisoner now. She pushed the edge of one of the rusted blades against his side, knowing how deadly a flesh wound could be in this sludge. She didn't want to threaten him but knew he didn't want to die yet. He took a step forward, enough for Onali to jab him in the shoulder with a numbing spike.

The shouts from the angry crowd overpowered the engines. They waved their arms, picked up rocks and chunks of metal, and flung them at the circular lift. Yara shoved Cyn forward, and Onali pulled him onto the center platform. Yara collapsed on top of him.

With a surge that forced Yara's body down, pressing it hard against the strong heat of Cyn, the lift shot up through the canopy, leaving the angry swell of people below.

Cyn looked at her, helpless and drugged. Even through his glassy expression, his eyes burned with his betrayal.

"I trusted you," he whispered, his voice weak and hoarse with the drug flowing in his system.

"I'm sorry," she offered one last time as her palm smoothed over the scar on his chest.

# 20

CYN SEARCHED THROUGH EVERY WORD OF EVERY LANGUAGE HE HAD EVER
heard and still couldn't find the words strong enough to equal
his rage. He fought the effect of the numbing agent as the lift
rocketed toward the canopy. If he took the five worst binges of
his life, shoved them together, and suspended himself under-
water, it wouldn't have equaled the slow, muddled feeling of
his body. But his mind wasn't as affected. His mind never lost
focus. The fetor and darkness faded away as the mid-cities passed
in a blur, and the bright light of the canopy stabbed at his eyes.

He knew he shouldn't have trusted her. The Elite always
turned back to their training. She was brainwashed, and he
should have seen it. He had shocked her, frightened her, and
like an animal running into the fire destroying its home, she'd
embraced her training instead of him.

The look in her eyes back in the shack had seemed so real,

so honest. He wasn't an easy man to fool, and yet she'd played him like a string of nines in ralok.

He shoved her with his shoulder to try to force her off of him as the lift slowed and came to a stop. He didn't want her touch. He couldn't even look at her.

One of the other Elite warriors yanked him to his feet while Yara fixed immobilizers to his wrists behind his back.

He stumbled and almost fell to the side, but the drug was wearing off quickly.

"Strip his weapons and toss him in the sterilizer," the tall woman commanded.

Yara stood in front of him, her expression hard, her eyes cold and dead. This wasn't the woman he knew.

It wasn't the woman he *loved*.

"Aw, shit," he grumbled. He loved her.

Yara glanced up, just enough to catch his eye. The Elite never permitted a man to look them in the eye. He studied her face. There was a tension there, something driving her. He'd seen the subtleties of her expression before, right before she made a move on the lattice back on the Touscari pier.

His rage burned deep in his heart, yet that ever-present bastard, hope, whispered in his mind.

What game was she playing? Or did she simply forget where they were for a moment?

She unbuckled his belt. A shot of pleasure lanced through his abdomen as he thought about the last time she had touched the waist of his pants.

With efficient speed, she stripped his belt, took Bug, who remained in stasis, and tucked him into a pocket of the clinging black pants he had given her.

What was she up to?

She stepped behind him, her fingers trailing over the edge of his bracers. He felt each quick tug as she unhooked the buckles. They cracked open and peeled away from his skin. The air touched his forearms, and it felt cold, much colder than it should have. That skin was never exposed, and now his arms were laid bare for all to see.

"By Fima, he's the blood of Cyrila?" One of the other guards exclaimed. "He's Cyani's brother, isn't he?"

"I'd say it's a pleasure, but it really isn't," he grumbled. Yara took one of his knives. She inspected the pristine blade before drawing it under his sleeve at the elbow and pulling it up toward his ear. The fabric split over the razor sharp blade, rending the shirt. He waited for the sting of a nick, a slice from the opposite edge, but she was careful not to cut him. The shirt fell from his shoulder, hanging down toward his waist, exposing the scar on his chest. She quickly slit the other sleeve, then pulled the torn garment away from his body, popping off the clasps in the front.

The tall one with the harshly controlled hair gasped. Her eyes went wide and a blush tinged her cheeks.

Cyn grimaced as Yara grasped his upper arm and shoved him into the sterilizer. It didn't take long for the pulses to cleanse him. They were set to such a severe level they stripped his hair of the last of the color he'd used to hide the iridescent sheen.

Completely exposed, he stepped out of the sterilizer. What was he going to do now? He had to escape custody. Once free, he could focus on gaining access to the com array.

He still needed a way to hack past the com security, but he'd figure something out. At least he was in the high cities, and within the Elite compound. Gaining entrance into the compound had always been a catching point in their plans.

"Take off your boots," Yara commanded. In the short time they had both gone through the sterilizers, she had transformed. The pure white garments of the Elite clung to her athletic frame. The high neck on the embroidered bodice gave her the air of stiff formality, leaving only her arms exposed to display her tattoos. He watched her hands as she fastened the last magnetic clasp under her chin. Her fingertips trembled.

He kicked off his boots. "You going to take my pants, too?" he challenged.

She glared at him. "Get over it."

"I'm afraid I can't." He had to steel himself. The revolution was on the brink. He had hoped Yara would see his side, help him prevent the bloodshed from within the Elite, but he had let his affection cloud reality. Dressed in her robes, he could see the truth. She was completely one of them.

He was on his own, and the people of Azra needed him.

Now all he had to do was survive long enough to start a war.

Tuz jumped out of the sanitizer, his thick fur standing on end. He fell into stride beside his master as they walked down a side corridor and entered the Halls of Honor.

A crowd had begun to gather at the feet of the towering statues of the Matriarchs. The sun lit the canvas awnings stretched above the corridor, casting the pure white monuments to Azra's finest Elite in an ethereal glow.

Cyn didn't bother to look at them. He knew their faces. He didn't glance at the crowds in his peripheral vision either. He let them fade into blurs, curious eyes, and the occasional pointing finger.

He could hear them well enough as their strange little parade marched over the shining white floor. His name whispered through their ranks like the slow hiss of the snake.

They passed the statue of Yarini, and Yara squeezed his arm tighter. He watched her as she looked up at her great ancestor. The statue bore a sad expression with softly closed eyes. Yara was the spitting image of the once-powerful ruler.

*And just as blind.*

He kept his head held high as they continued through the hall. The crowds grew louder and more animated. He could hear their calls for an execution.

"God, these people need a new form of entertainment," he grumbled.

Yara flinched.

He smiled to himself as they reached the end of the hall. He glanced up at the statue of Cyrila, and the statue offered him a subtle yet encouraging smirk.

They entered the throne room through one of the great archways circling the cathedral-like chamber. The Grand Bitch's throne rose above the milling people, suspended in the air by a carved branch that spiraled up from the center of the floor.

She descended the stairs with slow, deliberate steps. Cyn noticed a hitch each time she put her left foot forward. It seemed her crippling arthritis was getting the best of her. He wondered if she would recognize him as the Union liaison, Cyrus Smith, who had stood in this room and stolen her precious heir out from under her nose.

That conversation could be interesting.

The crowds hushed as the Grand Sister threw the edge of the mantle of power back over her bony shoulder. Her thinning white hair stuck up in short tufts, while her ice blue eyes glared at him.

"Cyn of Cyori," she announced, coming face-to-face with him. "The crimes of your family run deep."

"You'd know," he countered.

She whipped a blow across his face. Her sharp nails clawed into the skin of his cheek, scorching him. The crowd cheered.

He recovered from the blow and smiled at her, even as he felt the trickle of blood slide over the edge of his jaw.

"Do not dare defile me with your words, traitor." She placed a bony hand on the whip she always carried. "I will flay you thrice for every word you speak to me, and I will take flesh."

She turned her attention to Yara. "You have done well." Her hoarse voice didn't offer any love or even admiration for Yara, and yet Yara bowed her head in submission to the monster before her.

How could she be so blind?

"It is my honor and holy purpose to please the great and powerful leader of our noble planet," Yara droned.

Cyn wanted to reach out and shake her, kiss her, do something to find the woman he knew—the woman he loved. This machine beside him wasn't even a person. His anger returned, along with a very deep sense of loss.

He knew what he'd had in her. But that person was dead.

The warrior beside him was as lifeless as the statue in the hall.

The Grand Bitch held her skinny arms aloft, silencing the crowd. Oh great, a speech.

"Today is a glorious day for the people of Azra," she began. Cyn rolled his eyes. "The kidnapper who imprisoned Cyani,

our own Elite sister, has been brought here to face justice."
Her rasping voice echoed in the cavernous throne room.

*Kidnapper? Of Cyani? Yeah, that's what happened.*

If he didn't survive this ordeal, at least he could be proud
and satisfied that he had freed his sister from this bullshit. How
had she survived this hypocrisy for fourteen years?

The chants calling for his death grew louder. He ignored
them. The Grand Sister wasn't going to kill him yet. She wanted
Cyani. And there was no way she'd ever find her without him.

He wasn't going to give up the location of his sister, not for
anything. No pain, no torture would ever surmount the peace
in his heart when he thought of her happy and safe with the man
she so clearly loved.

"Patience," the Grand Bitch called out over the crowd. "The
prisoner must be interrogated, and I, with the power and strength,
the holy honor of Azra, will make him reveal the location of
our lost sister."

Yara slipped him a sidelong glance, but he knew what it
meant when the corner of her eye narrowed, even though the
change in her expression was so subtle he barely caught it. She
was up to something.

The tendrils of hope hooked in his heart, pulling at it.

"Follow me," the Grand Bitch insisted. She marched out of
the throne room through one of the eastern corridors, the ones
that lead to the holding cells for prisoners awaiting execution.

Yara pulled him by the arm, but the other two Elite warriors had remained behind in the throne room to prevent the
crowds from entering the passage.

"You're an arrogant bastard," the Grand Bitch insisted as
she strode down the hall, trying to hide that hitch in her step.

"Well, we know where I get it," he countered.

The old woman turned on her heel, and with a speed unnatural for someone in her condition, she unfurled her whip and snapped it across the front of his bare chest.

Yara pulled him back as the lash struck, but the pain of it shot through his nervous system, turning his body to fire. Yara had prevented the strike from tearing his flesh.

He glanced at her, but her face remained impassive.

The Grand Sister looped the whip in a coil and struck him across the cheek with it, a warning blow.

"The next time, I take flesh. I'll bleed that scar." The old woman let the whip slide on the smooth floor as she turned the corner and entered the long hall.

Four Elite guards stood sentinel at the arch, though no prisoners remained in this section of the complex. His aunt didn't keep prisoners very long before she either killed them or banished them.

Yara pushed him into the back half of a small room, and an energy shield immediately activated, slicing the room in half.

"Leave us," the Grand Bitch insisted.

"In my experience, he's a crafty fighter. I wouldn't lower the shield . . ."

"Do not presume to tell me, holy leader of Azra, what to do," the crone screeched.

Yara bowed her head in submission. "I seek forgiveness for my failings," she chanted.

"Go, leave the prisoner to me."

# 21

YARA KEPT HER PACE STEADY AND HER HEAD STILL AS SHE WALKED BACK OUT of the prison. Her heart beat so powerfully, she feared others could see the movement through her clothing and know her intentions. She wished she could have told him her plan, but Onali knew her too well, and the woman had eyes like a hawk. If Cyn showed anything but complete contempt for her, it could have blown their cover.

*Calm, serene. This doesn't matter to you.*

Oh, but it did. That was the problem. She was about to start something she couldn't take back, and it could cost her her life.

When the Grand Sister struck Cyn, she had to fight the urge to draw her dagger. She loved him. She couldn't deny it. Her gut reaction to seeing him in pain only proved what her heart already knew.

She would stand with him in victory, or in death.

Tuz followed obediently at her heels, though he watched her as he walked. He could sense her agitation, and he was ready for battle.

Good.

Yara nodded to the guards, then turned a corner out of sight, and locked herself in an empty interrogation room.

Furiously digging at her belt, she pulled Bug out from the items she'd confiscated from Cyn.

"Wake up," she urged, tossing the disc in the air the way Cyn had back on his ship. The lifeless bot fell to the floor with a nerve-jarring clang.

Tuz pounced.

Bug's aura flared to life, as blue charges shot out of his edge. Tuz puffed up into a ball of hissing and spitting fury.

"Enough," Yara commanded. Bug shot up off the floor and bolted around the room so quickly his aura left a jagged trail of light through the air. He stopped centimeters from her face.

"We're in the Halls of Honor. Cyn is in prison," she explained. Bug let out a shrill alarm.

"Bug, listen to me," she insisted. The edge of his disc glowed with a threatening blue charge. "I need your help. It was the only way to get him into the Elite complex so he could access the com array. I need you to help me break him out."

The pink in Bug's aura flared. "*Pip!*"

"All right," she ran a shaking hand through her hair. "Here's what I need you to do. Can you link into the com channels for Tuz's collar?"

"*Pip!*"

"Good." She lifted Tuz and held him close to her chest. "I need you to spy on Cyn's cell through the ventilation gap."

"*Brrrrrrr,*" the bot insisted as he rose in an affirmative way.

"Have you done this before?"

"*Pip!*"

Yara placed the old Union eyepiece she'd pilfered from the supply room where she'd dressed on her face and turned the holo-screen on. "Okay, link through the channel and send any images to my eyepiece."

The tiny screen broke up with static, then cleared, a perfect translucent image of her face. "Good work." She didn't have an ear set, so she set Tuz's collar to project the audio feed from Bug.

"He's in the third cell on the right side of the hallway to the north of us." She stooped and lifted open a filigree plate exposing the ventilation shaft. "I need to know when the Grand Sister leaves."

"*Pip!*" Bug flew into the tiny shaft, his aura illuminating the dark tunnel.

Yara's anxiety pounded in her head as she sat at the edge of the simple table in the center of the room. She didn't want to think about the weapons that usually lay on the table to intimidate prisoners, or torture them.

Cyn was in very real danger. The Grand Sister could do severe damage if she wanted, and Yara would have to watch.

By Fima, the thought made her sick. She felt so helpless. It had been bad enough knowing Cyn thought she'd betrayed him, but she couldn't risk giving them away to Onali and Esalin.

She trusted her allies but not enough to let them in on blatant treason. That, and she hoped Cyn's anger would give him strength.

"You're very crafty, Cyrus Smith." Yara lifted her head and focused on the holo-screen as the Grand Sister's cold voice filtered through Tuz's collar.

The dark image in front of her wavered, and then she could see Cyn, at least everything from his mouth down, through the filigree of a second vent shaft. All she could see of the Grand Sister was the edge of the mantle of Azra and the tail of her whip. Cyn crossed his arms, displaying his Azralen coloring.

"I wondered if you recognized me," he stated with the cool composure of someone sitting down for a mug of ale.

"I should have seen through your little disguise. You're the very image of your father." The Grand Sister sounded bitter as she stepped completely out of the frame. Cyn's lips quirked in his sardonic smile.

"Should I send your brother your regards?" he asked.

What?

The Grand Sister's whip snapped across the shield, sending surges of energy radiating out. The holo-screen blurred with the surge, then returned to normal.

Her brother? That would make Cyn her nephew. Her blood. How?

"Where is Cyani?" the Grand Sister insisted.

"Beyond your reach."

"Nothing is beyond my reach." The Grand Sister began to pace. "You will contact her, you will tell her to return, or I will kill you."

"We both know that isn't going to happen. If you kill me, then you really have no hope of finding her, and I'm your last living blood." Cyn shrugged.

"Then I'll make you wish you were dead."

"Too late for that."

Yara felt the impact of his words deep in her heart. She just wanted to get him out, to let him know the truth. She hadn't betrayed him.

"Cyani will sit on the throne of Azra. My blood will continue to reign. If she has been soiled by that sex slave, I'll get rid of any whelps and use her shame to regain her allegiance." Yara's head reeled as she listened to the Grand Sister. By Fima, the woman was as merciless as her ancestor.

"We both know the Elite will never follow Cyani. They're already looking to Yara to replace you. Cyani has nothing to do with the future of Azra." Cyn leaned forward, placing his elbows on his knees as he let his hands hang loose in front of him. "And Yara is too strong to control. That's why you've never supported her ascension. Your reign will end. The line of the Just will resume the throne, and you'll disappear into obscurity."

Yara felt her heart expand at his words. He thought she was strong. She had to believe it. If she hesitated at all, the entire planet would fall to ruin.

"Ah, Yara," the Grand Sister continued. "She's very pretty, isn't she?"

"I hadn't noticed," Cyn deflected. Yara felt herself blush. *Dirty liar.*

"I had plans for her. I knew she'd have to be removed for the others to support Cyani." Yara felt as if the Grand Sister

Jess Granger

had just slapped her in the face with the handle of her whip. "You didn't think I was going to waste your genetic potential on someone unworthy of you."

*What is she talking about?*

"You pulled this scheme before. I figured you'd try it again." Cyn's words held a bitterness he couldn't hold back. "Was that why you chose her for the bloodhunt?" Yara focused on his face. She could see the burning hatred in his eyes.

"Perhaps all I need is a little modification of my original plan." She paused, stepping in front of Cyn. The fraying hem of the mantle of power filled the small screen. "I intended to have Yara go to the ground to find you once Cyani was ready to ascend. She has a weakness for male flesh. Perhaps that's my fault. I wanted her broken in young. I set up an Alkar ceremony for her and some of the others with talent. I find it's best to hinder any ambitions toward the throne by ensuring I have blackmail material on each of the girls."

Yara fought to breathe. The loss of her vow? It had all been a scheme. She'd been manipulated by the Grand Sister. She wanted to blame herself for not seeing it for what it was, but looking back, it all made perfect sense. She had been immortal, untouchable, until that day. After that, the lingering fear that others knew, that someone could use it against her, always remained in the back of her mind.

By Ona, the Grand Sister had no limits to her obsession with power.

"So you planned to drug me so I'd seduce Yara, the way you drugged my parents so they'd conceive your heirs?" Cyn's dark voice broke Yara out of her thoughts and forced her to focus on what was happening now. The Grand Sister had drugged

272

Cyori? By the Creator, all the pieces were beginning to fall together in her mind.

Cyori was the most talented warrior any generation had seen since the great Matriarchs. Fira was older. She couldn't compete with Cyori's strength and legendary agility in battle. So instead of getting rid of Cyori by challenging her, Fira drugged Cyori and her own brother so Cyori would be shamed, and Fira's niece and nephew would be the offspring of the most skilled blood on the planet, the full bloodline of the Merciless and the Rebel.

According to Azralen law, Cyn's father would have been able to keep and raise the babies in the high cities if he'd claimed them. Instead, he disappeared. *He followed the mother of his children to the ground.*

So Cyori was shamed, and Fira assumed the throne, but she lost access to the babies she'd so carefully crafted through her deception. She lost her heirs, until Cyani returned to the high cities accused of murder.

No wonder the Grand Sister had shown Cyani *mercy.* She not only got her heir back, but she ensured Cyani would never betray her out of fear for her life and the life of her brother.

But Cyani did betray her. Cyn defied her even now.

"All I have to do is purge your blood of infertilizers, shoot you so full of Byralen stimulants you go mad, wait for the right time in her cycle for her to conceive a female, and then let you rape her, over and over." The Grand Sister's voice lowered, seething with hunger and malice. "Maybe this time I'll watch."

Cyn leapt at the shield, throwing his fists against it. "I will not!"

The Grand Sister threw her whip through the shield, catching him across the scar on his chest. He recoiled as an angry red welt rose on his skin.

"Oh you will, my nephew. Then, as soon as she conceives an heir, I'll have you executed for rape, and I'll keep the baby under my careful control this time. If Yara tries to rule Azra in a way I don't approve, I'll teach the child how to be strong through pain."

Yara clenched the edge of the cold table, numb and sick with shock. Fira had to be stopped. She was the only one with the power to stop her.

"Yes," Fira sneered. "I like that plan much better. Goodbye, Cyn."

Yara stood, gathering her resolve. She no longer thought about her fear. She no longer thought about anything but her pure rage. The reign of deception would end before nightfall.

The Grand Sister's footfalls clicked down the long hall. It was time to put her plan into motion.

"Tuz." Her cat snapped to attention, his long whiskers pricked forward as he watched her with a war-hungry look in his eyes. "I need you to work with Bug. You two have to cause a distraction in two places at once." She stroked his thick head as the cat grinned at her and purred. "A big one. Bug, when you hear Tuz's signal, wait fifteen seconds and then make as much noise as you can on your end."

"Yowwrrr," Tuz called and ran out the door. The holo-projection dipped in affirmation. Good. Between the two of them, they should be able to cause enough havoc to cover her.

Yara grabbed two injection spikes filled with a potent tranquilizer. She removed the eyepiece and returned it to her pocket.

With stalking strides, she exited the interrogation room and crept back to the corner.

A sudden cacophony erupted down the far hall, followed by an urgent scream. Two of the four guards ran past her, leaving two behind at the archway. Perfect.

She readied the injectors and counted, three, two, one.

An ear-piercing whistle sounded from within Cyn's cell.

Yara jumped out from around the corner. Both guards had turned their backs, looking toward the noise. Yara jabbed them simultaneously in the necks. They crumpled to the floor before they had the chance to turn around and see their attacker.

She didn't have much time. Dragging them into the nearest cell, she locked them behind the shield, then ran to Cyn.

He stood at the shield, the whip burn across his chest still bleeding. He stared at her in shock.

"Yara?"

She punched the release, and the shield dissolved. He rushed forward and took her by the arms.

"I'm sorry," she confessed. "It was the quickest way to get you into the Elite complex without suspicion so you could hack the com array. I couldn't tell you, or—"

Yara couldn't say another word before his mouth captured hers in a blistering kiss. He wrapped his arms around her, holding her so tightly she couldn't breathe as his lips, his tongue tangled with hers in a frantic, passionate release.

She pushed her arms up, circling his neck, tangling her fingers in his shining hair. Her rush of relief and arousal sped through her body on the wings of her coursing blood.

He gripped her, his strong hands holding her body to his.

She pulled away enough to catch her breath. "We don't have much time," she gasped.

He kissed her again, smoothing his hands up her sides and capturing her face.

"I know," he grunted, tipping his forehead against hers. "God, I love you."

Yara pulled him back and kissed him. Her lips felt tender, raw, but she didn't care. She nipped his lip then looked deep into his shining green eyes. "You'd better."

Bug rattled up against the grate. Yara pulled out of Cyn's embrace and opened the grate so he could fly out. He spun around Cyn's head and landed on his shoulder.

Tuz ran into the room with the spastic control and enthusiasm of an untrained kitten.

"Tuz, take Cyn to the linking station of the com array that is connected to the docking interface," she commanded. "Use as many of the thin branches as you can and scan for witnesses." She turned her attention to Cyn and placed her hand over the welt on his chest. "Don't get caught. As soon as you hack into the array, you're vulnerable. Get the cannons down, and your message out quick. If I'm unsuccessful, the people of Azra need to rise."

"What do you mean?" He caught her wrist, then tucked her hand against his heart.

"I'm going to give you your distraction." She let her fingers splay out over his warm skin as she felt the beat of his heart against her palm.

"Yara, what do you mean?" he asked again.

"It's time to light the fire in the temple."

# 22

CYN STEPPED BACK. "YOU CAN'T." HE STARED AT HER IN SHOCK. HIS FACE
paled. "You'll be in the path of the revolution."

"I know," she said, taking his wrist. Her fingers caressed the
snakes. "It's a sacrifice I'm willing to make."

"I'm not." His eyes shone with sincerity, but her mind was
made up.

"I'm going to challenge the Grand Sister. If I don't survive,
Azra must rise." She swallowed.

He took her hand and pulled her closer to him. "Fira will
cheat. She'll do whatever it takes to kill you, Yara. She's already killed three challengers, and they were younger, stronger,
and more talented than she is. Even if you defeat her, you'll
have to contend with Palar. She'll challenge you before you
ever step off of the platform. It's the only time you'll be vulnerable enough for her to strike."

"I know. It'll give you the time and opportunity to lead our people, Cyn. You have to take it. The access code for the com system is integrated into Tuz's collar. Bug should be able to find it." Yara let her body soften against his. She tilted her head up and kissed him one last time.

"Go," she implored.

He looked stricken as she backed away from him.

"Go." She turned her back and strode out of the hall. She didn't have much time. As soon as she lit the fire in the temple, all eyes would turn to her. No one would see Cyn in the chaos.

With the force of her conviction, she quelled her nerves and steeled herself for what was about to come. The beauty of the high cities passed by in a blur as she marched through the smooth white streets built over the arching branches of the eldar trees.

The serenity of the light filtering through the bright green canopy only hardened her resolve. This was her beautiful home, but Azra was more than just this. If things didn't change, the high cities would fall. The time of reckoning was upon them.

She turned the corner and climbed a flight of stairs. The open arc of the covered bridge rose before her, when a small boy in white prayer robes caught her eye. She paused, drawn to the little boy. He turned his enormous green eyes up to hers.

He was so young, so innocent. His sweet little face glowed as he gave her a hesitant smile. She was about to bring war to this child.

By Esana the Noble, what was she doing?

His mother grabbed him by the shoulder and yanked him around. "Get back! Lower your eyes!" she shouted at the boy.

Yara blinked in shock. The mother shoved the baby behind her and bowed in deference. "I am so sorry, Your Holiness. He did not mean to look at you. He knows his place." The mother shook as her skin paled. "I swear he knows his place."

Yara touched the woman's bare shoulder. She tensed, her fear so stark and raw. The Elite were supposed to protect the people. When had they gone so wrong?

She squeezed the woman's shoulder, then turned and entered the bridge to the temple. The bridge arched over the gap between eldar trees leading to the holy temple. Smooth, white branches wove up from the floor supporting the roof above her. The shadows of the twisted branches curled across the floor as they passed swiftly beneath her feet.

She knew what she had to do for all of Azra.

She climbed the steps to the towering doors of the temple. Two low-level orderlies greeted her with a sweeping bow, their faces masked by a white drape. She walked straight past them, over the inlaid floor depicting the glory of the Matriarchs, to the chewed-up wood of four support columns in the central sanctuary. In each column, daggers stabbed into the ancient pillars, grouped by loyalties among the Elite. She saw her own dagger. It hadn't moved in the four years she'd been away, and now even more daggers jutted out from the wood just below it than she had ever seen. Palar didn't have a quarter of the backing she did.

Would they support her in this?

It was time to test loyalties.

She took a deep breath and climbed the steep shrine stairs to the golden brazier burning in the heart of the temple. One of the priestesses gasped. She couldn't turn back now. Grasping the ceremonial torch, she dipped it in the fire.

Flames licked along the torch, warming her hand. She lifted it, felt the heat close to her face as she closed her eyes and prayed.

She prayed her heart was guiding her to the will of the Matriarchs. She prayed she had the strength to succeed and survive, but most of all she prayed for the future of Azra.

She opened them again, at peace with herself and her decision. The priestesses had gathered at the foot of the stairs, waiting. She turned and placed the torch in the center of the open hands of the statue of the Creator.

The flame burst to life, traveling down oil-filled channels carved along the edges of the temple. It barreled along its path, proclaiming to all those in the center of the temple that change, violent and terrible, was coming. It reached two pillars at the end and roared to life with a terrifying ferocity as the flames shot up through the center of the pillars to the crown of the temple above. Soon all of Azra would know what she'd done.

She turned and watched the crowd through the angry tongues of flame as she gripped the torch. The sounds of frantic conversation began to fill the temple. A stream of people flooded in from the doorway.

A hush fell over the crowd as the Grand Sister entered, the mantle of power swaying behind her.

"Palar!" she shouted. "How dare . . ."

Her eyes locked with Yara's, and Yara lifted her chin in defiance. Fira paled, her expression slack with shock. A moment passed, then two. Yara watched the Grand Sister's icelike eyes dart around, chased by the turmoil in her expression. The color returned to the old woman's face; she flushed red with it as she ascended the steps like a stalking cat.

"You were not to light the fire," she scolded then took another step. Yara tightened her grip on the torch.

"Yet I did." She took a deep breath, her resolve strengthening her. She would not let one woman torture Azra any longer. Fira's time was done. Yara welcomed the fight.

"Your High Holiness," someone shouted from the doorway, "the prisoner has escaped."

"What?" Fira shrieked, her voice cracking as she unfurled her whip. She sent it flying over the heads of the Elite. Then she rounded on Yara, climbing the last of the steps with her rage pushing before her like the wall of a great hurricane.

"You freed him. You have betrayed me. You have betrayed Azra," she accused Yara under her breath.

"The torch has been lit," Yara stated, even though her heart raced for Cyn. She sent a quick prayer that he wouldn't get captured or killed. "How do you answer?"

"Your blood will wash my feet!" The Grand Sister's voice boomed through the temple. The crowd gasped. The nervous current of whispers slid through the room. "Prepare yourself. I will meet you in battle."

"Find the son of the Rebel and bring him back alive," she thundered as the crowd parted and she exited the temple.

Yara let out the breath she had been holding and tried to keep her focus through the reeling in her head and gut. She couldn't lose her concentration now. She had to rely on the precision and cold certainty of her training.

It was in her. She couldn't fail Azra.

She took each of the steep white steps carefully. Her nerves made her feet uncertain, but she couldn't let it show. As soon as she reached the crowd, Onali grabbed her elbow. Yara glanced toward the columns as three of the young girls in training put their daggers with hers.

"Why?" Onali urged, squeezing her elbow tighter as they rushed out of the temple with urgent strides. "You have everything. Why are you doing this?"

Yara lifted her head, surprised by Onali's concern.

"Because it has to be done," Yara confessed. "Please trust me, Nali."

"You could die," Onali warned, blinking her eyes. Yara remembered the death of the last challenger. Penora had been so strong, so skilled, but in the arena it was as if her life just faded out of her for no reason. She seemed weak in battle. It was unlike her. They all took the loss hard, but it was the way of the Elite. "I don't want to lose another sister," Onali confessed.

*Sister?* Yara had spent her entire life not feeling connected to anyone, but the truth almost slapped her in the face. She had not connected to them, but it didn't mean they had not connected to her.

She looked away from Onali. "It's too late. I have to face her now." She didn't realize the depth of Onali's loyalty until this moment. She didn't want to betray it. What choice did she have? "I'll see you at the platform."

Onali left with a swift and angry stride. Yara swallowed her regret. She didn't have much time to focus. The Elite were already looking for Cyn. Her distraction would only work if she pushed things quickly.

It was time to face the Grand Sister once and for all and end the grip of terror.

Yara passed through the back branches, the thin sweeping arches bowed gracefully amid the foliage and ciera blossoms. In spite of the tranquil beauty, she felt the same way she did just before the spider attack on Cyn's ship.

She had fought through blood, horror, and agony, and she stood victorious. She pulled that memory to the forefront of her mind as she thought about being chained on the Kronalen ship. Her sheer will to live had kept her focused and calm. She felt that instinct rise as she stepped onto the final arching bridge that led to the platform.

The thin bridge swayed beneath her feet, and she thought about Cyn, the way they had fallen together through the lattice, then kissed.

She had something to live for.

She was more than duty. She was more than her training. She was Yara, blood of the Just, and a woman who would do anything to help and protect the man and the planet she loved.

She stepped onto the ceremonial platform. The gleaming white expanse hovered directly over the shadows below. Five thin arches led onto the platform. Each would be guarded by a group of Elite warriors. The only way off of the platform was the straight drop to ground below.

Spectator stands rose above them, separated from the arena floor, forming the deadly gap. Already the stands were filled with at least half the population of the high cities. They eagerly watched the projections above the platform. Everyone on Azra would be able to see the challenge through the com array.

Yara strode to the center of the platform, holding her fist high. A cheer rose from the crowd, heartening her. She had support. She had the love of the people.

The crowd suddenly hushed, and Yara felt the hair on the back of her neck prick up.

Fira smiled as two temple attendants removed the mantle of power and two more carried in the ancient ceremonial blades. The curving bone blades made from the rib of an ancient felam beast had been sharpened and hardened with a special resin and treated to make them as strong and sharp as steel.

They rested within their clean blessed cloths, the attendants forbidden to touch them.

Fira took the master blade and smiled. The bone had been stained with the blood of generations of challengers. "You're a fool, girl. And you're going to die."

"Not by your hand," Yara stated.

Fira chuckled, a chilling and ominous sound.

Yara grasped the two handles of her own bloodstained blade. Her skin tingled where she gripped the felam leather.

*Odd.*

She shook off her sense of foreboding as she held her blade out to the side by one handle and bowed her head. Fira did the same.

The temple attendants disappeared over the bridge as the hush of anticipation fell over the crowd.

Her palms itched. Yara felt weak. A rush of adrenaline shot through her as the Elite standing at the bridges shouted as one.

Fira swung her blade without missing a beat. Yara countered quickly, blocking the blow even as the force of it jolted her body.

The Grand Sister had probably taken enhancers along with her drugs. She'd be foggy. Yara had to wait for the right opportunity and strike quickly.

Fira lunged after her, a wild attack like an animal on a rampage. Yara used her skill and instinct to block. It was easy to see the old woman's next move coming. If she kept up this pace of attack, she'd run out of energy soon. Yara was younger and stronger. She'd outlast the aging tyrant.

Suddenly she felt as if a fire licked over the skin of her hands. She shouted, nearly dropping her blade. Fira laughed and took a swing at her head. Yara ducked, rolling out of the way as the blade whistled past her ear.

*What is going on?*

She glanced down at her palms. Her skin was raw and red. The fire moved through the muscles of her arms, even as her mind fought to focus.

She launched her own attack, using both hands to spin and strike with the elegant blade as she drove forward, pushing Fira back toward the edge of the platform. Yara felt hot, weak. Like her body was fighting the way it had when she had been poisoned.

*Poison.*

Glorious Creator, Fira had poisoned her. The tyrant screeched a shrill war cry, coming at Yara with fury and unnatural strength.

Yara deflected each blow, but it drove her back toward the center of the arena.

The pain was excruciating. It burned through her the way the Kronalen poison had. She wanted to curl into her body, ease the pain, but she couldn't. She would not give in. Not like this.

"You're stronger than I estimated," Fira growled as Yara locked blades with her, bringing them face-to-face. "But you should have learned long ago not to defy me, girl."

She had poisoned the other challengers, too. By the Mercy of the Matriarchs, she had kept her throne through murder. It was the most vile betrayal of the holy order they gave their lives to maintain. A murder for control of the throne had caused the end of the golden age. Azra would not survive that turmoil again.

Yara broke away, letting go of one side of the blade. The skin on her palm glared angry and red.

*The blade.*

She had poisoned the leather on the challenger's blade. No one else could touch it except someone in the ring. They'd never find the poison.

Yara shuddered as she ran across the arena, her feet skimming the floor as she pushed her body as hard as she could. Even poisoned, Fira would never match her speed. As she neared the northern bridge, she threw the blade. It skidded over the platform to the feet of Onali. Yara drew her daggers as Fira, the true blood of the Merciless, descended on her.

The crowd gasped as Yara used her two crossed blades to deflect an arching blow.

"Why aren't you dead?" Fira shouted.

She'd weaken soon. She didn't know how much longer she could go on like this. Yara heard the Elite at the bridge murmur something. She couldn't be distracted. It took all of her strength to fight through the pain.

Yara dodged, leapt. Blow after blow, she used her agility alone to spare her life, to give Cyn more time. Her strength flagged, she stumbled, but she recovered her balance as Fira lifted her blade.

The sound of an Elite cruiser caught her attention, and Fira turned. Yara backed away, spared for a second. She felt so hot, so weak. She couldn't hold on much longer.

Then Yara pulled her bleary eyes to the cruiser.

Two Elite warriors held Cyn. Blood gushed over his face from a wound to his head. His eyes met hers.

Yara felt her heart plunge as if she'd stumbled over the edge of the arena. It was lost.

They'd failed.

She fell to her knees, succumbing to the raging pain in her body and heart.

It was over.

# 23

FIRA SAUNTERED FORWARD, SWINGING HER BLADE IN A LAZY ARC AS SHE cackled. "It's a pity I have to kill you," she stated, lifting her sharp chin. "You would have birthed strong daughters."

Yara's body shook with pain and fever, but it hadn't given in. She was still awake, still alive. She could still *fight*.

Cyn shouted as Fira lunged forward. Yara dodged the blade by diving toward the old woman. As she somersaulted to Fira's left, she stabbed her dagger into the Grand Sister's foot, sinking it through flesh and lodging it in the floor of the arena.

Fira howled in rage, pulling against the pinned blade as Yara found the strength to rise.

"You're a murderer," Yara shouted, pushing all her strength into the call, but it didn't feel like it was enough. Her voice felt small and isolated at the center of the crowd. "You poisoned the challenger's blade. Isala, Onai, Penora, you poisoned them. That's how you defeated them."

The Grand Sister's eyes widened as she looked toward the Elite. Yara followed her gaze to see Onali bent over the challenger's blade.

"Fool girl. Your lies can't prevent the inevitable. You will die now because you are weak." The Grand Sister's voice echoed off the stands.

Yara lifted her single dagger. "So long as I live, I will defend Azra!" The rush of determination and adrenaline numbed Yara's pain as Fira yanked the blade from her impaled foot and flung it at Yara's head.

"Azra is mine!" she declared, her bony shoulders shaking with rage.

Just then the skies roared with a sound like the winds in a great sea storm. The crowds screamed as strange hovering ships, undersides glowing with pulsating blue and green light, rose above the spectators. Fira ducked, her eyes wide with panic.

*Yes!*

He did it! Cyn did it. He summoned the Nudari.

Yara stood taller, hope rising in her heart like a surging tide. Dischargers appeared from the sleek lines of the ships, aimed at the Elite on the platform.

The people in the stands cried and shouted, but they couldn't leave. At least seventy black Enforcer ships cut off passage, trapping the people at the arena.

Yara's heart thundered. She willed the vessels not to fire.

There had to be a way out of this.

As the shouting died down, the eyes of the Elite turned to her. She didn't know what to do, but Fira lifted her blade.

"Traitor!" she screamed. "You bring arms against Azra."

"Murderer." The voice came from the outer edge of the circle. At first Yara thought someone had shouted at her, but when she turned, she saw Onali walking into the center of the arena holding the challenger's blade with a cloth. "Yara was telling the truth. The challenger's blade has been poisoned with sanar. The Grand Sister murdered her challengers," she accused. "The blood of Isala, Onai, and Penora is on us if we do not seek justice. The proof is here." She threw down the defiled blade.

Yara listened to the dark murmurs among the Elite. It was as if the Nudari and the Enforcers had disappeared.

"They were unworthy of the throne," Fira shouted.

"The Creator determines who is worthy of the throne through battle," Yara defended. "To murder a challenger destroys the will of the Creator. The Creator will punish corruption with darkness."

Yara took a deep breath as the Elite stalked forward from their positions at the bridges. She fought the urge to give in to her pain as she spared Cyn a glance. He gave her a slow nod. She could feel the call of justice. It shone in the enraged eyes of all of the Elite.

"No one person determines the will of Azra," Yara called, stoking the flames.

Fira backed up, her fear plain on her face. She held the blade of the Matriarchs in defiance, as if the symbol of power could protect her from the will of the Elite.

The Elite continued their slow march forward, their ranks drawing together behind Yara. The sound of their feet on the arena floor reminded her of an executioner's drum. They pounded like the angry heart of Azra herself, until Fira stood only a meter from the edge of the platform.

"Get back," Fira shouted. "You are all unworthy. I know what you have done. Your sins. Each of you is tainted, weak. I am Azra!"

The light caught the spinning blade of a ceremonial dagger only a fraction of a second before it sank deep into the Grand Sister's gut. Yara flinched in shock, unable to believe what she was seeing.

Fira gasped, dropping the blade of the Matriarchs. It clattered to the arena like a dead limb. The old woman's bony hands closed over the hilt of the anonymous dagger lodged in her stomach. A dark red stain crept out from the wound, turning the tyrant's white robes the color of blood.

Yara held her breath. It felt as if her heart had stopped as a second blade flew out of nowhere, sinking into the Grand Sister's shoulder. And like harbingers of a pounding rain, the first two blades were followed by a hail of daggers. They flew through the air like a swift flock of birds, intent on a single target.

Fira stumbled backward, her thin body pierced by scores of blades. She wheezed, her hands still gripping the first blade. She swayed, then tripped over her injured foot. Her body fell back in a graceful arc. Time slowed as she crashed to the arena floor, but her hip landed at the edge. She twisted and slid over the rim, leaving a smear of blood on the gleaming floor. Yara watched her fall to the shadows below, condemned to death and the darkness.

It felt as if the world refused to breathe. Even the hum from the Nudari ships sounded subdued. The whole of Azra watched, waited. The other Elite looked to one another with emotionless masks then they all turned to her.

Yara took two solid steps forward, her adrenaline pushing her body with a will of its own. She grasped the blade of the Matriarchs and took it in her hands. The elegant arched weapon felt light and strangely heavy at the same time. Perfectly crafted, it was the eternal symbol of the Elite. She was more than someone who could wield a weapon.

She looked up at the Nudari ships, and the dark ships of the Enforcers. The fearful eyes of her people implored her to save them from the Azra that rose against them.

She didn't know if she could. She didn't know if there was anything she could say to douse the flame of revolution. For Azra, she had to try.

"A new dawn is upon us," she began, not knowing where the words came from. "Azra is free." She swallowed as she lifted her chin, and listened to the echo of her voice projected over the arena. All of Azra could see her, not just the high cities but the mid-cities as well. She had to speak to every Azralen, they had to find a way out of this together.

"Too long we have been divided," she continued. "Sea and land, ground and sky, women and men."

She paused, finding her strength as she realized she understood her world in a way she never had before. "That division will destroy us. Like a festering disease, it will eat away at the roots of who we are and eventually topple us. I will not let Azra fall. We are one people. Together we can return to the golden ages. No longer will we be torn apart, hidden from one another."

She looked to the Enforcers, standing in their open cruisers. "No longer will the canopy ignore the suffering of the innocent. Justice, not one person alone, will rule us. Together we will decide what is right and holy, and what is evil."

She lifted her face to the Nudari ships. "Justice will bring us vindication. Justice will bring us peace."

She held her hands out, the blade of the Matriarchs stretching out to the side. "I offer myself as your servant. I will honor my blood, and the noble bloodlines of all the great Matriarchs. We are one people, and as one, we will not fall."

The silence engulfed her, as she looked to her people. What were they thinking? Had she failed them?

She held the blade of the Matriarchs in front of her. "I am Azra!" she declared. "Do any dare challenge me?" Her voice rang through the still arena. If none met her in battle, she would become the Grand Sister, because she held the blade. If she survived, she'd earn her title through mercy and kindness, not war.

She looked to Palar, but the coward shrank back, her nervous eyes fixed on the Nudari ships. Had she been one of the conspirators?

Cyn shrugged off his stunned captors and leapt off the ship that had held him. He landed on the platform with the grace of a korcas. He rose, dark and imposing. A chant thundered from the cities around them, over and over, voices united by one purpose called his name until the sound felt like it could crush her. "Cobra, Cobra, Cobra," they chanted. The platform shook with the power of the noise, and the Elite around her looked to her in fear. They had all taken the will of the people of Azra for granted too long.

"I control those rising against you. Blade or no blade, I hold the fate of Azra in my hands." Cyn's voice boomed, dark and powerful. "The sea, the ground, they all follow me."

It was a message to all the Elite. There was no denying it. In that moment, Cyn was Azra, the Azra that had been ignored, defiled. The sisterhood silently parted for him, their eyes locked on his bare arms and the Rebel's snakes tattooed there. Never in her life had Yara seen the Elite so afraid. He was not a man, and they knew it. He was much more than that. He was the pain of Azra personified, and it was terrifying.

Cyn's face still dripped with blood as he stooped to pick up the poisoned challenger's blade and strode forward until he stood directly before her.

Yara swallowed, but did not back down. He could not lead Azra to peace. He could not rule Azra from the throne in the order of law. The traditions of their culture and law would have to be completely destroyed for him to rule.

"We rise against you," he challenged. "I will not allow the suffering of Azra to continue. How will you appease me?"

The Elite shifted behind him, aware of the dischargers trained on them, aware of the shift of power all around them. The son of the Rebel lifted the challenger's blade and swung it.

Yara countered, the bone blade crashing against tainted bone. She stared into Cyn's deep green eyes; the streaks of blood trailing over his face made him look fierce and wild. In this moment, she was Azra, he was the Rebellion. He was her enemy.

And she loved him anyway.

She twisted her blade down, pulling his down with it and kissed him with the force of everything she felt in her heart.

His mouth met hers, hot, hungry, and powerful. The kiss

itself was a battle, one that stole the strength in her legs, yet lightened her body until she felt she was floating.

He dropped the challenger's blade and captured her face as a thundering cheer erupted from the crowds ten times louder than the chant of war. Yara wrapped her arm around his neck, needing to hang on to him, to his solid strength as they battled with lips and tongue, heat and will.

He was her equal, and she couldn't rule Azra without him at her side. She could never do this alone.

He softened the kiss, soothing her lips with a tender caress as he brushed back her hair with his strong hands.

"I'm so proud of you, my queen," he whispered. He dropped to his knee before her, bowing his head in deference.

The deafening roar grew even louder.

Yara's emotion choked her. She would never be worthy of him, and she'd spend any moment they could steal alone showing him that he was the one who made all things possible for her. She was who she was because of him. If only the other Elite would accept him.

Onali stepped forward, the only Elite with the blood of the Pure. She sought her friend's gaze, begged her with a desperate and silent prayer to bless this union.

It was the only way to bring them all together.

And she loved Cyn. She wouldn't give him up for the throne.

Onali gave her a sly smile and pulled her last dagger from the straps on her arms. She knelt, sinking it into the floor at Yara's feet. "So be it," she declared.

One by one, the Elite fell to their knees, planting their daggers in the floor before her. She looked up at the Nudari, and the ships came alive with light and color before they slowly rose and then darted swiftly toward the horizon and their homes in the sea.

As the ships rose and disappeared over the crest of the canopy, the people stood, jumping and hugging. Their cheers rang over the tops of the trees.

*They did it.*

Yara bent and took Cyn's hand, she pulled him to his feet and raised their interlocked grip above their heads. The crowd went into a frenzy as she fought back her own tears of relief and joy.

"Let's get out of here," Cyn murmured as he leaned closer to her. "This blood is stinging my eye."

"It's a good thing you aren't wearing your contacts," she teased. The Elite rose and parted for them as they crossed over the bridge that led toward the Halls of Honor.

The chorus of cheers greeted them, rising up from the cities below, even as throngs of people gathered in the streets.

"This isn't over," Yara warned. "Change doesn't come this quickly. The Elite are unsure about this, and won't accept it easily. They just don't dare to start a fight now. There will be challenges, attempts on our lives."

"Sounds like fun," Cyn replied.

"We're talking about the future of Azra," she scolded, even as she held his warm hand tighter. "Can't you be serious?"

"Not until I've run through the cleanser and cracked a bottle of nilo." He waved to a little girl who shook ciera blossoms at him.

"The Elite aren't supposed to partake—"

"Then it is a damn good thing I'm not one of the Elite."

They entered the Halls of Honor as the sun broke through the leaves and cast the hall in golden light. The Matriarchs' still expressions seemed to smile, the light playing with the shadows of their lips.

Cyn lifted his gaze, taking in each of the statues. "You are Yarini reborn," he stated with conviction.

"No," she dismissed. "I'm just a woman, as was she."

He looked at her. "You're more than that to me."

They entered the throne room, and two of the temple attendants held out the mantle of power.

Yara stepped forward, her body weak, her mind numb, but her heart so filled with hope and love that she felt she could bear any burden.

They lowered the mantle on her shoulders, the heavy fabric pressing on her even as the secure weight warmed her. With slow and deliberate steps, she climbed the spiraling stairs to the throne.

CYN WAITED AT THE FOOT OF THE THRONE FOR HOURS AS YARA SET THE ELITE and the Enforcers to work. Everything she said, she said with conviction.

In spite of being weak and in pain, she cared for their people first. Tuz clearly enjoyed his perch on the high throne as he hung his head and paws over the edge and stared down at the throng of people below.

Bug brought him a med cleanser, and he used it to take care of the mess on his face. The cut at his temple had healed enough to stop seeping.

He thought he would shed a lot more blood than this, but she had stopped it.

He loved her so much.

After what seemed like an eternity and a week, the crowds in the throne room thinned, until only a pair of Elite guards remained, the same two that had dragged him up from the ground.

"Get her out of here," one of them commanded. "She needs to rest. We'll keep you safe."

He nodded to the Elite warriors, then turned his eyes back to her. She seemed to float as she descended the throne. With the gleaming mantle of power on her shoulders, she almost didn't seem real.

But he knew the woman beneath that mantle. And tonight he'd show her how he felt.

She stopped before him and took his hand. Her eyes looked sunken and weary, but she offered him a soft smile. He didn't say a word as he wrapped her arm around his neck and lifted her into his arms.

She tucked her head against his shoulder as he carried her out of the throne room into the suite for visiting dignitaries. He couldn't bring her into Fira's quarters, not until the place had been purged of the taint of his aunt. Even then, he wasn't sure if they should ever reside in that place.

He was free of Fira. His family had finally seen justice, and it was all due to the strength of the woman in his arms. He kissed her hair as he entered the bedroom. The low wall along the edge of the floor opened up to the shimmering leaves of the canopy. A flock of colorful parrots chattered from a patch of bright red fruit, while ciera blossoms clung to the branches just beyond the low wall. A white awning stretched above them while light glimmered in the weather shield that allowed the soft fragrant breeze in.

At their feet, a nest of pale blue pillows and light silky blankets sank into the floor, inviting them to curl into the cushioned nook and sleep. Cyn gently placed Yara's feet on the ground.

He removed the mantle from her shoulders and hung it on a stand. Now she was his, and only his. It was his time to care for her.

"How are you feeling?" he murmured, still worried about the poison, though she hadn't succumbed to it yet. Still, he could tell she was on the verge of passing out. His palms itched from touching the blade, but it wasn't affecting him as severely as her.

"Like a pile of sarba crap," she admitted. "I think the fever broke. Why didn't it kill me, or at least make me pass out?"

"Tola gave you my immunity, remember?" Cyn kissed her hand as he led her into the cleanser, then showed her his slightly irritated palms. "It takes a lot more than a little poison to kill someone from the ground." He smiled as he undid the magnetic clasps at her neck and pulled her uniform off her shoulders.

He stripped and she leaned into his body as warm air swirled around them, stealing the last of the evidence of their ordeal. "I find that ironic. The blood of the ground foiled the tyrant," she quipped, then placed a sleepy kiss on his scar.

"Yeah."

He carried her back to the bed, but she had given in to her body's urge to recuperate and heal before he reached the cozy nest. He stepped down into it, tucked her gently beneath the covers, then snuggled into her side. With reverent kisses, he used the art of Tanro to manipulate her nervous system so she would no longer feel any pain.

They had one hell of a mess to clean up. He was willing to bet there'd be some sort of formal call for his head in the morning, but he had faith that the Elite were smart enough to recognize him as a symbol and use him to appease the masses. He was fine with that as long as they were also fine with his plans for reform.

It would probably take them their entire lives, and the lives of several more generations, to undo the wrongs and the suffering of Azra. But for this moment they had peace. They had hope.

For the first time in his life, Cyn felt blessed.

# 24

"SO HOW DOES IT FEEL BEING THE VERY FIRST HOLY CONSORT?" YARA TRAILED a lazy hand over the fine hair on Cyn's lower abdomen.

She'd spent a busy day negotiating with a delegation of Nudari, then visiting the hospitals teeming with the innocents brought up from the ground. She convened the Council of Islands to maintain order on all the islands and to make sure everyone was cleaning up the ground cities.

A contingent of Bacarilen traders were due in the morning, and Yara had to battle with her newborn prejudice against them. She may be the blood of the Just, but she was still human. She'd deal with them fairly as long as they agreed to her new rules for facilitating trade on Azra.

She leaned over and kissed Cyn, the caress lazy and comforting after a stressful day.

"Consort?" Cyn laughed. "That's how the Elite decided to justify our little arrangement?"

"*Holy* Consort." Yara playfully tapped his nose. "It's taken them seven months to work out a way to deal with you. You should have heard the creative interpretations of the writings of Ona the Pure to come up with that one."

Cyn slid his hands down her bare sides. "I think I like being a consort."

She considered him. Cyn had been busy as well. The people of the ground, the Nudari, and the people of the mid-cities all embraced him as a national hero, and so far the Elite hadn't tried to pull anything for fear of upsetting the masses. He had worked tirelessly to organize the rescue efforts for those on the ground and to create a fair trial system for those who perpetuated heinous acts there. Then he'd been the primary contact to the Nudari, drawing them out of their homes on the bottom of the ocean to become more integrated in the political discourse in the canopy. Some of the Matriarchs had done far less for their people than he had, and he was just getting started. "I wonder if future generations will look back on you as the first Patriarch of Azra."

"What would they call me?" he teased. "Cyn the Handsome?"

"I prefer Cyn the Pliant." She smoothed her hands down his chest.

"No you don't." He grabbed her around the waist and rolled her beneath him. He entered her in a swift hard stroke that stole her breath as she clung to his shoulders.

*By Ona, this was pure.*

He surged into her again. "How about Cyn the Insatiable."

She gasped.

"No?" His fingers trailed over her breasts, playing her like the strings of his precious guitar.

"Ona, forgive me, yes!"

He collapsed on top of her laughing, his eyes crinkling in the corners. She kissed him on the nose. "Perhaps you'll be Cyn the Honorable."

He propped himself up on his elbow and looked away. "I don't deserve that."

"I heard the speech you broadcasted when you hacked into the array," she murmured as she enjoyed the feel of the slow flexing of his muscles beneath her hands. She kissed him on the chest, then the neck, reveling in the sweet and salty taste of his skin and the feel of him settled peacefully inside her.

His skin flushed. "I didn't intend for you to hear that."

"Follow her, for she is the true queen of Azra? Only Yara can bring us justice, prosperity, and peace?" She pressed her palms to his chest as he pushed deeper within her, moving again. His love felt like the constant crash of the sea against the cliffs. That wasn't the half of what he had said about her. When she listened to the recording, she couldn't contain the love that swelled in her heart. "Trust her because I trust her?"

"I know what I said," he growled. He pulled away from her, flipped her over with a strong arm, and surged into her from behind. She let her upper body collapse against the soft bedding, completely dominated by him. "I haven't forgotten."

"And I won't ever forget," she gasped as he thrust deep and hard. Her core ached as he buried himself in her. The cool bedding kissed her heated skin as the breeze from the open arch to the canopy slid over her bare back and hips.

His hands stroked her, igniting her nerves, heightening her pleasure as he pushed her closer and closer to the edge. Hot, slick, and wanton, she abandoned herself to the pleasure of his body.

She was his woman. *Consort* didn't begin to describe what he was to her. He was her equal, her man, her king. "My Cyn."

He unleashed his passion as he grasped her with firm hands and thrust within her, over and over. She fisted her hands in the bedding, holding on to anything she could as her pleasure built until it erupted in wave after blinding wave of ecstasy.

She cried, overcome by the power and the pleasure of it as his breath came in short gasps. The intensity blinded her, thrilled her. He gasped, shouted, then clung to her, shaking as he released.

They collapsed together, sated and reeling from the power of their love.

He rested his head on her chest, idly trailing his fingers over the sensitive skin just below her breast.

Yara frowned as she stroked his hair. The high cities hadn't quite embraced him as a peer, but generations of sexism didn't die in a matter of months. They'd fight the prejudice for the rest of their lives, as would the generations that followed, but Yara held out hope that his presence here with her was the beginning of the end of the separation that had nearly destroyed Azra.

"Onali asked if I was going to change my name," Cyn murmured, then turned his head and kissed her breast.

Yara laughed. Normally when a man was given to a woman, he kept the suffix of his name and added the prefix of hers. "What did you tell her?"

"That I refuse to be called Yarn."

They both laughed. He kissed her, a deep and hard kiss filled with the promise of endless nights just like this. Maybe *consort* wasn't so bad after all. He ended the kiss with a teasing nip and gazed down on her, admiration shining in his gorgeous eyes.

"I think it's about time men kept their names. Their bloodlines are just as worthy as ours," she mused. *Her merciless rebel.* She thanked the Matriarchs for his blood. It had awoken the woman within her, and saved them all.

"Save it for the throne, Pix," he teased. She laughed then tugged a lock of his shining hair.

"Have you heard from Xan?" she asked. She owed him her life.

"The Kronalen know a prince is out there, but they haven't identified him yet," he answered. His brow creased with concern.

"We'll be there when he needs us," Yara offered. "It's up to him now."

Cyn lifted her hand to his lips. "It's up to all of us."

"I love you, Cyn." She touched his face, letting her fingertips linger at his jaw.

He took her hand and kissed the back of her knuckles. "I love you, too."

# Beyond the Shadows

*Berkley Sensation titles by Jess Granger*

BEYOND THE RAIN
BEYOND THE SHADOWS

# Beyond the Shadows

## Jess Granger

BERKLEY SENSATION, NEW YORK

**THE BERKLEY PUBLISHING GROUP**
**Published by the Penguin Group**
**Penguin Group (USA) Inc.**
**375 Hudson Street, New York, New York 10014, USA**
Penguin Group (Canada), 90 Eglinton Avenue East, Suite 700, Toronto, Ontario M4P 2Y3, Canada
(a division of Pearson Penguin Canada Inc.)
Penguin Books Ltd., 80 Strand, London WC2R 0RL, England
Penguin Group Ireland, 25 St. Stephen's Green, Dublin 2, Ireland (a division of Penguin Books Ltd.)
Penguin Group (Australia), 250 Camberwell Road, Camberwell, Victoria 3124, Australia
(a division of Pearson Australia Group Pty. Ltd.)
Penguin Books India Pvt. Ltd., 11 Community Centre, Panchsheel Park, New Delhi—110 017, India
Penguin Group (NZ), 67 Apollo Drive, Rosedale, North Shore 0632, New Zealand
(a division of Pearson New Zealand Ltd.)
Penguin Books (South Africa) (Pty.) Ltd., 24 Sturdee Avenue, Rosebank, Johannesburg 2196,
South Africa

Penguin Books Ltd., Registered Offices: 80 Strand, London WC2R 0RL, England

This book is an original publication of The Berkley Publishing Group.

This is a work of fiction. Names, characters, places, and incidents either are the product of the author's imagination or are used fictitiously, and any resemblance to actual persons, living or dead, business establishments, events, or locales is entirely coincidental. The publisher does not have any control over and does not assume any responsibility for author or third-party websites or their content.

PRINTING HISTORY
Berkley Sensation trade paperback edition / May 2010

Library of Congress Cataloging-in-Publication Data

Granger, Jess.
    Beyond the shadows / Jess Granger.—Berkley sensation trade paperback ed.
        p.  cm.
    ISBN 978-0-425-23415-0
    I. Title.
    PS3607.R36285B495    2010
    813'.6—dc22                                                    2009053187

PRINTED IN THE UNITED STATES OF AMERICA

10  9  8  7  6  5  4  3  2  1

*To my friend Rose.*
*Keep fighting. I have many more stories to tell you.*